# Lovebirds

Three Couples. Two months. One lodge. And too many *secrets*.

Chani Harris Kartobi

ISBN: 979-8-218-83923-9

# CONTENT WARNING

This novel gradually introduces mature themes and potentially disturbing content that may not be suitable for all readers. Content appears in both the present narrative (late-2019 to mid-2020) and in flashbacks presented throughout the novel. It includes:

- Intense psychological manipulation and gaslighting
- Depictions of severe emotional trauma and PTSD, and how it can lead to destructive decisions
- Complex, unhealthy, and taboo relationship dynamics, including family trauma
- Explicit sexual content
- Infidelity
- Severe mental health struggles and substance abuse
- Vehicular manslaughter
- Extended confinement
- Violence, physical and emotional (on-page)
- Death, including that of minors (off-page)
- Mentions of child abuse and predation

**This novel is NOT for everyone.** Please use discretion if you plan to continue beyond this page, and consider your emotional well-being if you have trauma related to any of the bullet points.

# Prologue

*'Cause I Really Need Somebody*

## 19 June 1998- South Boston, MA

Squeals and laughter filled M Street Park as kids ran, jumped, and tussled on the playground. Somewhere, an ice cream truck warbled out a tune that was half lullaby, half nightmare.

Kelly O'Connor didn't care for lullabies.

At just 6 years old, she walked like she had just stepped off a stage and expected the spotlight to follow her. Her fiery red curls bounced as she marched to the sandbox, where a blond boy sat alone drawing lines with a twig. A '96 Camry drove by, Aaliyah's "Are You That Somebody?" playing loud through the radio.

She plopped down right beside him without invitation. Her emerald-green eyes narrowed as she observed him.

He looked at her, his blue eyes wide, like she'd just descended from a spaceship.

Finally, she spoke:

"You're new here."

The boy nodded, his cheeks flushed from the sun. "We moved here three days ago."

Kelly's eyes narrowed further, assessing him. "What's your name?"

"Kevin," he said softly, blinking at her.

Kelly grinned then, the gaps in her little teeth showing. "You have a 'K' name, too! I'm Kelly."

She offered her tiny, freckled hand like a businesswoman making a profitable deal, the charms on her Claire's bracelet clinking together.

Kevin looked at her hand, blinked again, and then took it into his.

By sunset, they'd climbed three trees, skinned two knees, and declared one war on the meanie boys who wouldn't let them into their fort. Before their moms took them home, they promised to be best friends forever.

**New Year's Eve 2019- Atlanta, GA**

Raven Quinn was sprawled out on the king-sized bed in the middle of the high-rise's bedroom, the black of her silky robe matching the sheets. Her acrylics sparkled as she scrolled through her Instagram notifications. She smirked when she saw that her latest post had already garnered 25k likes.

Damien King packed a charcoal-colored suitcase with military precision: hoodies, joggers, sweatshirts, loc sprays, silk durags, and the freshest sneakers. It was so neat, it could be a magazine ad.

"You know we leavin' out tomorrow, right?" he asked, his deep voice resonating through the spacious room. He was shirtless, his pecan-brown skin glowing under storytelling tattoos, a pair of silver dog tags glinting against his chest.

Raven looked up from her phone and narrowed her eyes at him. "Gimme a break, King. I won't be able to check this beautiful app for two months. Eight weeks. Sixty days. I *deserve* this."

"Aye, *you* the one that said you wanted an adventure," he said, his dark eyes looking over her. Even after two years, Raven's beauty amazed him.

She sat up then, her robe falling off her left shoulder, baring a small tattoo on her collarbone: *Damien Maurice King.*

"Fine, I'll *paaack,*" she drawled out, crouching on the bed so that she could reach underneath it and pull out a massive skull-patterned suitcase.

Damien couldn't miss the opportunity to smack her voluptuous ass while it was up, making it ripple like water under his palm. Raven let out a sultry giggle, flipping over on her back and using her powerful legs to pull him atop her.

They kissed passionately on the bed; her fingers in his locs, his gripping her hips- the letters *RAVEN* inked across his right hand, *QUINN* across his left.

"Two months of this," he whispered against her berry-painted lips. "Can't *wait* to be a dad when it's over."

Raven laughed so hard she threw her head back, which he took full advantage of.

### Pittsburgh, PA

Laney Cohen smiled as she zipped up her beige suitcase. "*And* we're all set," she said, her left hand tracing her swollen belly through her cashmere sweater.

Michael Cohen's glasses-covered eyes were glued to his MacBook, his fingers typing almost inhumanly fast, his breathing somewhat labored from how intensely he was focusing.

Laney placed a hand on her hip.

"Uh… earth to Cohen?"

Michael continued typing, keyboard keys clicking like a constant percussion. "No way in hell I'm letting these *children* on League think I went AFK 'cause they bested me." He pressed 'enter' with the most dramatic of flairs. "Had to protect my clout before we revert to pre-civilization."

Laney snorted. "You calling two months without internet 'pre-civilization' proves that we *need* this trip."

Michael got up then, hugging his wife affectionately. "No, you carrying a whole ass *human* is why we need this trip."

Laney smiled and nuzzled his neck. "It really *is* perfect timing. No distractions for our last few months as a family of two."

Michael smiled, trying to lose himself in the moment, even as the mere *idea* of going that long without Wi-Fi made him feel sheer dread.

"I'll enjoy every minute."

**Brooklyn, NY**

Fireworks went off faintly in the distance as Selene Brown packed a lavender-colored suitcase with almost ritualistic precision: perfectly folded yarn-knit sweaters, cozy leggings, fuzzy socks, and her *best* yoga mat just in case the floors were hard.

Her gold-ringed fingers hovered over a zipped lining pocket almost lovingly before she zipped the suitcase closed.

Caleb Brown's navy-blue suitcase was… well, it didn't look like his wife's. Compression shirts, shorts, joggers, and massive jugs of protein powder were just kind of thrown in. "Babe, where's my creatine?" He called out, looking around the bedroom with a squint.

Selene smiled softly, not even looking up at him. "Already in your suitcase."

The well-muscled man paused, picked up a half-thrown towel from the bag, and there it was. "What the hell would I do without you?" he asked lovingly with a smile.

"Immediately implode," she responded with a wink, gently placing a raw citrine in a teal-colored toiletry bag beside an array of different essential oils. "I can't believe we're both Scorpio suns with Capricorn risings. We're so *different*."

Caleb rolled his eyes and chuckled, sweeping the small woman up like she weighed nothing at all, making her squeal and giggle. "*I* can't believe I'm gonna spend two whole months in the mountains with the most gorgeous woman on the planet."

Selene quirked a brow, her full lips smirking. "Planet?"

"*Cosmos*, sorry," he chuckled, gently putting her down.

Selene lifted her hands and placed them on his cheeks, her golden-brown eyes looking between his blue-green ones. "This will be our honeymoon."

Caleb smiled, gently tracing her wedding rings, his own gold band glinting under the room's dim lighting.

"And it'll be the best honeymoon ever."

The two of them stood there, gazing into each other's eyes like there was no other place they'd rather be.

But for a second-

Just a split second-

A pang slashed through Selene's heart.

Without even thinking, she glanced over at the window to look at the rising moon- a waxing crescent this evening.

She whispered, so low that only she could hear:

"Wish us luck."

Then, she looked back at her husband, kissing him like it was the last time she'd ever truly be able to again.

# Chapter 1

*My One True Love*

## New Year's Eve 2006- Queens, NY

The small Tudor house smelled of cinnamon tea and burning sage, the kind of scent that seemed stitched into the walls. A string of gold star garlands looped around the living room windows, and the TV flickered with muted images of Times Square preparing to drop the ball. Outside, faint pops of fireworks sounded early, distant like promises.

In the middle of the living room, Selene, 11, was putting on a *show*. She had the iPod dock blasting Panic! at the Disco through tinny speakers, her jumbo box-braids bouncing with every spin. She clutched a hairbrush microphone, stomping dramatically in her socks across the Beni Ourain rug.

*"Now I'm of consenting age!"* she belted, squeaky but determined, her dimples flashing as she pointed toward her imaginary crowd with a wide grin.

Her 6-year-old sister Athena sat cross-legged on the couch, eyes wide with hero worship. She clapped and kicked her small legs, the silver bangles on her wrists jingling. *"To be forgetting you in a...* um... *cab or ray!"*

At the kitchen table, Lashawn Freeman-Amrani, their mother, leaned back and laughed, her curvy frame wrapped in a loose batik dress. Her thick locs were tied back with a scarf, deep mocha skin glowing in the lamplight. "L-Lena, baby, you gon... gonna wear yourself out before the New Y-Year even gets here." She smirked warmly, revealing deep dimples as she sipped from a mug of lavender tea, which she'd brewed patiently over months from her backyard garden.

Beside her, Youssef Amrani, their father, small-framed and thick-mustached with deep-set, golden-toned eyes that could enchant the dead, chuckled in his thick accent. "She is *just* like her Tatie. All performance, all the time." He leaned toward his wife, whispering in mock seriousness, "We should start charging admission."

Selene struck a final dramatic pose, clutching her brush to her chest. "Thank you, thank you. For my New Year's resolution for 2007, I've decided I'm starting a band. Like Panic! at the Disco. But *better.*"

"Better?" Lashawn teased, raising her brows. "You g-gonna show Brendon Urie what's what?"

"Yes, ma'am," Selene declared with utter seriousness, and both parents laughed.

Athena piped up suddenly, springing to her feet. "My resolution is better!"

"Oh yeah?" Selene teased, ruffling her little sister's fluffy curls. "What is it, Thena?"

Athena puffed out her tiny chest, her big brown eyes sparkling. "I wanna meet my soulmate at a mountain lodge. Just like Troy and Gabriella in High School Musical!" On the family computer against the wall, Athena's *Virtual Magic Kingdom* avatar rocked Gabriella Montez's iconic red dress.

Lashawn snorted into her tea. "A soulmate at six y-years old? Girl…"

Athena ignored her mother, spinning in a circle with arms wide. "And then, after the lodge, we'll lose each other… but then we'll meet again somewhere else and fall in love! Like *destiny*!"

Selene rolled her eyes, but a smile spread across her face. "That's not a resolution, Thena. That's a Disney movie."

"It's my *dream!*" Athena shot back, grinning as her eyes twinkled with hope.

Youssef leaned down and kissed the top of her head, his thick brows softening with adoration. "Then may the New Year bring you destiny, *binti.*"

The four of them laughed together as the fireworks grew louder outside.

Selene climbed onto the couch beside her sister and cuddled her close. Lashawn raised her mug, Youssef lifted his glass of Maghrebi mint tea, and they toasted softly in the warm glow of the living room.

"*Bismillah,*" Youssef murmured.

"To love, to music, and to dreams," Lashawn added warmly.

Athena clutched Selene's hand and whispered into her ear, hope all over her little face:

"And, to soulmates."

**New Year's Day 2020- Inara, UT**

The Mercedes-Maybach that picked Selene and Caleb up from Salt Lake City International started to slow down along the winding driveway.

There was a large, gorgeous wooden sign that read:

**Evervale Lodge.**

"Okay, this *already* feels like a damn movie," Caleb said, his golden-toned waves tousled after the flurry of travel.

Selene just smiled, her eyes widening as she looked out of the clean windows, Melanie Martinez's "Class Fight" playing through her AirPods. The mountains were absolutely *breathtaking;* tall, rugged, and snow-capped.

The car continued to swerve through the winding drive, and the excited couple traded gasps until it finally came to a stop.

And the newlyweds *froze*.

Because the lodge? It wasn't just some mountain lodge.

It was a *fairytale come to life.*

Tall and sprawling with timber wood, tall arched windows that reflected the firelight within, castle turret-shaped chimneys that puffed out smoke, steep gables, and a wrap-around balcony that looked like it *begged* to be stood on. The mountains surrounded it in a way that made it look mythical.

"You gotta be fucking kidding me," Caleb whispered, eyes wide.

He looked at the driver's partition, which was closed when the car picked them up, and hadn't opened once since.

"Uh… driver… are we good to get out?"

Nothing. Not even a breath.

Selene looked at Caleb, who looked at her in return.

Then, she shrugged. "Let's just get our luggage." With excitement coloring her features, she opened the car door and stepped out into the crisp mountain air, taking a deep inhale like it was the first time she could truly breathe in years.

Caleb followed her out, and the trunk immediately opened.

"Guess it's invisible hosts *and* invisible drivers," he muttered, taking out both of their large suitcases. He turned around to face the lodge in all its glory. Even from feet away, it smelled faintly of cedar and cinnamon.

Selene smiled and led him to the large double doors, excitement twinkling within her eyes.

As they stepped up the gorgeous stone steps, they met a sign:

**No internet access beyond this point.**

She turned to Caleb with a teasing smirk. "You got anyone you want to say goodbye to before we seal our fate?"

Caleb winced from her words. "Sheesh, don't say it like that. And no, of course not. You know I have no family."

Something passed across Selene's face as her eyes softened.

She squeezed his shoulder. "Well… you want to go in?"

Caleb took a deep breath for a reason he couldn't explain and opened both well-shined handles of the door.

And their breaths were taken a second time.

The cedar/cinnamon scent hit them *hard,* now. The wooden ceiling was unbelievably tall, with a large antler chandelier hanging down. The windows were just as tall, showcasing the otherworldly mountains and pines beyond.

There was a large stone mantle that held a dancing, crackling fire, which cast an orange glow onto the most inviting setup: multiple plush couches and poufs, a massive Beni Ourain rug, and a thick mahogany coffee table.

On that table sat six ornate mugs, a copper pot of hot cocoa, and a single golden envelope that seemed to sparkle where it sat.

Caleb stood rooted, his mouth agape. "This is *home* for two months?"

Selene's honeyed eyes glowed as she took in her surroundings, twirling slowly in place like a Disney princess who'd just moved into her castle.

She then walked over to the table, grabbed the wooden handle of the copper pot, and poured the decadent, milky liquid into two beautiful hand-thrown mugs- a lavender one and a teal one.

Caleb froze for a moment as the scent of the beverage hit his nostrils. "That smells like your aunt's hot chocolate. Is that…Is that *orange blossom?*"

Selene froze for a second and then took a sip from the lavender mug. She hummed, delighted. "Oh my God- it *is!* I guess it makes sense, though; we filled out that questionnaire with all our favorite meals and drinks. You *know* I had to add Tatie's recipe to the list."

She then picked up the golden envelope, surprised by its weight and by how it shimmered. She opened it gently, humming curiously at the handwritten letter inside.

With a deep breath, she read aloud:

"Welcome! We're so happy you've made it safely to our lodge. The other two couples will be joining you shortly."

Caleb exhaled, a hint of unease growing behind his cyan eyes as he glanced at the front doors. "All I hope is that they're cool enough to not ruin our honeymoon for us."

As if right on cue, the front doors flew open.

And the energy in the room *completely* changed.

The man was a *force-* towering, broad, dressed in black from Balenciaga beanie to Timbs, with a natural swagger to his step that made him look like he'd *been* in the limelight.

The woman at his side? She didn't step in; she *strutted.*

Her knee-high boots clicked against the gleaming hardwood floors like applause. Her hair, impossibly black and silky, swung to-and-fro against her back with every sway of her full hips.

She looked around the luxurious yet cozy space and quirked a perfectly arched brow like she wasn't impressed by what she was seeing but might be willing to be.

The man paused when he saw Caleb and Selene.

"Y'all the hosts?"

The newlyweds were both frozen in place from the second couple's grand entrance, but Caleb shook it off and gave a charming smile. "Nah, we're one of the couples. The hosts are supposed to be 'invisible', remember?"

"Right," the man muttered, his deep-set eyes scanning the perimeter like it was second nature.

He then stepped forward and offered his large hand.

"Damien."

Caleb noticed the *RAVEN'* ink spanning the man's hand and quirked a brow.

He took it confidently and firmly, meeting Damien's eyes. "Caleb."

The two men were a *vision-* both tall, broad-shouldered, and visibly strong. Caleb wasn't used to seeing men who could go toe-to-toe with him like this- he'd spent the past seven years making sure he *never* would- and he didn't know how to feel about it just yet.

He dropped Damien's hand and gestured to Selene, who was walking up beside him. "And this is my wife, Selene."

Selene smiled warmly as she extended her hand, delicate gold bracelets glittering on her small wrist. "It's nice to meet you, Damien."

Damien's eyes flicked over her before he took her hand- much more gently than he'd taken Caleb's. "Same." He noticed that the woman's scent, sweet and warm like vanilla and sandalwood, fit the vibe perfectly.

Before he could introduce the woman he'd arrived with, she sauntered forward confidently and extended her alabaster-toned hand, which was adorned with thick silver rings and a large Celtic knot tattoo.

"Raven."

Selene froze, just for a second, and then she took the black-haired beauty's hand. "It's nice to meet you, Raven."

Raven's wine-red lips curved as she turned to Caleb. She removed her sunglasses, revealing her mesmerizing green eyes.

"God damn, look at *you*," she said bluntly, looking back at Damien with a teasing smirk. "You worried, soldier?"

Damien rolled his eyes and plopped down on one of the plush couches, legs spread, eyes still scanning the opulent yet homey space with part curiosity, part suspicion. He immediately clocked every exit.

Raven sauntered to where he sat and plopped down on his strong lap like she belonged there, her eyes scanning the room with similar suspicion. "If the next couple's hot, we're *definitely* being filmed."

Right on time- the front doors opened again.

In stepped the final couple- an average-height man with messy brown curls, round-framed glasses, and a thick hoodie that read *'I Paused My Videogame for This'*; and an average-height pregnant woman with identical glasses to the man's, a beige parka over a baby-blue sweater dress, and *very* recognizable golden tresses.

Laney.

Caleb *froze*.

Every part of him tensed- from his jaw to his shoulders. His breath caught audibly in his throat, and his heart rate skyrocketed.

Laney looked around the space in awe, and when her hazel eyes landed on Caleb-

She froze the exact same way.

"…Caleb?" she barely managed to whisper out.

Selene narrowed her eyes, looking between the unfamiliar woman and her husband.

"Caleb… do you *know* her?"

Caleb stood frozen for a couple more seconds, pure panic settling behind his eyes, and then cleared his throat, attempting to gather his bearings.

"She's… yeah. Sh-she's my half-sister."

The "half" made Laney wince like she'd been slapped.

Selene looked between them, confusion and a hint of betrayal in her eyes.

Michael looked at Caleb like he was seeing a ghost in real time.

And Raven and Damien? They gave each other a look that said, *'So this trip might be interesting, after all.'*

# Chapter 2

*Golden Skans*

## 2 November 2011- West Philadelphia, PA

Laney, 22, cleaned the tiny kitchenette for what had to be the third time that day, her long, pink-highlighted hair swinging around her sculpted waist. She wore a hot-pink, trippy mushroom top that revealed her belly-button piercing and a miniskirt that showed off her fishnet stockings.

Michael, also 22, in a red "Science!" ThinkGeek tee, quirked a brow. "Lanes, I swear to God, Caleb will appreciate the free Wi-Fi much more than your lemon-fresh insanity." His bushy curls brushed his shoulders, a pimple visible on his cheek.

Laney smirked. "He's my little brother. Sue me for wanting him to live in a clean, good-smelling home." The apartment was tiny, but full of life- namely, the colorful, *completely* mismatched Goodwill furniture and a loud, rickety heater that was barely holding on.

Michael snorted. "I wonder if he'll actually talk to us. He's always been *kinda-*"

Right on time- one tentative knock sounded from the other side of the front door.

Laney *squealed.* She reached the chipped door in three giant steps, her septum ring glinting as she opened it wide, as if a gift were sitting on the other side.

Caleb, 18, scrawny with too-big glasses over his hollowed, dim eyes, stood at the doorway, his hands holding measly trash bags full of ill-fitting clothes.

Laney didn't even wait. She *jumped* into his arms, squeezing him tight. "Finally! God, I missed you. Happy birthday, Cabe."

Caleb immediately tensed, feeling awkward with affection. "Thanks."

Michael strolled up to the door, placing a heavy hand on Caleb's shoulder, making the willowy young man rock back and forth from the motion. "Welcome to Haunted HQ, dude."

Caleb blinked, his expression muted. "Huh?"

Laney rolled her eyes at her live-in best friend's antics and ushered her younger brother in like some kind of VIP. "The canon is, Cambridge Pines is haunted. Every July 1st, some crazy off-the-wall shit happens that no one can explain."

Caleb blinked again. "July 1st? Like, your *birthday*, July 1st?"

Laney nodded and smirked, her pink lip gloss shining. "By all means, that was *probably* a sign that we shouldn't have moved here. But we were broke college grads, and rent's cheap as fuck."

Caleb actually managed a tiny smile at that. "Still better than mom's."

Laney gave him a look of pure understanding then. "You can say that again. I swear, the minute I left that cunt's house, my life improved in every possible way. Now that you're here, I'm gonna pimp your wardrobe, get you one of those haircuts that all the girls love, teach you how to dance…"

She went on and on, and Caleb couldn't help but smile, excited about this fresh new start he'd been given.

The dining room was *immaculate*.

Tall arched windows lined with arabesque curtains, colorful yet warm paintings of bustling markets and souks, a chandelier made of colored glass that cast a gorgeous rainbow around the space, yet *another* crackling fireplace, and a long oak table that held a feast fit for royalty:

Chilled bottles of Château Margaux, Dom Pérignon, Perrier, and Badoit surrounded by impossibly clean crescent moon-etched glasses; thick-cut bourbon-glazed lamb chops, cornbread muffins baked to a perfect gold, creamy gouda mac and cheese, candied yams glistening with brown sugar, a deep dish of collard greens simmering with turkey necks, a still-bubbling dish of peach cobbler, and a plate of cantaloupe cut into perfect hearts.

And at the center of it all, like a whisper waiting to be opened, sat another golden envelope- neat and crisp, as if it had been placed there with complete care.

"Jesus *Christ,* "Michael breathed out, his brown eyes wide behind his glasses. "It's like a fucking Studio Ghibli film- comfort food edition."

Damien let out a breath. "I put soul food in my preferences, but I ain't even expect them to do it *this* good. This almost smell better than my grandmama's."

Raven's lips stayed parted until her mouth went dry. "Alright. I wasn't sure before, but I think we had the right idea coming here." She picked up the bottle of Margaux and sniffed, her eyes rolling back. "Ohhh, yeah. That's the *good* shit."

Caleb and Laney admired the dishes, but the weight between them didn't lift even an ounce.

In sync, they glanced at each other- just for a second- then turned away like it burned.

Selene's eyes lingered on the half-siblings for a bit, shifting between them observantly. Then, she walked to the envelope.

With a soft, forced smile, read aloud:

"Welcome officially to Evervale Lodge, lovebirds. Every day, breakfast will be served at 9 a.m., lunch at 2 p.m., and dinner at 7 p.m.; always fresh, always homemade. Don't worry about cooking or cleaning; we'll always take care of that. When you are finished eating, head upstairs to your personalized master suites."

Selene looked at everyone with raised brows and a smile, then continued: "You won't have to look hard; your door will be carved with your and your partner's initials. Oh, and by the way, get used to these letters; they're how we'll be communicating with you during your stay."

She paused, then, her breath catching in her throat.

Damien blinked. "So *that's* what they meant by 'invisible'."

Raven cackled, drinking from a glass that she'd already filled to the brim. "It's like 2000s reality TV. Except," she looked around the dining space with a suspicious squint. "I don't see any cameras."

Selene giggled nervously, her fingers tightening around the paper. "At least they're paying us 100k for this. I can deal with some weird envelopes and possible surveillance for two months if *that's* at the end."

She continued reading, her bearing a bit tense now: "For now, let's do some icebreakers. As a couple, answer these three questions: how did you and your partner meet? How long have you been together? What are you hoping to get from this retreat?"

She set the envelope down slowly, her eyes roaming the room and the five unsuspecting faces before her.

They eventually settled on her husband, who still looked like every bit of life had been sucked from him the moment his eyes met Laney's.

She sat beside him and squeezed his hand under the table, putting on a comforting smile. "You wanna go first, babe?"

Her eyes flicked, just for a second, to Laney, before they focused back on Caleb.

Caleb snapped up as if pulled from a haze. He cleared his throat, his jaw still tight, and nodded at Selene with a smile, though his posture gave away his discomfort.

She gave him a look that screamed, *We'll talk about this later tonight.'*

Then, she put on a warm smile, gently placed the card with the questions in front of her on the table, and cleared her throat.

### 1.     How did you and your partner meet?

"Caleb was my personal trainer two and a half years ago," she began, her shapely eyes glittering from the lights overhead. "I knew it wasn't right; he was my *trainer* after all; but the minute I saw him… well…" she giggled. "Y'all see him."

Raven smirked, her emerald eyes glinting as she looked Caleb up and down in silent agreement. Damien rolled his eyes at his girlfriend's shameless antics.

Caleb smiled, the tension in his features softening a bit. "I knew I was in trouble when she walked in, honestly. That smile made me stop breathing for a second."

Selene smiled on cue, dimples deepening as a flush rose to her cheeks.

Then, she turned to Raven. "What about you guys?"

Raven stretched out in her chair like a cat, fully revealing a choker tattoo around her neck and a bear paw on her cleavage beneath Damien's full name. She looked at her boyfriend with a wicked smirk.

"He was my bodyguard. Couldn't resist me. It was a scandal."

Laughter bloomed throughout the dining room, and Damien just smirked, shaking his head as he continued to eat.

"I guess we *both* ended up with men we hired," Selene said with a cheeky smile as she put some candied yams on her plate with a pleased hum.

Slowly, everyone's eyes, except for Caleb's, turned to Michael and Laney.

Laney wasn't 'there' at all, her eyes focused somewhere no one else could see, her hand tight around the hem of her dress. But when she felt the eyes on her, she snapped up with a slight jolt.

She managed a small smile, then. "Michael and I met in college. We were just best friends until after we graduated, though, even while we lived together."

Michael smiled, nodding, his mouth still full of peach cobbler. "I was in the friend zone for *four years*. It was worth it, though. She was amazing even then. Her energy, her wit, her care. Especially for her broth-"

He stopped speaking abruptly, realizing the *massive* mistake he'd made.

Laney paused her hand over her fork, her heart rate picking up.

Caleb's jaw tensed visibly, his fingers tightening around his own fork.

Selene noticed it all, a sadness settling within her.

Then, she cleared her throat and smiled. "Let's go to the next question?"

### 2.     How long have you and your partner been together?

She looked up at Caleb with a warmth in her eyes, the love she had for him evident despite her confusion. "We've been together for exactly two years, married for 18 months. Today's our anniversary."

Raven's perfectly sculpted brows rose in surprise as her hand paused over her wine glass.

"Today's *our* second anniversary, too."

Selene's brows lifted in surprise. "What? You got together *two years ago today*?"

Raven nodded lazily, finally sipping from the glass. "Romeo over here," she gestured toward Damien with a sharp acrylic, "made things official when the clock struck midnight."

Selene gasped, lightly gripping Caleb's arm. "Caleb asked me out the same way! Well, actually, he never asked me out at all; he straight up *proposed*," she said with a slight giggle. "We moved… pretty quickly."

Caleb nodded, but his jaw was tight.

Only Selene noticed the way his eyes darted quickly to Michael and Laney.

Michael chuckled in complete disbelief. "Well, I'll be damned. I asked Laney to be my girlfriend when the clock struck midnight on New Year's Eve, too, but that was, like, *seven* years ago- not two like you youngins. And we got married on New Year's Day the next year."

Laney managed to nod despite her tension, her voice quiet, apprehensive.

"It's *our* anniversary, too."

The six of them looked at each other with a mix of awe and apprehension. The massive lodge suddenly felt *too* quiet- even the fire seemed to freeze.

Then, Selene let out a light chuckle, attempting to thin the air. "Either this is the wildest coincidence… or it isn't a coincidence at all."

Raven huffed, throwing the rest of her wine back like it was the most natural thing in the world. "They definitely picked us specifically for that reason. Probably wanted to creep us out just for shits."

Selene laughed softly, smoothing her burgundy turtleneck down over her trim stomach. "*Or* they wanted us to all celebrate all of our anniversaries here. It's kinda romantic, in a way."

Damien dug into his collard greens like a man who hadn't eaten in days, moaning lowly under his breath from the decadent flavor. "Shit's gettin' weirder and weirder, but God *damn* they can cook. I *swear* this feel like home."

Selene smiled softly at his enjoyment. Then, she turned to Caleb, who still looked… far away, his posture screaming *'I want to be **anywhere** else'*.

"Last question?"

### 3.    What are you hoping to get from this experience?

She squeezed Caleb's hand under the table, attempting to steady him. "We got married right when our careers started picking up- yoga teaching for me, personal training for him- so we didn't get to have a honeymoon. We were kinda hoping to use this trip as one."

Raven pouted her lips in a mock swoon. "How adorable is that?"

She turned to Damien, who had cleared every single crumb on his plate. "You answer this time, daddy."

Damien, satisfied, leaned back into his seat.
"Somethin' new."

Raven rolled her eyes. "Jesus. At least *try* to compete with the honeymooners."

He smirked then. "We from Atlanta. Used to the hustle and bustle of workin'. Figured we could use some time alone in the mountains. Reconnect and… shit."

Raven smirked and kissed his jaw, leaving behind a crimson-colored lip print.

Everyone then turned to the final couple.

Laney smiled this time, tracing her round belly. "Time together as a duo before we become a trio."

Michael nodded, lightly squeezing her shoulder. "And, if we're honest with ourselves, the money doesn't hurt, either." Everyone chuckled in agreement.

Selene looked down at Laney's belly curiously, then back at her face with a genuine smile. "How far along are you, mama?"

Laney smiled, though her shoulders were still tense, her neck strained. "Around seven months. Due three weeks after this."

Selene's breath caught for a second, and then she shook it off and smiled. "Wow, *seven?!* You're brave, cutting it so close."

Laney nodded, her conservatively cut hair swaying slightly. "It just felt like fate. Like we *needed* this."

Michael nodded. "It's our last hurrah."

Everyone continued eating, the air warm, the food delicious, and the discomfort ever-present.

# Chapter 3

*Dreamt About Them Days*

## New Year's Eve 2007- Rex, GA

Fergie's "Glamorous" boomed through the iPod Video docked on the mahogany entertainment center, but it couldn't quite drown out the raucous happening two feet from it.

"I'm Goku, you Krillin," laughed Damien, 13, as he body-slammed his 12-year-old brother onto the gold Persian-style rug, making the younger boy yell out. Both of their heads were freshly cornrowed, parts immaculate and Blue Magic-smelling.

"Man, shut up. Just 'cause you older don't mean you ain't soft," strained Xander as he tried- really, *really* tried- to flip them over.

A beautiful girl- deep caramel skin, box braids with gold beads, and a sparkly Baby Phat dress- giggled on the fluffy suede couch. "Xan, I been watching you and D fight for almost a decade. You ain't won, *once.*"

"Shut up, Jasmine! You only sayin' that 'cause you in *looove* with him," Xander shot back, sticking his tongue out at her from beneath Damien, who kept him pinned without mercy.

Jasmine made a look of mock-disgust, but she blinked rapidly in succession. "Ew! I am *not* in love with the homie since I was 5."

"Well, he definitely like *you*," Xander said with a smirk and eyes locked directly on Damien, who flipped him onto his stomach and pinned him there in revenge, making the younger boy groan. "Man, stay in a child's place," Damien said, his voice deep even then.

Just then, from the arch leading to the hallway: "What y'all NOT gon' do is tear up my house!"

Tonya King stood behind the leather sectional, arms crossed beneath the soft sleeves of her burgundy robe, which hugged her voluptuous curves like it loved them. Her cheetah-print bonnet framed her gorgeous ebony-toned face.

The boys separated immediately and jumped up in formation, like they knew they'd been raised better than this. "Sorry, ma," they said in unison.

Tonya's brown-glossed lips curved into a smirk as she shook her head. "Xander, come help me boil these crab legs," she said, already turning around.

And then, so slightly that it could've been missed, she winked at Damien.

Damien smirked softly as Xander huffed and walked out behind his mother, gripping the waistband of his sagging jeans. All that could be heard was Tonya telling him to "put a damn belt on."

Damien stretched like he was trying *hard* to appear casual and plopped down on the couch beside Jasmine. He rocked a long white tee, baggy jeans, and a very fake but very shiny gold chain.

Jasmine looked at him and gave a soft smile, deep dimples forming in the smooth skin of her cheeks. "Xan is doin' the most as usual," she said casually. But her knee wouldn't stop bouncing, and her hands wouldn't stop playing with her dress.

Damien smirked just slightly, his eyes tracing her features. Even then, he had the most breathtaking dark brown eyes.

He looked right into her eyes with them. "He wildin' but… Ion' know…" He didn't finish his statement; just kept looking at her.

Jasmine's breath caught in her throat. "You don't know… what?"

Damien looked out of the window at the already-booming fireworks, took a deep breath, and then looked back at her.

"Ion' know if he wrong about me likin' you."

Jasmine let out the softest gasp without even meaning to. Her pink-polished hands played with the hem of her dress even faster, now.

Then she looked up at him again.

"He not wrong about me, neither."

The two new teens looked at each other for a good five seconds before Jasmine started nervous giggling.

"When… how long… You know?"

Damien smirked. "You want me to be honest?"

Jasmine nodded, smiling with teeth now, her braces shining.

Damien flashed his iconic crooked smile. "Day you walked into Ms. Brackett and Ms. Orr's class."

Jasmine's already-large brown eyes got even wider as memories flashed within her mind. "Kindergarten?! Like, the day we *met?*"

Damien nodded, eyes nostalgic but certain. "Thought you was cute as hell witcho afro puffs and Minnie Mouse jumper."

Jasmine snorted at the thought. "Why didn't you say nothin'?"

Damien tilted his head and looked at her, as if to say, *'Really?'*

"You had a new boyfriend every week. Was never checkin' for me like that."

Jasmine gasped. "Only 'cause you had a new chick literally every *day!* I didn't have time to be wastin' my time."

Damien snorted, leaning back casually. "Ay, don't hate the playa."

They laughed for a few seconds, and then things got quiet, quiet in a way they'd never gotten before between the childhood best friends.

It was Jasmine who spoke first. "So… we boyfriend and girlfriend, now?"

Damien looked at her, his hand slowly reaching out to hold hers, and smiled.

"Let's get together at midnight. We gon' have the best anniversary date ever."

Jasmine giggled, squeezing his hand, her heart fluttering. "Let's do it."

☽

Damien and Raven were the first to head upstairs, of course, needing the bedroom for… reasons.

Raven's eyes narrowed with amusement at the tall, *D&R*-engraved wooden door. "Okay. Bougie as hell. Let's see if they got us right."

Damien pushed open the door, bracing for threats even now.

And both of them stood still for a second.

The room was *stunning*. Dark stone walls, golden sconces making the stone glow gold, and a massive, low-profile king bed framed in black lacquer. The bedding was a mix of crimson silk sheets, plush matte-black pillows, and thick faux-fur throws folded neatly at the foot. A large abstract oil painting hung above the bed; a crow mid-flight against a muted red sky, with what looked like flames at the bottom.

On each nightstand sat a pair of black matte glasses and a brand-new bottle of Jack Daniel's.

Raven walked further in, letting her fingers graze the edge of the bed. "Okay… they *snapped* with this. It's literally my aesthetic made domestic."

Damien's dark eyes scanned the place. "Well, 'cept for the Jack. You *hate* that shit. And there's *two*."

Raven froze in place for a moment, her eyes drifting to the bottles. Flashbacks started to form in her mind, but she shook them away physically, making a mocking gagging noise. "Yeah, you can have those to yourself."

But still, she continued gazing around the room, awe in her eyes.

The back of the suite held tall, freshly-polished glass doors that opened onto a private balcony with a view of the backyard. Damien stepped over and unlatched them, letting in a whisper of crisp mountain air into the spacious suite.

The moment they stepped outside, they stopped in their tracks, amazement identical in their eyes.

The mountains stretched out endlessly beneath a sky full of huge, twinkling stars. The trees below were dusted in snow that shimmered like it had been sprinkled with diamond powder. A frozen lake reflected everything above it like glass.

Raven blinked, lips parting slightly. "God *damn*."

"Yeah," Damien murmured, wrapping an arm around her waist. "This ain't *real*."

She pulled a weed pen from her coat pocket, took a slow hit, and exhaled into the night. Then she passed it to him. He took it just as casually.

After a moment, she asked, "So. What do you think of our little 'roommates'?"

Damien snorted, leaning his thick forearms on the balcony rail as he continued admiring the stars. "We in for a weird ass stay, that's for damn sure."

She barked out a laugh, taking a hit so big it lowered her lids. "I'm trying to give Caleb the benefit of the doubt. Poor guy looked like he saw a *ghost* when Laney walked in. That family drama is gonna be a *mess*, and you *know* I'm here for it."

"Facts," Damien muttered, chuckling slightly at the memory of the golden-haired half-siblings acting like being in a room with one another was psychological torture of the highest order.

But his jaw shifted as his thoughts drifted elsewhere-

To the roommate whom he considered even stranger.

"But it's his *wife* I'm weirded out by."

Raven tilted her head, eyes narrowed as she attempted to puff out a ring. "Selene? The tiny little yoga teacher? Why?"

He shrugged, taking another vape hit.

"Ion' trust her."

Raven blinked, leaning in slightly like he'd just shared spicy gossip. "You *don't?*"

He shook his head slowly, replaying dinner in his mind- from Selene's poised princess-like posture to that perfect dimpled smile to those eyes that he, a man who'd been *trained* to read people, couldn't decipher.

"She too polished. Prim, proper. Sat up at that table like she had a stick in her spine. Ate like she was tryna get graded on every bite. Even the way she *laughed* was rehearsed as hell."

He blew out vapor, leaning against the railing.

"I know when people got somethin' to hide. That broad? *She* got somethin' to hide."

Raven studied him. Damien was always casual, always cool, and was so even now, but the suspicion, the slight hint of discomfort in his bearing, was there.

She smirked then, nudging him teasingly as she took another pen hit. "You're paying a *lot* of attention to that dude's wife."

He cut her a look. "You think I'd be with *you* if I liked chicks like *her?*"

Her mouth dropped open in mock offense as she nudged him harder, now. "Excuse me?! The hell do you mean by *that?!*"

"I'm just sayin'…" His lips curved into a slow crooked grin, one that still managed to make her hot after two years. "You *real.* Ion' ever gotta worry about you fakin' *nothin'.*"

"Damn right," she said, stepping closer to him with low, seductive lids, her eyes tracing his features. It almost *bothered* her how handsome he was.

He didn't move an ounce; just took her in.

"You *fire*, baby."

She looked at him for a heartbeat and then grabbed the collar of his hoodie and pulled him into a kiss- slow, deep, and claiming, a hum rising in her throat at the feel of his succulent lips. Damien kissed her back just as fully- his hands, still rightfully inked with her full name, pulling her flush against him like instinct.

Raven smirked against his mouth, leading him back in without breaking the kiss.

☽

Caleb reached for the brass handle on the wooden door engraved with *C&S* and turned it. The door creaked open slowly, like it wanted them to savor the reveal.

Selene gasped.

It was a *dream*.

The room was bathed in orange light from a crackling fire in a gorgeous stone mantle. A massive four-poster bed sat in the center, layered in plush cream bedding so soft it looked like it had never known a wrinkle. Oversized pillows in velvet and linen lined the top, and the headboard was carved with an intricate sun-and-moon design that made Selene's heart melt.

To the left of the bed was a wide bay window with a cushioned bench, overlooking snowy peaks that didn't even look real. Terracotta pots of lavender and eucalyptus lined the windowsill, and the whole room smelled like calm.

On one dresser were individually wrapped almond cookies- Selene's favorite. On the other were thin mints- Caleb's favorite.

Selene slowly stepped into the room, exhaling in awe as she twirled. "It's like they took my daydream and *built* it."

Caleb set their bags near the tufted ottoman and whistled under his breath. "They really got *everything* right. I don't even remember putting thin mints in my preferences."

Selene stayed quiet, looking down contemplatively, playing with her wedding ring. After a moment, she finally turned to him, her expression soft but serious.

"Why didn't you tell me?"

Caleb blinked, his shoulders stiff. Suddenly, all the awe in his features was replaced with what could only be described as dread.

Selene's eyes didn't part from him, her brows furrowing in concern. "About Laney. Or... that you had any family at all."

The suite remained silent, nothing but the sound of distant laughter and... other things... from Damien and Raven's suite next door.

Caleb lowered himself to the edge of the bed, leaning forward with his elbows on his knees, like her question genuinely *exhausted* him.

After a few heartbeats, he inhaled deeply. "I haven't spoken to Laney- or anyone in my family- in seven years." He finally looked up at her, his teal eyes flickering with something she'd never seen in them before. "It's not something I talk about. Not because I wanted to keep it from you. I just... I didn't know *how*."

Selene walked over and sat beside him. She took his hand in her much smaller ones, her bracelets clinking softly.

"You don't have to tell me everything tonight," she said gently, her eyes looking back and forth between his like she was trying to find answers within them.

"But you *will* tell me."

He met her eyes. For a second, something heavy passed between the two of them.

Selene had always cared deeply about transparency, so Caleb knew he *would* have to tell her eventually, whether he wanted to or not.

He gave a small nod and a forced smile. "I promise I'll tell you. Just not tonight. Tonight, I just want to be with my beautiful wife in the beautiful honeymoon suite of this beautiful cabin."

Selene studied him- the tension in his jaw, his shoulders, his hands.

Then she nodded. "Okay. But I'm holding you to it."

His lips curved, and then, without warning, he scooped her up bridal-style into his sculpted arms, making her squeal, her giggle echoing like sunlight in the room.

"Caleb!"

"This bed looks *way* too soft not to test out," he said, already walking them over.

☽

Michael opened the *M&D*-engraved door with dramatic flair, his arm around Laney's waist as they stepped in.

Laney let out a breathy, "Oh *wow.*"

The room was straight out of a luxury bed-and-breakfast catalog: soft tones, warm light, and thoughtful touches that made it feel like someone had asked them both what "home" meant and somehow made it feel like luxury. Creamy walls, buttery oak floors, a low platform bed dressed in sage green linen with a thick ivory knit blanket folded at the base.

To the left of the bed was a bay window with sheer linen curtains and a cushioned bench beneath it. A pale wood rocking chair sat nearby with a folded throw over the back. On the nightstand sat a vase of jasmine and lilies, so fresh that they were fragrant.

Next to them was a tray with lemon-ginger lozenges, a bottle of belly oil, and a note that read, '*Just for you, mama.*'

Laney walked over slowly, her hand resting on the curve of her stomach. "Okay, this is…" She blinked. "This is *insane.*"

Michael gave a low whistle. "I feel like I'm in a spa and a nursery at the same time. They really knew what they were *doing* with this."

Laney sat slowly on the bed and exhaled. It dipped beneath her gently, as if it were built for her weight exactly.

Michael joined her, but his expression shifted as he looked around. He leaned forward slightly, his elbows on his knees, his jaw clenched.

"So… we're not gonna talk about the fact that your *brother*, who we haven't seen in I don't know how many years, just happens to be in this massive mountain cabin with us?"

Laney's smile faded, her forest-floor eyes suddenly somber behind her round glasses.

"Seven," she said softly. "To this day."

Michael paused, his eyes widening. "Yeah... he *did* leave New Year's 2013. I remember 'cause I wanted us all to go out and celebrate you and me finally getting together, but he was MIA."

He leaned back, his voice distant. "It was so *random*. He was living with us, seemed cool as hell with us both, and then... poof. Like he never even existed at all." He looked over at her. "And now he's all... jacked? And hot? And *married?*"

Laney didn't laugh. She was staring at the window now; her arms folded tightly across her belly. There was a look in her eyes that Michael couldn't quite place, which was rare; her eyes *always* reflected her feelings clearly.

He reached over and set a hand on her shoulder. "I know how much you loved him. You two went through *hell* together growing up. Maybe in time, he'll tell you what happened. Maybe us all being here is some weird kinda fate."

Laney nodded, just once. "Maybe." But her white-knuckled grip on the sheet said something else.

Later, after they had both showered and changed into soft cotton sleepwear laid out for them in the closet, Michael collapsed into the bed and exhaled like a man finally relaxing after a 10-hour shift. Within minutes, he was snoring, sprawled sideways with one hand still resting on the curve of Laney's belly.

Laney's eyes, however, stayed open, unblinking.

Just like the night Caleb left.

# Chapter 4

*I Wonder*

**Thanksgiving 2007- Queens, NY**

The Tuscan-style kitchen smelled like cinnamon, cornbread dressing, fried turkey, candied yams, and collard greens simmering on the stove. Outside, light snow had already begun to fall over Broadway-Flushing, dusting the Tudor roofs in soft white powder. But inside, the kitchen was warm, comfy- Kanye West playing from the tiny CD boombox on the counter, and *Kirikou et la Sorcière* playing from the TV in the living room beyond the archway.

Lashawn, her locs a regal crown against her heart-shaped face, blue-beaded earrings swaying with each movement, stood at the small counter, her soft, shea-buttered hands slicing fruit with a calm yet intense focus. She looked down beside her, a smile on her plush lips as she continued slicing like she'd done it all her life.

"Baby, not so much pressure. L-let the knife glide."

Selene, now 12, stood beside her, mimicking her mother's motion as best she could. She wore a beige Southpole sweater dress, her thick curls brushing her shoulders, hands small but steady as she attempted to cut a heart into a piece of watermelon.

Athena, now 7, with her curls in a high ponytail, was on the other side of their mother with her tongue poked out in concentration. She was trying- *and* endearingly failing- to carve a flower into a pineapple slice.

Lashawn glanced at both of her girls with pride, plates of perfectly cut mangoes and strawberries sitting before her like edible arrangements. "Y'all gonna… thank me when you grow up and everyone's asking how you learned to do this."

Selene grinned, nudging her mom lovingly. "I already do, Mama."

Just then, a black-cherry LG Chocolate on the counter vibrated and lit up.

"Uh oh! Th-that's probably one of my mamas. She's really far along. I… knew she would have a… holiday baby."

Selene and Athena looked at each other and gasped in excitement, their little feet dancing in place. They loved it when their mother delivered a baby; it felt like a new family member had arrived.

Lashawn checked the caller ID. "Ohh! It's your Tatie!" she said, smiling wide. She flipped the phone open and pressed the speaker button.

"Inas?"

From the other side came a rush of joyful energy. "Lala! *Lhamdullah!* You cooking, yes? I smell it through the phone!"

All three women (and little women) giggled at once. Selene leaned close to the phone with a big smile. "Bonjour, Tatie! Happy Thanksgiving!"

Inas let out a joyful gasp, the love she had for her niece audible. "*Lena habibti! Sana sa'ida, a zin!* Give me my Thena, where is she?"

Athena bounced up and down, a pineapple star falling to the ground. "I'm here, I'm here!"

"Ohhh, *binti zwina*! You cooking like your sister? And is my useless *khūya* helping you?" Youssef and Inas had a… lovingly aggressive sibling bond.

"Baba is buying food at the store! And yes, I've been cooking all morning!" Athena announced proudly, her glasses falling slightly down her little button nose.

Lashawn laughed, her cocoa-toned eyes glassy with warmth as she leaned her pear-shaped figure against the counter. Her skin glowed like she was health incarnate, her stacked wooden bracelets matching the board of the incense burning on the counter behind her. "Told you I'd raise them… right, Inas."

"You did, chérie. They are *jewels.*"

Selene took the phone and held it closer to her lips. "Tatie, I saved you a strawberry heart. If you were here, I'd give it to you first."

From the speaker, Inas gasped dramatically. "*Ya Latif,* you the sweetest girl in New York. When I see you this Christmas, I will make the big couscous with olives and lamb. And the chocolat chaud with orange blossom. And the almond cookies. Just for you."

Selene beamed, her eyes twinkling with love and excitement. *"Deal."*

## 2 January 2020- Evervale Lodge

Breakfast's golden envelope led the group through couples' competitions in the lodge's indoor pool room, attempting to bring the six together while strengthening their bonds with their partners. By the time dinner rolled around, they were more at ease…

Well, at least on the surface.

When they came down to the dining room at 7 p.m., they stopped in place when they saw what was on the oak table:

Multiple plates of juicy, perfectly roasted lamb sat at the center, skin crisped and gleaming with lemon oil. Briny green olives dotted the platter like peridot jewels. Bowls of warm, buttered couscous steamed softly beside trays of roasted carrots glazed with pomegranate molasses. To the side was a plate of heart-shaped strawberry slices that screamed one thing: *This dinner was made with love.*

But what really caught their attention was what sat at the far end of the table:

An entire marble tray of top-shelf liquors-whiskeys, flavored vodkas, mezcals, and a few bottles of high-end gin. Alongside them, a dozen crystal shot glasses, a glass pitcher of chilled water flavored with sliced oranges and cucumbers, and a single stack of sleek black cards that looked just-manufactured.

Selene reached the golden envelope first, of course, unfolding it with the grace of someone who'd opened every envelope in her life like it meant something. She wore a black turtleneck and jeans that hugged her round hips this evening, her long, thick curls half pulled back to show off her blue-beaded earrings.

"The competitions aren't over just yet, lovebirds," she read aloud, her voice smooth with amusement. "This time, we're going back to college with a game of Never Have I Ever. The couple who drinks the most wins the imaginary 'Most Interesting Couple' award. Have fun."

Raven smirked and cracked her knuckles, looking ravishing in a lacy black crop top over a push-up bra that did its job, and sleek black leggings. "Oh, it's *on.*"

Michael chuckled, already reaching for the gin. He rocked a red flannel and grey sweats tonight, finding he was surprisingly at ease despite the lack of Wi-Fi. "Most interesting couple? *That's* a challenge if I've ever heard one."

Laney rested a hand on her bump, wearing one of Michael's flannels and high-waisted maternity leggings. "You're drinking for both of us, babe."

"Say less," he said, already filling a shot glass with the darkest drink he could find.

Everyone settled into their seats. The mood was relaxed, even *giddy,* like they were back in someone's dorm room.

Well, except for Caleb and Laney continuing to avoid each other's eyes like they'd turn to stone if they didn't, of course.

Raven unconsciously reached for the whiskey before freezing- just slightly- and moving on to the vodka with an uncharacteristically tight jaw.

Selene's eyes lingered on her for a bit before focusing on the cards.

She pulled one from the stack and read aloud with a little smirk:

"Never have I ever… done it in a public place."

Raven and Damien clinked glasses and drank at once, like another Thursday.

Caleb followed with a sheepish smile, cutting Selene a knowing look.

She raised her brow, shock coloring her features. "Babe?!"

He chuckled then; his cheeks flushed from inebriation already. "I mean, technically, the locker room... *counts*. Doesn't it?"

She laughed, her own cheeks flushing from the memory, then took a sip.

Raven smirked over her glass. "Knew you two weren't *completely* boring."

Laney then nudged Michael to drink for her.

Michael quirked a brow. "With *me?*"

Laney snorted, her cheeks flushing despite the lack of alcohol. "No. You remember how I was in college. It was... well, I did it everywhere."

Raven's brow lifted, her green eyes widening in almost pride as she tried to imagine the wholesome pregnant woman doing that. "Laney was a little *slut?!*"

Caleb cringed without meaning to.

Laney's cheeks flushed. "I... had fun."

Michael rolled his eyes. "And *I* had to deal with it." Everyone cackled in response.

The following cards were... expected.

"Never have I ever sent nudes" (Damien, Raven, and Laney drank immediately; Michael cheekily asked if his man-boobs counted).

"Never have I ever used a toy with a partner" (Damien, Raven, and Laney again drank instantly; Caleb and Selene looked at each other, curious if they should jump on the bandwagon one day).

"Never have I ever hooked up with someone more than ten years older" (Again- Raven, Damien, and Laney drank without hesitation; Michael said he was beginning to feel jealous- not that Laney had been with others, but that he didn't lead anywhere *near* as wild a life).

But it wasn't until one of the later questions- "Never have I ever been in love with someone who broke my heart"- that the tone began to shift.

Damien drank first; his hooded eyes focused on the flames flickering within the stone mantle to his right, his shoulders extra broad in his pale grey fleece hoodie.

Then Raven drank right after him, looking at him knowingly.

Selene tilted her head at the seemingly unbreakable pair. "Wait, really?"

Raven just shrugged, her eyes becoming distant. "It happens."

Damien said nothing, but his gaze didn't leave the fire.

Michael looked around, sensing that the air had become thicker, less loose, and reached for another card. "Okay, let's shake it off- next one."

He read, brow raised: "Never have I ever… only been with one person."

Selene blinked, slowly, then raised her glass and drank, looking directly at Caleb.

Caleb drank too- but something shifted behind his eyes, his fingers tightening around his glass.

Raven squinted at the 20-something pair, the shots making her sway already. "No fucking way?"

Selene nodded, smiling almost too brightly as she grabbed her still-new husband's hand. "Caleb and I are each other's first *everything*."

There was a heartbeat of silence, nothing but the crackling fire and amazement.

Laney's brows lifted in surprise, and then her expression became very soft, almost sympathetic. "That's... kind of beautiful."

"Y'all rare as hell for that," Damien added, not touching his shot glass for once.

Caleb looked away, his expression hard to read. His fingers tapped the table unconsciously.

Selene said nothing, but her large eyes narrowed at him.

Then, without pulling a card, she looked around the table and asked, very gently-

"Never have I ever done something I hope no one in this lodge finds out about."

The room went *still*.

Raven was the first to reach for her glass and drink, her eyes getting that same distant look. Selene's eyes lingered on her a bit longer than necessary.

Damien followed afterwards, eyes set on the ground.

Then Michael, shoulders tensing *hard*.

Caleb and Laney drank almost in sync, their eyes glancing at one another so quickly that no one, not even Selene, noticed.

Selene stared into her glass of vodka for a long, long moment.

She raised it to her mouth, the rim brushing her plump bottom lip.

Then, she lowered it again without taking a sip, smiling softly to herself.

Caleb's eyes narrowed at her this time, one of his brows lifted. She did a mischievous, identical brow lift in response.

Michael chuckled nervously. "Phew, the tension is *thick* at this table."

Selene smiled then, light, her eyes twinkling as the vodka was *hitting*, now. "Let's lighten the mood, then. Never have I ever… gotten arrested."

Then, to everyone's shock, Michael and Laney *both* drank.

*"No,"* Raven whispered dramatically. "The slut stuff, I can come to terms with. In time. But *this?*"

Michael leaned into his expecting wife with a proud grin. "It was *her* fault."

Laney smiled smugly, cheeks flushed despite not drinking any liquor. "And the cop was into it."

Laughter bloomed around the table as the tension began to melt like ash.

# Chapter 5

*Ruby Lights*

**25 April 2010- Rex, GA**

"Man, STOP!" Damien, now 15, coughed out in his bedroom as Xander, 14, practically drowned him in Axe body spray at 3 a.m. "You tryna kill me?"

"I'm tryna *help* you," Xander said, continuing to spray like it was something that simply *had* to be done. "You 'boutta get some, gotta be smellin' like it."

Damien finally shoved his younger brother away, shaking like a wet dog to get the extra spray off. "Man ain't nobody talk about gettin' some. I just wanna give her a lil' mixtape, that's it."

Xander tossed the now-empty bottle on the bed and plopped down on it, relaxing like he'd just done good, honest work. "Everybody know what come after a mixtape. Jus' don't make ma a grandma, she gon' kill *me* for bein' *related* to you."

Damien scoffed out a chuckle before he looked in the full-sized mirror. Low-fade clean, fake diamond studs sparkling in his earlobes, white tee crisp, jeans low enough to show his boxers but not low enough to slow his stride.

Jas wouldn't even know what hit her.

He grabbed a small Adidas drawstring bag and turned to his 1-year-younger brother. "You coverin' for me, right?"

Xander nodded with a smirk. "I gotchu. Jus' hope you do the same for me when *I* start pullin'."

Damien snorted, dabbing Xander up before opening the bedroom window and climbing out like he'd done it a hundred times. Which, he *had*, but not quite *this* late.

Luckily, his bedroom was on the first floor, so it wasn't a jump. When his brand-new Air Force Ones landed on the grass, he glanced around for witnesses- especially their neighbor Miss Bertha, who was somehow deep in the business of *everyone* on the block and beyond- before heading down the Amberwood street.

Eventually, he reached a green-shuttered brick ranch with a driveway hoop and a scooter tipped over in the yard. He glanced around again before going behind the house to a large, lightly curtained window.

He went into his bag and pulled out a Blackberry Bold with a screensaver of himself and Jasmine, taken in the mirror of his bathroom right after they'd gotten together and shared their first kiss upon 2008's arrival.

He scrolled through his recent calls, the most recent being *'Lil Mama <3'*. He clicked it, heart fluttering a little quicker than he'd expected it to.

"You here?"

"Yeah, I'm out here."

Slowly, the window opened, and there she was.

Hair freshly relaxed and pressed, swinging down her back like it had its own opinion. Huge gold bamboo hoops that brought out the shine of her skin. A baby-pink camisole over light-wash Apple Bottoms shorts that showed off her smooth, freshly shaven legs.

Damien blinked, his dark eyes flicking over her. "Jesus, ma."

Jasmine's full, freshly glossed lips smirked before she reached out her hands, jelly bracelets on each wrist. Damien took them, and she helped him inside, excitement glittering behind her brown eyes.

The two teens stood together, face to face, hand in hand, in her formal living room. The house was quiet and homey, walls lined with photos of Jasmine's family- here, and in Jamaica.

They never approved of her bond with the Black-American boy. She never cared about their approval.

"Happy birthday, boo," he said, pulling her flush against him with a soft peck on her lips. He relished the scent of her Victoria's Secret Love Spell lotion.

Jasmine savored the feel of the boy she'd loved for almost a decade and then coughed out a laugh. "Did you drown yourself in Axe or somethin'?"

Damien sighed. "You know Xan, man…"

But Jasmine wasn't finished.

Slowly, she gripped the hem of his tee and lifted it over his head, baring his torso and his unbelievably smooth, cinnamon-brown skin.

"That's better," she said with a sparkle in her large eyes.

Damien froze in place, heart thudding so hard it was visible at the base of his neck. "Jas…"

Jasmine smirked, taking his hand and leading him upstairs to her bedroom. "Shhh, if you don't want my parents to hear you."

Damien scoffed out a disbelieving laugh, shaking his head side to side. "You wild, girl."

It was around 3 a.m. when Damien stirred, limbs stiff against the hardwood, dreads messy.

Raven was sprawled across his chest, one of her creamy bare legs draped lazily over his hips. Her body was wrapped in the plush throw blanket that now covered them both with care.

Slowly, he remembered they'd gotten so drunk from the game that they went to the living room together for a game of "I Spy" and ended up falling asleep right there on the floor.

He frowned slightly, shifting on the wood.

The fire had died sometime during the night, leaving only a few faint embers glowing like dying stars in the massive stone hearth. Outside, the world was sunk deep in the hush of witching hour, black and crystalline. Tall floor-to-ceiling windows looked out on nothing but darkness and snow, the mountains reduced to jagged silhouettes against a velvet sky. A thin crescent moon hung low, its pale curve caught between the peaks, while a scatter of sharp, icy stars glittered overhead, refusing to yield to sleep.

Inside, the cabin felt warm and intimate by comparison, even without fire in the mantle. Soft golden light from a single lamp pooled across thick rugs and heavy timber beams. The air carried the faint, comforting scent of pine, smoked cedar, and the last traces of last night's drunken heat.

However… the blanket hadn't been there last night.

Neither had the fluffy pillow beneath his head.

He frowned slightly, shifting just enough to glance around the living room.

Then he heard it:

*Thock. Thock. Thock.*

At first, he assumed it was the hangover in his skull playing tricks on him, but when he heard it again, he carefully slid out from under Raven's arm and stood.

The sound drew him down the hallway, his heart thudding as he wondered if he'd actually catch a glimpse of the 'invisible' hosts.

And then… he saw *her.*

Selene stood at the kitchen island, bathed in soft golden light. She wore a silky ruby-toned robe that hung open just enough to reveal the supple swell of her cleavage and a hint of black lace beneath. A matching satin bonnet covered her hair, the deep red fabric framing her face like she'd stepped out of a dream. The robe clung gently to her curves as she moved.

She hadn't noticed him yet. Her thick-lashed eyes were focused on the wooden cutting board, where she was slicing fruit with quiet precision. Watermelon into perfect circles. Pineapple into tiny stars. Kiwi into delicate crescents. Each piece arranged with care on a tray, like she was composing something beautiful.

Damien stopped in the doorway, arms crossed, eyes narrowing slightly. He was still half-asleep, still wary of this performative woman… but he couldn't look away.

Finally, he cleared his throat. "Couldn't sleep?"

Selene jumped, pressing a hand to her chest like she was surprised. The motion caused her robe to shift, offering a fleeting, innocent glimpse of lace and skin before she quickly pulled it tighter around herself, cheeks warming with embarrassment.

"Oh my God," she breathed, a soft laugh escaping her. "Damien, you scared me."

She glanced down at her robe, then back up at him with a shy, self-conscious smile. "I didn't expect anyone else to be up."

Damien's gaze lingered for half a second longer than it should have. "Didn't mean to creep or nothin'. Just woke up… saw the blanket… heard the noise…"

Selene's expression softened at the memory. "You guys looked so uncomfortable on the floor. I figured I'd try to help."

"You put the pillow there too?"

She nodded, going back to her mango, carving another perfect star with steady hands. "I couldn't not. Those floors are *hard.*"

He studied her for a bit, then stepped further into the kitchen, his large, socked feet quiet against the warm wood. His eyes drifted to the cutting board- little bursts of color and symmetry.

"You do that a lot?" he asked, voice low.

Selene looked up, aureate eyes catching the light as she offered a small, serene smile. "It's just something that calms my mind."

She looked down at the fruit, then back up. "You want some?"

Damien couldn't help the faint smirk that tugged at his lips. "You gon' make mine look pretty too?"

Selene's smile deepened, soft and genuine, as she handed him a tiny sage-green plate of honeydew hearts.

Raven stirred awake grumpily, looking down at the fluffy blanket draped over her body with utter confusion, squinting around for Damien.

Right on cue, the bodyguard walked from the kitchen toward her with a tight smirk.

He stopped in front of her and handed her the plate.

Raven blinked up at him, her inky hair messy with sleep. "What the fuck?"

Damien snorted below his breath, whispering out, "I woke up, went to the kitchen, and that girl was doin' *this* shit."

Raven blinked at the plate, then up at him. "Selene?"

He barely nodded, looking over his shoulder to make sure the yoga instructor wasn't listening in. "Said she was makin' hangover smoothies 'cause she knew we would be hurtin'. At *three* in the damn morning."

Raven deadpanned.

"Okay. You were right. This bitch is fucking weird."

Damien pointed to the pillow and blanket. "She's the one who gave these to us, too. Just… saw us and put it on us. Like some creepy nanny or some shit."

Raven blinked down, then back up. "Oh my *God?*"

The power couple laughed and whispered in baffled confusion as they headed upstairs to their suite, leaving the pillow, blanket, and plate of fruit hearts behind.

The living room was too quiet- nothing like the cozy, lively space it had been just that morning, when the four of them sliced fruit hearts together to celebrate the day.

They could still hear Sade's "Smooth Operator" playing softly from the boombox as Lashawn and Youssef danced like newlyweds in the middle of the warm-toned kitchen, their laughter lighting the air like moonlight behind clouds.

A small sage-green plate of honeydew cut into perfect hearts- cut by Lashawn, of course- sat on the counter like a reminder.

Selene, 14, sat on the floor in her pajama pants and hoodie, legs crossed tightly, arms wrapped around 10-year-old Athena's trembling body. Her little sister's face was buried in her chest, her sobs sharp and breathless and endless.

Selene rocked them gently back and forth, her face pale and wet but set in stone.

"They're not coming back?" Athena asked between gasps, her little voice shaking.

Selene swallowed hard as her arms tightened.

"No, baby. They're not."

The words felt *wrong* in her mouth, *unfair,* like something only a stranger should ever have to say. But no one else was there to say it.

It had been two hours since the police left. Two hours since the whole world cracked open.

Their parents had gone out to dinner to celebrate their 15th anniversary. They were dressed up nicely. They had kissed them both goodnight before they left.

And now... just like that... they were gone.

Killed by a drunk driver who slammed into their Kia Soul head-on.

Athena's sobs came harder, her small fists curling into Selene's sleeves. "I want Mama. I want her to come back. I want to hear Baba's laugh again."

Selene buried her face in her sister's curls and held her as tightly as she could, her voice cracking with a stifled sob. "I know. I know you do. I do, too."

They rocked like that in the dark, the kitchen clock ticking way too loud in the background. The silence behind Athena's crying was *enormous*.

But Selene didn't let go.

"Listen to me," she whispered into her sister's hair. "Tatie is already on the plane from Fez. She'll be here soon. She's gonna move in with us. We won't be alone."

Athena whimpered, her voice hoarse. "What if she can't come? What if they don't let her?"

"She's coming," Selene interrupted. "No matter what."

She pulled back just enough to look Athena in the eyes, brushing her tear-streaked face with shaking fingers. Her own tears were still falling, but her voice was stronger now.

"You have *me*," Selene said, trying to will her tears to stop. "I'm gonna take care of you. Okay? I don't care what happens. I promise, Thena, I'm gonna take care of you forever."

Athena nodded slowly, eyes too wide for her face.

Selene pulled her back in, kissed her forehead, and held her tighter than before.

# Chapter 6

*Where the Light Won't Find You*

**New Year's Day 2003- South Boston, MA**

"No more change, I'ma change, what you call range. Tear this mother-father roof off like two dogs' cages!" Kevin rapped… or well… *attempted* to rap, his voice still squeaky. He wore a baggy tee plastered with Eminem's face in different expressions, baggy jeans, and a Red Sox cap that he, like the cool kid he decided he was, wore backward. From the Sony boombox his parents had bought him for Christmas, the instrumental version of the *8 Mile* soundtrack played out.

Kelly, 10 now, cackled on the living room floor of his triple-decker, her long red curls tied up with a couple of colorful scrunchies. "Kev, *please* choose another resolution."

Kevin looked at his best friend of almost four years like an enemy. "You're just jealous. *Everyone* can see I'm meant to be the next Slim Shady."

Kelly barked out another laugh, flipping her ponytail behind her. Her green eyes were even more piercing now, her freckles many, but endearing. "And *I'm* meant to be the next Rose from Titanic because I'm beautiful with red hair. Right?"

Kevin rolled his eyes and then plopped down beside her. His face suddenly turned serious, contemplative.

"Kells, we're gonna be *middle schoolers* this year. That's like… *grown.*"

Kelly stopped laughing immediately, processing his words like he'd just said something profound.

"Yeah. We can't let this year go to waste. We have to do something *big*. Something *no* other kid at Southie can do."

The two almost-preteens kept lying on the carpet, thoughts doing somersaults in their heads.

Then, Kelly gasped. "I know!"

Kevin lifted a brow. "You *know?*"

She stood up then, so quickly that Kevin didn't know how she didn't feel dizzy.

She grinned.

"We become the most popular kids in school."

Kevin looked at her for three seconds. "You act like we're not *already* the best kids at Southie."

Kelly shook her head, her sparkly Limited Too *'Drama Queen'* top matching her eyes. "No. That title belongs to *Saoirse Sullivan* and *her* crew." She said the blonde girl's name with scorn, resentment coloring her features.

Kevin sighed, his blue eyes suddenly glazing over. His once light blond hair was dirty-blond, now. "Saoirse is seriously the most prettiest girl I've ever seen."

Kelly kicked him in the shin, harder than she wanted to, making the boy groan. "What?! Have you *seen* her? You know it's true!" He wheezed out.

Kelly rolled her eyes. "Fine. I have an idea."

She looked at him then, something dancing in her eyes. "We get you with Saoirse Sullivan. *You* get your little crush, and *I* get to be best friends with the most popular boy in school. Before 6th grade, *everyone* will know our names."

Kevin grinned, wide and genuine. "*Now* you're talkin'!"

Kelly laughed, but a small pang slashed through her.

◐

Breakfast's golden envelope told the group to dress in their finest for dinner, as it would be a special one.

When they arrived in the dining room at 7 p.m., the transformation was nothing short of cinematic.

The tall windows were veiled with rich velvet curtains, casting the room in near-darkness. The only light came from dozens of electric candles scattered across the space, flickering to cast slightly eerie shadows along the walls.

Everything felt both intimate and theatrical. From speakers they couldn't see, Tears for Fears' "Everybody Wants to Rule the World" played out, giving the room a nostalgic yet haunting glow.

And the group? They came dressed to *kill.*

Raven shimmered in a skin-tight burgundy dress that hugged every curve of her hourglass figure like it loved it; her jet-black hair was slicked back into a low ponytail, revealing silver hoops. Her porcelain skin was unbelievably uniform, and, paired with her evergreen eyes, she looked *otherworldly.*

Damien stood proudly beside her in a fitted satin black button-up, top buttons undone, dog tags glinting against his lightly-haired chest. The sharp lines of his jaw were freshly edged, and his locs were tied back stylishly, revealing a tiny gold hoop in his left ear.

Selene wore a plum-toned long-sleeved silk dress that wrapped around her graceful frame like it was made for it. Her thick curls were set into a classy updo, revealing a pair of hanging lepidolite earrings that matched her dress perfectly. Her radiant golden skin shone even more than usual. In her hand was a mid-sized lavender clutch with teal accents.

Caleb stood at her side in a deep navy blazer over a white shirt, his golden hair combed back classily. His eyes, always a breathtakingly vivid Caribbean-sea color, absolutely *sparkled* under the dim lighting.

Michael kept it classic in charcoal slacks and a crisp white dress shirt, tucked and rolled at the sleeves with casual cool. His curls were just as messy as always- partly because he'd never really known what to do with them, and partly because he didn't really feel like trying, as the lack of Wi-Fi had officially begun to get to him.

Next to him, Laney stunned in a bump-hugging forest-colored gown that made her hazel eyes pop even beneath her glasses. She tugged at her neckline, muttering something about regretting wearing heels- but unlike her husband, she wore a genuine smile.

The table was always set for royalty, but tonight's dinner was something *else*.

On the freshly-shined oak sat roasted duck breast drizzled with pomegranate glaze, a glistening rack of lamb, truffle mashed potatoes, wild rice pilaf, endive and blood orange salad with champagne vinaigrette, platters of fresh figs and soft cheeses, tall flutes of sparkling chilled rosé and Dom, and fresh mango cut into tiny yet somehow still crisp star shapes.

And of course, a golden envelope lay at the center, as if it *knew* it was the most important thing in the room.

Selene reached for it with an excited little 'ooh', her full lips painted plum.

She opened it slowly, reading aloud in her usual smooth, gentle tone:

"You see each other, but can you see *through* each other? You *know* we couldn't host a group in a lodge without at least *one* murder-mystery dinner. Each of you needs to get into character and act your asses off. Just focus on that, for now. On the table are six small envelopes, and inside them are your character cards."

She paused and scanned the table, where six tiny, crisp, silver envelopes were placed before the seats, each of them carrying a different guest's name in handwritten cursive.

Raven breathed out. "Okay. I *still* don't know who the hell these people are, but they take this shit *seriously*. You *gotta* admire it."

Michael chuckled, though his internet withdrawals were still in full swing. He fidgeted with his collar uncomfortably. "I'm just glad there's booze," he muttered before throwing one of the full flutes of champagne back like nothing. Laney rolled her eyes at him.

Damien sat at the head of the table where his envelope rested. He opened it to reveal a sleek steel card that shone like a polished knife. His dark eyes squinted a bit as he scanned the engraving on it.

"I'm the detective. The one figurin' this shit out, I guess."

Raven sauntered to the seat beside him, where her envelope lay.

She opened it half-bored, read the steel card, and let out a dramatic gasp.

"Excuse me? The detective's 'meddling' wife? I was not informed I'd be in a *supporting* role."

Damien grinned and leaned close, nibbling her ear seductively, making her purr. "You the real boss anyway."

Selene smiled, excitement growing behind her eyes as she took the seat at the other end of the table across from Damien, near a plush bench. She opened her envelope and read:

"The femme fatale. Sexy, tempting, dangerous… and sleeping with the heiress's favorite bodyguard."

Caleb found his place beside her, pulling his card out with charm, though his jaw was tense as he slowly started to realize he might have to talk to… certain others.

"The heiress's favorite bodyguard. Apparently sleeping with the femme fatale… and the heiress."

Laney took her seat directly across from Caleb, jaw equally tight, and opened her envelope. When she read the role, she let out an exasperated sigh.

"The heiress. Why am I *not* surprised."

Michael plopped down in the seat right beside her, sighing in dread as if he *knew* his wouldn't be good. "Please be something sexy, please be something sexy…" he took out his card, and his face immediately contorted in genuine annoyance.

"The heiress's opportunist fiancé who's being cheated on? Oh, come *on!*" Everyone chuckled at that, but they couldn't deny that this was kind of exciting.

One by one, they stepped into their roles.

Laney cleared her throat, raised her chin, and tossed her golden waves over one shoulder like she was trying to embody the *epitome* of a prima donna. "As heiress to the Virelli estate," she said with a mock British accent, "I *demand* to be seated at the *center*. I refuse to dine in shadows like the *help.*"

Michael pulled his chair closer to hers and took on the stiff-backed charm of a yes-man. "Of course, my love. Anything for my fiancée. Your comfort is my priority. Well... and the prenup."

Laughter rippled around the table.

Caleb, seated right across from Laney, took a slow sip of Dom and leaned back. His voice was low, quiet, but sharp enough to cut.

"Kind of a shame I'm protecting someone who cares more about her *image* than her safety."

Laney's expression faltered. She blinked once, then smoothed her napkin in her lap, forcing a smile that still came off cold as glass.

"Even *more* of a shame that I have a bodyguard who doesn't know what *true* protection means."

The room went still. Selene glanced between them, sipping from her flute.

Caleb lifted his glass again but didn't drink, his expression stone.

"Hard to protect someone who's completely fine leaving someone else with shit they never asked to carry."

Laney didn't look at him directly, cutting her duck a bit harder than she meant to.

"It's hard *not* to leave someone with shit they brought entirely on themselves."

The candlelight danced between them like a fuse burning. Everyone looked at each other as if asking, *'Are you seeing this, too?'*

And then-

**Click.**

Every single electric candle blinked out at once.

Darkness swallowed the room *whole*.

Everyone gasped, genuine *fear* rising in the too-quiet air.

"Hello?" Raven said quickly, reaching beside her. "Babe?"

"I'm here, baby," Damien's deep voice answered as he squeezed her thigh protectively.

"Okay, what the hell-" Michael started, reaching blindly.

"Thaaat's not creepy at all," Laney said tightly, one hand on her belly, the other on Michael's knee.

There was a heartbeat of silence, and then a muffled thud.

"Selene?" Caleb's voice, tense now. "You there?"

No answer.

Just… silence.

And then-

**The electric flames flickered back on.**

And there, draped over the velvet bench behind the chair where she was once sitting, lay Selene, eyes closed, lips slightly parted, her silk dress folded neatly around her like she was ready for burial.

Everyone gasped, petrified.

Caleb nearly *lunged* toward her, but then-

Her eyes cracked open just a bit.

"My card told me to play dead when the lights went out," she whispered with a slight smirk on her lips.

Everyone let out the collective breath they didn't even realize they'd been holding.

Then-

"What the hell is *this?*" Raven muttered, looking down. Everyone followed her gaze to the table.

In front of each plate was a sheet of parchment, aged at the edges like it had been pulled from an antique desk. In ornate script at the top of each page read:

**Updated Character Details**

Beside them sat a large sand-filled timer- already draining.

And beside that? A *new* golden envelope.

"Oh, *hell* nah," Damien said, already rising to his feet.

He moved to the side of the table and inspected a wooden door behind it.

He turned the knob.

*Locked.*

"Guess our 'invisible' hosts watchin' from in there," he muttered, eyes narrowed in suspicion.

He returned to the head of the table and opened the new envelope with a tight jaw. He read:

"A murder has taken place. One of you is the killer; it will say so on your sheet. Do *not* tell anyone. Your sheet also has updated details on your relationships. You have ten minutes to figure out who the killer is. Good luck, lovebirds."

Everyone reached for their sheets. The room was sheathed in an uneasy quiet.

Then, one by one, they began to speak.

Caleb's voice was hard to decipher. "Apparently, the heiress recently found out I was also sleeping with the femme fatale." His eyes cut, just once, to Laney.

Laney let out a dry laugh. "And I wasn't even surprised. You've always been rather… *messy.*"

Caleb's jaw tightened as he forked his duck.

Michael raised an eyebrow. "My sheet says the femme fatale was my boss, and she fired me recently. So… it's safe to say I wasn't a fan of hers?"

Raven leaned back in her chair, lifting her parchment with casual ease. "Mine says the femme fatale and I recently got into a physical fight. But not why." She set the paper down. "All I know is, I definitely laid her ass *out.*"

Selene remained lying down, but she couldn't stop herself from smiling.

Damien flipped his paper, tone cool. "Mine just says: lead the investigation. So… leggo I guess."

He stood tall, dark eyes scanning the group with the sharp suspicion of a true detective.

"Which one of y'all had beef with Selene?"

Raven snorted. "Let's be real. Selene was *everyone's* opp. She fired Michael, fought me, and was fooling around with Caleb, who was Laney's side dick."

Caleb raised an eyebrow, clearing his throat. "Apparently, my character had… *flexible* standards."

Laney scoffed. "Flexible? Try *trash.* You were fucking your boss and her *fiancé's* boss? Who *does* that?"

Caleb leaned back with a shrug. "Maybe I like a challenge."

Laney's eyes darkened. "Maybe you like blowing up lives."

Another weighty, uneasy silence.

Selene couldn't help the small smile that curved her lips. She leaned forward on the bench, the low neckline of her dress catching the candlelight.

"Maybe the *real* question," she said softly, eyes flicking to Damien, "is who *benefits* from me being out of the picture."

Damien's gaze locked onto hers for a beat. His dark eyes narrowed slightly, trying to figure out exactly *which* kind of role the woman was playing now.

His voice dropped low. "Or *maybe* you was just collectin' secrets like you collect titles. Boss. Side chick. My wife's opp." He smirked. "Ain't no *tellin'* what else you was doin' in the dark."

Selene's eyes sparkled with mischief. "Careful, Detective. You're sounding less like you're trying to investigate, and more like you're trying to *scapegoat.*"

Raven gave Damien a playful smack on the ass. "Yeah, babe. Why're you sounding so pressed about a dead bitch's affairs?"

Damien chuckled, but his eyes stayed on Selene a moment longer. "Just doin' my job."

The timer continued to drain. Accusations flew back and forth.

Finally, the last grain of sand fell.

Damien stood, pulling the parchment from his pocket with a dramatic flair. He held it up for the group to see:

**YOU ARE THE MURDERER.**

Gasps, groans, and laughter exploded around the table.

"Noooo!" Raven shouted, clutching her chest in mock betrayal. "You? You? *You?!*"

Damien popped his collar, a prideful half-smirk on his lips.

Selene giggled, fixing the strap of her dress. "Go on. Read the reason why!"

Damien cleared his throat with a grin and read from his character sheet:

"You were having an affair with the femme fatale. Not just any affair- a deep, passionate *love* affair. When you found out she was also sleeping with the heiress's bodyguard, jealousy consumed you. You killed her during dinner prep… right before the main course."

Raven's mouth dropped. "THAT'S why I beat her ass!"

Selene snorted. "My character *clearly* had her fun, I see."

Damien, still grinning, sat back down and collected everyone's character cards, tucking them into his pants pocket like souvenirs. "I'm keepin' these. Framin' em or somethin'. I *killed* that performance. Pun and everything."

Raven plopped down on Damien's lap with a pout. "You better not ever cheat on me in real life. I *will* fight."

Damien snorted, squeezing her ass. "Havin' to deal with you every day got me goin' grey already. No way in *hell* I'm addin' another chick to the roster."

Laughter rippled around the table, everyone so tickled that they completely forgot about the locked wooden door at the side of the room.

# Chapter 7

*Slow Down for the Dip*

## 17 June 2012- Panola Mountain State Park

Crickets chirped like a thousand tiny violins, and the trees whispered above in the soft wind. A fire crackled at the center of the campsite, casting flickers of gold and orange against the night. On a large log, two brothers sat listening to Ice Cube's "You Know How We Do It" through a sleek new iPod Touch, a bag of marshmallows, chocolate, and graham crackers between them.

Xander, now 16 and already his big brother's height, leaned back on his elbow as he roasted a marshmallow to golden perfection. He nudged Damien with his shoulder. "Told you I could build a better fire."

Damien, 17, chuckled, shaking his head as he took the marshmallow and sandwiched it between chocolate and graham cracker. "You ain't built a better fire, bruh. You just found the dryer logs."

"Man, it's called *strategy,*" Xander said with a grin. "You be thinkin' too much."

They sat in silence for a few heartbeats, watching the fire crackle and pop as they made another round of s'mores.

Then Xander spoke again, his voice quieter this time, his gaze not leaving the flames for a second.

"You ever think about how *real* fire is?"

Damien took a bite of his s'more, shaking his head like he'd completely expected this. "Here yo poetic ass go."

Xander nudged him, focusing even more deeply on the flames. "Nah, for real, man. It don't fake nothin'. It's warm, bright, it dance, it *live*. But it can destroy shit, too. It don't apologize for what it is. *That's* what love suppose to be like."

Damien glanced at him. "Aight, man. What you tryna say?"

Xander's dark eyes were still fixed, his handsome features illuminated. He took another bite of his s'more, his voice soft, genuine.

"I know you still heartbroken over Jas. But y'all ain't have a *fire* love."

Damien's jaw tightened. "Hell you mean?"

Xan leaned back, a new softness in his eyes. "What y'all had was sweet. Cute. But it wasn't *fire*. It wasn't what ma and pops got. What our *parents* got? That shit is fierce. *Real.* It ain't always sunshine, and lord *knows* it ain't always cute. But you know they gon' haunt the *world* if they ain't buried holdin' hands."

Damien let out a laugh that was more like a nose exhale at the thought of their parents, who radiated love even when they argued and bickered.

There were a few more heartbeats of silence as the two brothers watched the flames dance and finished their s'mores.

Eventually, Damien leaned back with a soft sigh, the pain seeping right back in.

"I thought she was the one, man. We talked about weddings. Kids. I wrote *songs* about that girl."

He let out a shaky breath, tears beginning to pool in his hooded eyes despite himself. "And now she posted up with some other nigga like I never meant shit."

Xander leaned back, shaking his head slowly in disappointment at the actions of his brother's childhood love. "Man, he prolly gon' cheat on her before midterms."

Damien snorted. It was humorless, but it cracked something open- something that had been closed since he went on Facebook, saw that the love of his life had blocked him, then heard from a mutual friend that she'd posted that she was in a relationship with a football player at the college she was going to.

Just a week beforehand, she'd asked for a break to "figure themselves out since they were going to college now and needed to find who they were."

"Forreal, though," Xander continued, "All them college girls gon' be throwin' themselves at him tryna get clout, and I heard Georgia Southern got *fine* ones too. He gon' fold like a lawn chair."

Damien chuckled sadly. "Ion' feel like *me* right now."

"You don't gotta," Xander said. "That's why you got *me.*"

For a few heartbeats, there was nothing but the sound of cicadas, squirrels pitter-pattering, and crackling flames.

Then, Damien leaned back, eyes distant.

"You think that 'fire' kinda love out there for everyone?"

Xander nodded, more serious now.

"Yeah. But you gotta be open to feelin' the burn first. Carryin' matchin' scars, too."

Damien went quiet for a while, the flames painting his face in orange shadows. Then, slowly, he nodded.

The sun had barely risen above the treetops, casting a pale gold light across the tall, snow-dusted windows.

The dining room, as always, looked like something out of a dream- gleaming oak table, decadent dishes laid out in perfect balance, fruit cut like edible arrangements.

But something about this morning felt… different.

The air, usually laced with laughter or teasing, was quiet.

Not cold; not tense; just… still. *Heavier,* somehow. Like the walls themselves were waiting for something to drop.

The six filtered in one by one, dressed in varying shades of sleep and softness. The smell of warm biscuits, sizzling sausage, sweet, buttered grits, and cinnamon pancakes topped with strawberry roses should have made the room feel lively.

Instead, it felt almost *sacred,* like a hush had fallen across the table even before anyone had spoken.

In the center, beside a pitcher of Selene's signature hangover smoothie, sat the ever-present golden envelope.

She, as usual, reached for it, opening it gently. She read aloud:

"Good morning, lovebirds. For the last couple of days, you've had fun. However, fun is only *part* of what builds connection. The other part is *vulnerability.*"

She stopped then, glancing around at the others.

"*Shit,*" Raven, in a fitted black sweater dress that hugged her curves this morning, muttered under her breath. "Knew *this* was coming."

Selene bit her lip and then continued: "Today will *not* be easy- we can promise you that- but we can also promise that it will be worth it. After you eat, head into the sunroom; it's already unlocked. For now, let's open your hearts just a bit: Tell everyone what scares you the most about your relationship."

No one spoke right away; everyone wondered if they were really in the mood to crack themselves open at 9 a.m.

Finally, Selene spoke again, this time not reading.

"I trust Caleb," she began, turning slightly to glance at her husband. She wore a soft baby-blue sweater over leggings this morning, her fluffy curls cascading over her chest. "More than I've ever trusted anyone. That's why what scares me most is… being blindsided by him."

Caleb's brows twitched, just a little.

Selene went on: "I took his last name. Brown. That meant… God, that meant a lot. My father's name, Amrani, meant a *lot*. And I *still* gave it up because I wanted to belong to this new identity with Caleb. If it ever turns out he isn't who I think he is… I don't know what it would do to me."

Her voice had dipped into something fragile, cracking, tears filling her eyes.

Caleb held her hand tightly in his. "You have *all* of me," he said so low that only she could truly hear it. "Every part. I would never blindside you. Ever."

But his jaw was tight- his shoulders stiff.

Then he exhaled. "Honestly… I'm scared I don't deserve her. Selene's like… *perfect*. And I'm… not." Selene's eyes softened as she squeezed his hand.

Across the table, Laney swallowed and shifted in her seat.

"I worry about the same thing," she admitted, voice quiet. She wore a white cashmere dress that hugged her bump this morning, her golden hair in a low ponytail. "That I'm not enough. That Michael is so good and I'm…" she couldn't even finish, shame coloring her features.

Michael blinked and sat up straighter, wearing a blue flannel over sweats. "Laney. That's crazy. I feel the same way about *you.*"

She looked at him, startled.

He continued, jaw tight. "You… you know I'm addicted to the internet. And… and it makes me check out sometimes. And… I don't think I can stop. I don't think… I don't think I can *change.*"

Laney squeezed his hand, her eyes soft. "Michael, it's already been *four days*. You've done just fine without it. I've had *so* much fun with you here."

Michael smiled, but his shoulders were tense, his knee bouncing in a way it only did when he was *struggling* inside.

Damien and Raven shared a look- knowing, sympathetic.

"Yeah," Raven said first, "We got the same fear."

She inhaled, continuing. "We've both had our hearts broken by people we thought were our forevers. People we thought would never, *never* hurt us. That kind of break *changes* you. I don't think… I don't think I could survive it again."

Damien nodded. "Same here," he sighed out, wincing from the memory.

"But," he added, "Since we both know what that pain feel like, it keep us from ever puttin' the other through it. I'd *never* forgive myself if I broke Rae's heart. I think I'd rather *die.*"

Raven looked at him, pure love in her gaze. "Same here, baby."

Selene looked between them, hand tightening just so on her fork, before she continued eating.

# Chapter 8

*Let's Turn Forever, You and Me*

**19 June 2005- South Boston, MA**

The near-Summer air was thick with the smell of grass and the hum of cicadas as Kelly and Kevin, now 13, walked side by side down the quiet street. Neither of them spoke much; their shoulders bumped now and then, but instead of laughing it off like they used to, both went a little quiet afterward. Gorillaz' "Feel Good Inc" played through the earbuds they shared on a lime-green iPod Mini.

They ended up at M Street Park, where they had first met seven years beforehand.

The swings creaked in the breeze, and Kelly sat down on one, curling her sparkly-polished fingers around the cool chains.

Kevin stood for a second, shoving his hands in his pockets, before finally taking the swing next to hers. His once-blond hair was now a medium brown, making his azure eyes look even more striking.

Kelly tried *hard* not to notice them.

For a while, they rocked gently, back and forth, staring at the ground.

Kelly's heart thudded in her ears. This was crazy. She *knew* this was crazy. But the thoughts had been torturing her for the past three years as she watched her best friend and his girlfriend rule the school, and she couldn't take it anymore.

"Kiss me?" she blurted out, looking right at him with forced confidence.

Her red curls were longer now, reaching her mid-back. Her body was beginning to fill out in a way she wasn't sure if she liked or disliked yet.

Kevin? He'd been trying *hard* not to notice those... changes.

His face grew bright red at her blunt words. "Kells... *What?* I-"

"Saoirse... I know..." she began, kicking the dirt with her sticker-covered Converse.

"But... you need to practice, right?"

Kevin's face flushed even more, his eyes blinking rapidly. "Kells, Saoirse's parents won't let us kiss till we're 16."

Kelly stopped swinging, a flush growing on her own cheeks as she made direct eye contact with him.

"Even more reason to practice with *me.*"

The two new teens were still for a good ten seconds.

Then... almost at the same time... they leaned in.

The kiss was quick- barely a peck- but it made both of their hearts thunder in their chests, and both of their breaths pick up speed.

Kevin blinked as he pulled back, eyes dazed as they locked on her equally dazed ones.

"*Whoa.*"

Kelly giggled, her heart fluttering so fast it shook her breath.

"Whoa is right."

There were ten more seconds of silence.

Then-

"You wanna... do it again?"

She barely got the sentence out before Kevin leaned in again, catching her lips in a way that had both of them melting.

When he pulled back, he chuckled, blushing. "So… are *you* my girlfriend now?"

Kelly grinned.

"It's about *time* you figured that out."

◑

The sunroom was soaked in late morning softness. Pale sunlight drifted in through the floor-to-ceiling windows lining three walls, casting soft beams across the stone floor. Beyond the glass, tall pines swayed gently in the wind, the sky above them still tinged with early golden blue.

The group entered quietly, Raven leading. Something about the room, or maybe the day itself, felt *raw*. Like they might not go to sleep that night the same.

At the center of the room sat a round table, surrounded by six plush chairs.

On the table lay a golden envelope.

Selene, as custom at this point, stepped forward and opened it gently, her voice soft as she read:

"You'll complete two exercises together, lovebirds. First, answer the three questions below, aloud, with full honesty. Then, look into the mirror across the room and describe exactly what you see staring back at you."

Everyone turned to the right side of the sunroom, where a tall gold-framed mirror lined a window.

Raven scoffed with an eyeroll. "Of *course*."

Michael chuckled nervously. "Wouldn't be a couple's retreat without baring your soul to complete strangers."

Selene, used to being the soft-spoken leader from her yoga classes, sat down first. "Might as well just… get it over with."

**1.      What is your greatest regret?**

She looked down, pain evident in every one of her features, hands wringing nervously on her lap as if she needed to do something- *anything*- to distract her from her thoughts.

Finally:

"Not protecting someone I love."

She blinked, tears forming behind her eyes.

Caleb, recognizing what she was referring to, immediately squeezed her thigh.

Damien sighed, his hand tightening on his knee.

"Same."

Selene looked up, something genuine in her eyes. Damien met them, and they maintained eye contact for a few seconds before looking down in sync.

Raven sighed then, eyes shut.

"Trusting someone who would end up *destroying* me."

Her usually sharp green eyes suddenly looked dazed as they gazed beyond the windows at the mountains. Damien squeezed her hand knowingly.

It was Michael's turn to sigh, now.

"Ever getting into that… fucked up shit. It's…
It's *ruined* me."

Laney gasped, not having expected that from her husband.

He didn't even meet her eyes, his knee bouncing even faster now.

Laney looked down, then, gripping the hem of her dress.

"July 1st, 2012."

She said it so softly, it could've been a whisper.

Caleb winced, visibly, like he was hurt. And then:

"Same."

Selene looked between the siblings, something hard to read in her gaze.

## 2.  What is your greatest fear?

Raven exhaled. "I said this at breakfast, but yeah. Getting my heart broken again would kinda fucking suck."

Damien's gaze dropped to the table, his hand tightening into a fist on his knee.

"For me, my greatest fear ever is actually somethin' different. It's… It's lettin' someone I love down again. Doin' 'em wrong, especially after promisin'."

Selene nodded slowly.

"Me too."

Their eyes met for a second time.

Laney glanced at Caleb, then back at her lap, then, tentatively, back at him again.

"Becoming like our mom."

Caleb gave a slight nod, cringing slightly as if the thought *alone* affected him physically.

"Yeah. It… keeps me up at night."

The golden-haired siblings made eye contact again. Selene glanced between them both.

Michael sighed before responding, his usually goofy expression *gone*, now.

"That I won't win. That…the *demons* in me will."

Laney looked over at him, shock and a hint of confusion in her glasses-covered eyes. She couldn't imagine what her husband of six years could be referring to.

He didn't even meet her gaze.

### 3.    What is the worst thing that ever happened to you?

Caleb opened his mouth, but the words caught in his throat. His hands tightened into fists, and his face dropped toward his lap.

Selene rubbed his shoulder, worry flashing through her eyes. She'd never seen him like this.

Laney looked down. "We've been through things we're not ready to say out loud yet."

Caleb gave a grateful nod, leaning back into his chair.

Raven's voice cut through.

"Literally *everything* from that shitty May night."

Damien lifted her hand to his lips and kissed it, understanding exactly what his girlfriend referred to.

Selene looked at them with something heavy in her gaze, her knee bouncing unintentionally.

She closed her eyes for a moment, trying not to break down right then and there.

Then:

"Losing someone who meant *everything* to me."

Damien looked at the wall beside him, fingers gripping his dog tags. "Same."

Michael tapped the armrest.

"Ever starting that… mess. Because now… now I can't stop."

A heavy weight hung over the sunroom after that.

Then, Selene slowly stood up. She stepped in front of the mirror first, shoulders back, head high. She took a breath so deep it was audible.

Then:

"I see someone who's been through a lot. Things that almost broke her completely." Her voice wavered ever so slightly on the last word, as did her posture. Unconsciously, she rubbed a specific spot on her forearm.

She rolled her shoulders back.

"But she stitched herself back together… and now she's just trying to take her life back her own way."

No one said a word; there was a gravity in her voice that didn't need a response.

She stepped aside, and Caleb approached right after.

He stood tall, hands in his hoodie pockets at first, then pulled them out as he looked at himself.

"I see a guy with a great physique," he said with a smirk, earning a few chuckles.

But his face sobered just as quickly. "I also see the reason I had to become this way. I see the old me... the one I used to be ashamed of. Sometimes, still am."

Across the room, Laney shifted slightly, the movement so small it was barely visible. Her heart started to thud in her chest.

Raven stepped up next, her strut confident but her eyes not quite meeting her own reflection at first.

"I see a lot of armor," she said after a few seconds of silence. "The kind I was forced to put on after experiencing something I never thought I'd go through."

Her voice didn't shake, but her fingers twitched slightly. Selene's eyes lingered on her a bit longer than necessary.

When she stepped aside, Damien replaced her.

He stared at himself for a while before he spoke, something almost *vulnerable* in his dark eyes.

"I see a failure," he said at last, his voice lower than usual.

Selene gasped softly under her breath, tears stinging the backs of her eyes for a reason she couldn't quite explain.

He took a deep breath and continued, his impossibly clean dog tags glinting against his chest. "It don't matter how many brands I wear, how many people I protect... I probably always will."

He stepped away with a rare heaviness in his gaze. Raven immediately grabbed his hand, as if knowing exactly what he was referring to.

Michael came next, his hands stuffed into the pockets of his hoodie as he stood in front of the mirror. He tilted his head a little and gave himself a half-smile.

"I see someone who's funny, easygoing. The class clown, y'know?"

He paused. Then, "But under that, I see someone with demons. The kind you don't shake. The kind that eats you up from the inside out."

Laney furrowed her brows, knowing she'd have to ask him about this later. Selene gave him an unreadable look.

Then, Laney walked toward the mirror slowly, almost reluctantly. She folded her hands in front of her belly and stood still for a long time before she said anything.

"I see someone who tried really, *really* hard to run from her past."

She blinked once, then again, slower.

"But I think the past caught her a long time ago."

When she stepped away, her eyes were glassy with tears.

Caleb's were, too.

## 1 July 2012- West Philadelphia, PA

The birthday banner over the kitchen arch still hung from the party, pink foil letters spelling out '*Happy 23rd, Laney!*' in cheerful script. The apartment should have felt festive, celebratory, even.

It didn't.

It felt cold. Bleak.

*Haunted.*

Caleb stood frozen, his face pale as a ghost's, staring at a red-stained pile of broken glass on the ground like it could swallow him whole.

Laney stood across from him, one hand clutched over her mouth, her other arm wrapped tightly around herself. Her blue-highlighted hair was a mess. Her face was pale, blank, as if her mind had disconnected to protect itself from what had just happened.

Her gaze was fixed on the same pile of broken glass.

After ten more brutal seconds of silence, Caleb finally swallowed and spoke, his voice cracked.

"Lanes… I… I don't know… I don't know what just-"

"Don't," Laney interrupted, quietly yet firmly.

She didn't look up for a second.

Caleb looked at her with a pained look in his eyes. He hadn't seen his older sister like this since they were living in their mother's hellhole.

Finally, she met his eyes. "Please, just… don't finish that."

He shook his head; shame etched into each of his now-handsome features as he looked at the glass again- sharp and knowing.

"I… I don't know what came over me. I… I just… couldn't control it. It's like I… blacked out or something."

Laney didn't respond right away; her eyes locked on the ground again, her breath coming in a little faster, though it was obvious she was trying to calm herself down. She looked at her hands, which were shaking and slightly red-stained.

Then, suddenly, she moved. She blinked, once, hard- like snapping herself out of a trance- and turned to him.

"It's my birthday," she said, simply.

Caleb looked up at her, eyes confused.

She took a deep breath, jaw clenched, brain clearly working.

"July 1st. Remember what I told you? Every year on that date, something... unexplainable... happens in these apartments. *Every* resident has a story."

She paused then, suddenly, breath catching in her throat.

Caleb didn't say a word, but his fingers twitched at his side as his eyes roamed around the room like he was trying to confirm what his sister was saying.

"I never believed it," she continued, eyes downcast. "All that haunted apartment bullshit. I thought it was just rumors. But this? This is *proof.* There's something *in* here."

Her voice trembled for just a second, eyes shifting around nervously. "What just happened? It wasn't... you. *You* didn't cause it. It was-"

Caleb sighed. "Laney... you're in denial right now. That wasn't a ghost or a spirit. That was-"

"Stop talking," Laney interrupted, her voice suddenly much sharper. "You don't know what you're saying."

Then, without even looking at him, she left for her bedroom, locking it behind her, not to come out for the rest of the night.

# Chapter 9

*The Fairytale Life*

**19 March 2011- Queens, NY**

The bedroom smelled faintly of African Pride Braid Sheen spray and strawberry lip gloss. On the bed sat Selene, 15, her fingers deftly working through two sets of thick, fluffy blow-dried hair. On the small TV across the room, *The Cheetah Girls* played softly- the girls performing "Cinderella" with that empowering energy that always made them feel unstoppable.

It was both Athena and her best friend Imani's 11th birthday, and the three of them had turned the night into a mini slumber party. Athena sat cross-legged between Selene's knees, almond eyes glued to the screen as she snacked on star-shaped pineapple. Imani, beautiful with her chestnut skin and long hair, sat on Selene's other side, singing along under her breath.

The sky outside the small window was unusually clear for New York. A large, glowing supermoon hung low and bright, bathing the room in silver light.

"You're getting better at this," Athena mumbled, still watching the performance.

Selene smiled faintly, separating another section of Imani's hair with careful, practiced hands. "Because I have two test dummies, duh."

Imani giggled. "Hey! I'm not a dummy!"

Athena huffed, pretending to be insulted, then leaned back just enough to look up at her sister.

"What will your babies' names be?"

Selene blinked, caught off guard. "Huh? That was random."

"Me and Mani *always* talk about our babies' names," Athena said matter-of-factly as she nudged Imani's arm. "It's like… part of being a girl."

Imani nodded eagerly. "Yeah! My daughter will be Ruby, and Thena's daughter will be Sapphire. We planned this out *ages* ago."

Selene chuckled and went back to braiding. She was quiet for a couple of heartbeats as her brain contemplated. And then:

"I want Greek god and goddess names. Like what Mama gave *us.*"

Athena sat up straighter, suddenly excited. "Ooh! If you have boy/girl twins, you should name them Artemis and Apollo!"

Selene snorted incredulously. "That's *way* too on-the-nose. My kids deserve something more creative, more *niche.*"

Athena twisted her neck to give her sister a mock glare. Imani laughed, covering her mouth.

"Fiiiine," Selene relented with a grin. "Luckily, twins are rare."

They sat in that warm rhythm for a while-Selene braiding, the girls swaying slightly to the Cheetah music, giggling to themselves as they remembered when this first aired on Disney Channel and how starstruck the three of them were.

Then Athena said, quieter this time:

"I'm jealous of your name."

Selene paused, braid half-finished in her fingers. "Why?"

"Because Selene is the goddess of the moon," Athena responded softly, eyes still on the screen. "Athena's just the goddess of wisdom. *Boring.*"

Selene smiled softly. "Wisdom isn't boring. Wisdom builds kingdoms. Wisdom changes the *world.*"

Athena shook her head. "Yeah, but… the moon is better."

She turned toward the window and pointed with a small finger.

"Look at it."

Selene followed her gaze. The supermoon was still there, full and sparkling and impossibly big.

"The moon connects *everybody,*" Athena said softly. "Even if we're far apart, we can both look at it and know we're looking at the exact same thing."

Selene's breath caught in her throat. She stopped braiding unintentionally as her gaze settled onto the glass.

Imani nodded, eyes soft.

"And maybe, somewhere out there in heaven… Your parents are looking at it, too."

Selene felt tears sting the backs of her eyes, sniffling just slightly as her parents' presence suddenly felt tangible in the bedroom.

Then, she forced out a giggle as she hugged both girls' shoulders from behind. "You guys are getting *way* too deep for 11-year-olds. You need to act your little age."

Athena laughed, playfully swatting her big sister's knees. "You know it's true, moon girl."

Selene smiled, taking another look at the ever-connecting sphere outside.

# 7 January 2020- Evervale Lodge

The lodge was quiet in that holy, suspended way only 3 a.m. could bring. A fire crackling low in the mantle cast a glow across the wide-planked floor of the living room, but that wasn't the light Selene was focused on.

She stood before the grand window, her silhouette illuminated. She wore a silky champagne-toned robe that brushed the tops of her thighs, a thin gold anklet glittering above her right foot. Over her hair was a cheetah-print satin bonnet.

Outside, the trees stood frozen beneath a dark, navy sky, the moon lighting everything in an ethereal glow. It was a waxing gibbous this morning; so luminous, Selene could've sworn it was sparkling.

She was so focused on it that she didn't hear the stairs creaking behind her.

Damien came down slowly, wearing one of his old Army shirts, grey joggers, and black socks, his dreads down and slightly wavy around his face.

He paused at the landing when he saw her.

Selene stood perfectly still before the tall glass wall, arms wrapped around herself, gaze lost in the night. Her breath had fogged a small, perfect circle on the glass. The moonlight painted her in silver, softening the edges of her petite frame and making her look almost ethereal.

Damien stiffened slightly. That lingering distrust still sat heavy in his chest- the feeling that this woman was too polished, too *intentional.*

But something about the quiet way she stood there made him hesitate.

In the end, he continued down the stairs and settled into the large leather chair by the stone mantle.

The moment his eyes found the fire, they softened, drawn in by the dancing flames the same way hers were drawn to the moon.

The silence stretched between them, comfortable in its own strange way.

Finally, Selene startled, turning toward him with a soft gasp.

"Oh… hi."

Damien glanced over, his expression guarded but not unkind. "Couldn't sleep again?"

She let out a gentle laugh, tucking a curl into her bonnet. "I told you- I rarely ever do."

Her eyes drifted back to the window. "The moon helps. When my thoughts get too loud, when everything feels too heavy… I just look at her. She's always there. Steady. Quiet. Like she *understands.* "

Damien was quiet for a long moment, watching the fire flicker and pop. The flames reflected in his dark eyes, alive and warm.

"Fire does the same for me," he admitted, voice low. "When the noise in my head won't shut up… I just need to watch somethin' *burn.* Reminds me I'm still here. Still movin'."

Selene turned to him fully then, surprise flickering across her face. For the first time, she looked at him like she was really *seeing* him- not Raven's adoring boyfriend, not the imposing bodyguard, but the person carrying his own quiet burdens.

"I guess we all have something," she whispered, a small, genuine smile touching her lips.

They maintained eye contact for a second. Damien couldn't help but smile when he realized she was wearing the same bonnet his mother always wore.

For the next twenty minutes, the two insomniacs simply existed in the same space- her gaze fixed on the silver moon hanging above the mountains, his locked on the living flames in the hearth, the silence between them oddly comforting.

# Chapter 10

*Down to Mars*

## 1 July 2012- Rex, GA

The sun had just started climbing over the rooftops, casting a soft amber light across the dew-covered grass.

The house was quiet; everyone else had already said their goodbyes, offered hugs and tears, and given last-minute advice in hushed, emotional tones. Even Keisha "Kiki" King had come back from studying abroad to say goodbye to her oldest little brother.

But this moment wasn't for anyone else; this was for Damien and Xander.

They stood at the edge of the driveway, arms crossed, matching tension in their jaws, matching barely hidden sadness behind their dark brown eyes. Neither said anything at first.

"You really doin' this," Xander finally said, voice quieter than usual. "You really goin' away. For real."

Damien nodded, his duffel bag slung over one shoulder, already dressed in his issued hoodie and fatigues. His head, which had been covered in an unkempt, lopsided afro since Jasmine left, was freshly shaven- ready for a world where he wouldn't be able to check her socials and see her kissing another dude.

"Yeah. Shippin' out tomorrow, but you know Pops wanted to spend some time alone with me first. He probably already put on some damn OutKast in there." He looked back at the black 2009 Nissan Maxima behind him, and Andre King, his "high yella" skin making him *very* visible through the tinted glass, was already bopping his head to "Roses".

Xander let out a snort. "Man, you bet' not let basic turn you into one of them serious ass dudes who can't even laugh no more."

Damien smirked. "Please. I'll still clown your ass any day of the week, uniform or not."

They both chuckled, then went quiet again as the weight of the moment settled in.

Xander shifted on his heels, scratching the back of his durag-covered head.

"Aight. So... if you pass basic-"

"*When*," Damien corrected, eyes narrowing with a cocky edge. "*When* I pass."

Xander rolled his eyes, letting out a scoff. "Fine. *When* you pass..." His expression became more serious, more genuine.

"I'ma enlist."

Damien's thick brows furrowed, his entire body freezing in place. "What the hell you talkin' about?"

"I *refuse* to be the soldier's loser brother," Xander stated with a casual shrug. "If you go out there and crush it, I ain't about to sit around here while you get all the glory. Fuck that. I gotta do it too."

Damien let out a short laugh, his lips curled. "Yeah right. You just love me and wanna be around me. Don't lie."

"Please," Xander scoffed, then leaned in a little. "I just heard there's a whole stereotype that military dudes cheat on they girls a lot. Know what that *really* mean? That mean they get *hella* play in them barracks. I ain't missin' out on that."

Damien threw his head back laughing, loud and full-bodied. "You so damn dumb, man."

"I'm sayin' though!"

They laughed together until it softened into silence.

Damien looked his brother dead in the eyes like he wanted him to remember these words:

"If you join, you know I got you, right? Ion' promise much, but long as you with me in there? I *got* you."

Xander smirked. "You ain't even gotta tell me that, bruh. It's common sense."

Damien smiled then and pulled the 16-year-old into a strong hug.

"Take care of Ma," he said into his shoulder.

"I got her. Now, take care of *you.*"

They pulled back. Damien gave one last nod, then turned toward the car.

◐

The storm had rolled in just before sunrise, swallowing the once-crisp mountain air in shadow. Rain danced relentlessly against the tall windows, fogging the glass and making the unsteady pines outside blur into gray watercolor.

Every few minutes, thunder growled low in the distance, a slow warning rumble that made the floorboards almost tremble.

And with each crack of it, Selene flinched- just slightly, but enough that Caleb noticed, squeezing her thigh in reassurance.

She sat near the end of the table, curled into herself in all-black- a turtleneck and leggings- and her hands were wrapped tightly around a teal-colored knit hat.

She gripped it like letting it go would cause the thunder to swallow her whole.

Damien, seated on the opposite side, didn't flinch at the thunder, but his jaw tensed every time it hit, his fingers twitching. At 6'3, 220 lbs., he was usually the one shoveling food into his mouth at breakfast, but he hadn't even put a *biscuit* on his plate today.

Raven was the quietest she'd been since arriving. She moved like she was underwater- slow, dreamlike, her eyes distant even when she reached for food. Her lids were low, her jaw slightly slack.

Every three seconds, Damien leaned over to her, kissing her temple, whispering, "You ok?" in her ear. She always reassured him that she was, even as every crack of thunder made her look like she didn't want to be in her own body anymore.

The cracks affected Damien too, but he put his training to use, pushing down his own feelings for the greater good- which, for him, was always Raven feeling safe.

Even Michael, who was usually the one cracking jokes over breakfast, was quiet. The storm pressed against all of them like something physical.

At the very center of the table, right where it always was, sat a golden envelope.

Selene didn't have it in her to reach for it this time, her eyes trying *hard* to avoid the storm that raged behind the massive windows, so Caleb went for it, opening it with steady hands.

He read aloud, his voice a little lower than usual:

"Good morning, lovebirds. The past couple of days have been full of sweet activities with your partner, but we think it may be time for a twist. You will be switching partners for a day. Your partner and activity today are as follows: Caleb and Laney in the ballroom; Michael and Raven in the yoga studio; Damien and Selene in the art studio. After all, you can't *truly* know what you have until you experience something different."

Caleb froze, jaw tightening visibly when he realized he'd have to be alone with his estranged sister for the first time in seven years.

Before he knew it, an image of broken glass on linoleum flashed through his mind.

Laney looked up at him from her seat with quiet disbelief.

"…Oh."

Caleb's mouth tightened.

"Well. That's… unexpected."

"Very," Laney muttered, then glanced down at her plate, focusing *hard* on her eggs.

Michael scratched the back of his neck, glancing toward Raven.

"Guess I'm your yoga buddy, Morticia."

Raven didn't even look at him, her eyes glassy, unfocused. "Cool."

Damien squeezed Raven's thigh before whispering, "You gon' be okay?"

"Yeah, King. I'll be fine."

But her head nodded to the side despite herself, and she shook it just to wake herself up.

He leaned in close, protective. "If there's ever a minute where you don't feel okay, I'll be there, aight? Call my name. I'll be on high alert."

Raven nodded, eyes gazing towards the lightning flash beyond the window.

Damien looked over at Selene then, jaw tight. He felt a little more comfortable with the yogi after their late-night moment, but this was new territory.

"Guess it's you and me?"

Selene gave the smallest nod.

"Art studio, then."

Outside, the thunder cracked louder this time, deep and jagged. Selene flinched again, and Damien shut his eyes.

# Chapter 11

*An Unlocked Place*

## New Year's Day 2013- West Philadelphia, PA

Laney stood frozen in front of the full-length mirror, her arms wrapped around herself, eyes wet and red-rimmed. Her shiny, golden hair was beautifully done up; so beautiful that it looked almost *sinister* against the dark air of the bedroom. Her makeup was immaculate. Her navy-blue halter dress sparkled like the starry sky beyond the small bedroom window.

Fireworks were still going off in the distance. People were still up partying, still celebrating 2013's arrival that had happened three hours beforehand.

But Caleb and Laney?

They had *nothing* to celebrate.

The silence stretched until finally, Laney spoke. Her voice was low, almost a whisper, but the pain behind it was unmistakable.

"I… I know it's the apartment. I know it's the ghosts. But Cabe…"

She looked at the 19-year-old young man, now taller, broader, and better dressed because of how well she'd been caring for him for over a year now, tears falling freely from her green-flecked eyes.

"I can't handle this anymore."

Caleb's head turned slowly, eyes narrowing.

"What? W-… What are you saying?"

She looked away, like she couldn't stomach seeing the look on his face after she said the words. She swallowed so hard it was visible.

"I'm sorry… but I think you need to leave."

He winced like she'd slapped him.

"You're kicking me out? You're putting this on *me*?" His voice cracked with betrayal.

"Laney, *I'm* not-"

"I *know!*" She said, much louder than she meant to, still looking at the ground. "I know it's not you, and I'm not blaming *you*. But… but God, there's only so much of this I can *take.*"

Her eyes finally moved to meet his. They were red, pure heartbreak in them, like she didn't want to say these words, but she knew she had to.

"Caleb, tonight, at the NYE party… Michael…"

Caleb's face suddenly went pale, his eyes widening in horror.

"No. *No.* Does… does he-"

Laney shook her head, quickly, too quickly. "No. God no, thank God, no, he doesn't. But he-"

"But he *what?*" Caleb asked, his eyes narrow. "But he *what,* Laney?"

Laney started crying harder now, tears spilling down her chest.

Caleb scoffed out a chuckle then.

"Oh. Of *course.*"

He looked right at her, betrayal deep in his eyes. "Of *course.* Because why *wouldn't* you do this? Why *wouldn't* you care about your image more than what actually matters? You're mom's *daughter,* after all."

Laney flinched like he'd just slapped her.

"Fuck you, Caleb. *Fuck* you."

She stomped past him then. She put her hand on the doorknob, staying there for about five seconds, before opening her mouth, her voice low and final.

"Before Michael wakes up in the morning… You need to be gone."

◑

The half-siblings walked into the spacious, fairytale-like ballroom like they'd have preferred to be *anywhere* else.

On the sleek grand piano in the center of the room was a speaker, and next to it was a handwritten note that simply read:

*"Dance away."*

They stood awkwardly for a second, not knowing how the hell they were going to go from seven years of silence to… dancing.

After five more seconds, Caleb finally turned to her. "You… doing okay?"

She looked at him, surprised that he'd even asked.

She gave a small nod. "Yeah. Actually. I am."

She tilted her head, studying how much he'd changed over the years. "You?"

He hesitated for a heartbeat, then shrugged. "Getting there."

The silence came again, but it wasn't as sharp this time.

Caleb glanced down, fingers tapping the impossibly clean surface of the piano.

"Did you… Did you get my email?"

Laney looked at him more fully now, her eyes softer. "Yeah. I got it."

Caleb exhaled through his nose, his jaw tight.

"Didn't even bother to respond?"

She gasped slightly, hurt in her eyes.

"You didn't get my response?"

It was Caleb's turn to gasp then, the resentment he'd been carrying for 18 months melting in one moment. "No… I… I didn't."

Laney let out a quiet sigh, smoothing her palm over her belly. Her face suddenly held a tension that wasn't there before, her feet shifting onto her heels.

"It was probably for the best that you didn't."

After five seconds of the loudest silence they'd ever heard, Laney turned to the speaker with the tiniest smile. "Remember that dance routine I taught you for your prom? Had to be like… God, 2010 or something. I came back from Penn just to teach you."

Caleb snorted. "Ellie Goulding. 'Lights', I think."

Laney let out the softest smile, then. "Wanna… do that again? Just to I don't know… pass the time?"

Caleb smiled, though he couldn't deny that he felt a ton of relief. "Let's do it."

## New Year's Day 2013- South Allentown, PA

The chipped paint on the porch peeled like old sunburn. The storm door let out a long, shrieking whine as Caleb stepped through it and into the suffocating warmth of the trailer. A baby screamed somewhere in the back. Someone else laughed in that grating way only people plastered before noon could manage.

He set his duffel down in the corner, jaw clenched like he already regretted this. Then:

"What a *surprise.*"

Deborah Miller walked in holding a half-lit cigarette, her tangled bleached-blonde hair up in a messy bun, wearing a leopard-print robe over a stretched-out tank top. Her face was leathery- far too aged for just 37 years old.

"You got a phone, don't you?"

Caleb blinked, his face already contorting in annoyance. "Yeah."

"Well, let me see it."

He stared at her, eyes narrowed. "Why?"

"I need to make sure you're not bringing any *bullshit* into my house."

The "house" she spoke of was currently filled with precisely that: two random homeless-looking men nodding off on the couch. Kids ran screaming down the hallway. The smell of weed, stale beer, and body odor mingled in the air.

Caleb gave a dry laugh. "Right. Wouldn't want to pollute this *sanctuary.*"

Her green eyes narrowed. "Don't get smart. Gimme the damn phone."

Caleb's hand tightened around it. "Dude, this is *my* business-"

Deborah snatched the phone with surprising strength and began scrolling with a cracked nail on her finger, smoke curling from her lips.

Caleb stood still, eyes closed, jaw tense, shoulders high. Then-

Deborah's piercing, *horrified* scream filled the stale air.

# Chapter 12

*If I Give All My Love*

## 22 May 2010- South Boston, MA

The gym lights cast a golden glow on the shiny streamers and balloon arches that screamed "prom night." The DJ was spinning some kind of mashup of every hit song of the time- mostly Ke$ha, naturally.

Kevin adjusted the crooked crown on his head with a grin. His hair had darkened to a debonair chestnut brown over the years, and it was swooped in the ever-trendy "Bieber" cut. His eyes, though, were the same heartbreakingly deep blue that Kelly had loved since the moment she first saw them in that sandbox and claimed him as her best friend.

"This feels fake," he muttered, laughing as he tugged at the collar of his rented but crisp black suit. "I thought I'd feel more… I don't know. Royal?"

Beside him, Kelly, 18 now, glowing in a champagne satin dress that hugged her now striking, curvaceous figure, lifted her own sparkly crown and gave him a sideways smirk. "Fake? Kev, we've been royalty since *6th grade*. The *adults* just finally caught up." Her hair was somehow even redder now, straightened so that it flowed down her back like a waterfall of lava.

The crowd cheered around them as the principal, a short, stocky, bearded man who looked like he'd just come back from the pub, finished announcing their names through a staticky microphone.

"Let's give it up for our 2010 Excel High Prom King and Queen- Mr. Kevin Murphy and Ms. Kelly O'Connor!"

The gym erupted in claps and whoops. Someone shouted, "Southie's golden couple!" while another added, "It's like a movie, I swear!"

When they made that New Year's resolution to be the most popular kids in school… well, they meant it. He was the star quarterback. She was the head cheerleader. If you weren't on K&K's good side? You were *nothing*.

The high school's golden couple took their slow, practiced walk down the makeshift stage- his arm slung comfortably around her waist, hers wrapped just above his elbow. Both of their heads were high like they'd completely expected this. Because, naturally, they *had* expected this. They'd worked for it, after all.

Students on both sides snapped photos with digital cameras and iPhone 3s, calling out compliments like they couldn't even help it:

"Kev, you clean up nice!"

"Kelly, you're legit glowing!"

"They're gonna have the most beautiful children, oh my God."

"They're *wicked* perfect together!"

Even Saoirse Sullivan, Kevin's ex "girlfriend" whom he dated from age 10 to 13 (until Kelly so *rudely* stole him away with a kiss), couldn't help but clap, a reluctant but real smile on her doll-like face.

K and K made their way to the dance floor as the opening beats of Drake's "Find Your Love" started playing, and Kevin snorted.

"Really? *This* is our slow dance song?"

Kelly rolled her eyes fondly. "It's *2010*, Kev. What'd you expect, Sinatra?"

Kevin laughed, pulling her in gently, his hands resting on her round hips. He couldn't believe what a breathtaking young woman the fiery 6-year-old girl from the playground had grown up to be.

"You know," he said, voice dropping a little lower as he kissed her ear seductively, "We really are *that* couple, huh?"

She smirked, resting her chin on his broad, football-trained shoulder. "Yeah. The ones in the yearbook everyone remembers."

Kevin smiled teasingly. "*Or* the ones people say peaked in high school."

She laughed into his neck. "Speak for yourself, Murph."

They swayed together, oblivious to the camera flashes and whispered envy around them, their lips meeting like magnets every now and again.

◐

The yoga studio was even nicer than Raven thought it'd be:

Tall windows that had a stunning view of the pines, even with the heavy storm making them thrash violently; lanterns glowing warm orange hanging from the high ceiling, an array of plush lavender and teal mats, paintings of the moon in different phases, and freshly watered plants scattered throughout.

Michael stepped onto a mat, looking up at the poses the hosts taped to the mirrored wall for them to follow. He wore a T-shirt and sweats, not having exactly prepared for stretching.

"Okay… Warrior Two?"

Raven blinked from across the room, where she sat slouched on a mat, legs crossed lazily. She managed to dress for the occasion in a crimson sports bra and biker shorts set, but she didn't look like she was even *close* to capable of stretching at the moment.

Michael smiled, trying to ease the vibe. "That's the one where we look cool and strong like ancient statues, right?"

Raven didn't answer right away- like there was a lag somewhere deep within her.

After five too-long seconds, she muttered, "Sure. Whatever you say, yoga king."

He furrowed his brow but didn't push. He moved into position, arms extended, and looked at her again.

Raven didn't move at all.

He hesitated. "You okay, goth queen?"

Raven shrugged. "I'm just tired. The fucking bed here is…" She yawned, a soft, eerily blank smile spreading across her face. *"Amazing."*

Michael gave her a long, concerned look. "If you want to just chill, we can. No one's grading this."

She gave another languid shrug. "No, I'm fine."

They moved into a different pose- Triangle. Michael shifted with slow care, but Raven's movements were sluggish and uncoordinated. She winced slightly as she bent forward, and he looked at her worriedly.

# Chapter 13

*Crystal Raindrops*

## 1 May 2013- Queens, NY

Selene, now 17, sat cross-legged on her twin bed, her comforter folded neatly beneath a sea of psych textbooks, highlighters, and fraying index cards. The radio, as always, was on her parents' favorite station, and Grover Washington Jr.'s "Just the Two of Us" played out softly, now.

"Lena… focus…" she muttered under her breath as she zeroed in on a passage. If she really wanted to go to NYU for psychology and publish her own research articles on love and relationships? She *needed* to focus.

She was so locked in that she didn't notice her bedroom door opening until-

"Lena?"

Selene glanced up to see Athena, now 13 and getting prettier and prettier each day, standing there, her curls freshly straightened, schoolbag still slung over one shoulder, cheeks flushed from the spring chill.

"What's up, Crystal Queen?" Selene asked, setting her pen down and smiling warmly at her sister.

Athena stepped inside slowly, the raw amethyst around her neck matching the rims of her cat-eyed glasses, the silver heart pendant of her bracelet reflecting the soft light.

"I was wondering… Do you think…" Her tone was hopeful yet hesitant, like she knew she might not like the answer.

"Do you think you could come with me on my band trip to Disney this weekend?"

Selene's heart tightened at that. She reached out and tugged her down beside her on the bed.

"I would love to," she said gently, "but my finals are next week, Thena. I need to get all the studying I possibly can *done* this weekend."

Athena's face fell a little, but she nodded. "Yeah. I figured."

Selene studied her little sister's face. She had their father's deep-set eyes, their mother's upturned nose, and a mixture of their skin tones, giving her the loveliest bronze glow.

Selene's eyes softened; she wondered how their parents would react to seeing them both so "grown up", now.

She sat up straighter and reached for the small shoebox tucked in the corner of the closet. "Okay, then come here."

Athena raised a thick brow as Selene opened the box and pulled out two carefully folded knit hats. One was a soft lavender, the other a lovely teal- Athena and Imani's favorite colors. One hat was stitched with a moonstone cut into a waxing crescent, the other with one cut into a waning gibbous. Together, they made a full moon.

"I was gonna give these to you and Mani when you came back to celebrate your big performance, but… here."

Athena's eyes widened in pure awe. "You *made* these?!"

"Me and Tatie," Selene said with a grin. "She did most of the stitching. I chose the yarn and the stones. Those moonstones are the real deal, too. Burned my whole Starbucks paycheck on them."

Athena squealed. "Oh my God, this is real moonstone?! Like, *real* moon magic?!"

She held both hats against her chest, then picked up the lavender one and placed it proudly on her own head.

"I'm giving *you* this one," she then said firmly, handing Selene the teal hat.

Selene raised a brow. "I don't even *wear* hats."

"You do *now*," Athena said with a pleased smile. She stood about four inches taller than her 5'1 older sister now, having taken more after Lashawn in height, while Selene had taken completely after Youssef's diminutive side.

She rolled her eyes fondly, tugged on the beanie, and posed dramatically. "How do I look?"

Athena squealed. "Oh my God. Wait a second."

She darted out of the room before Selene could ask what she was doing. Selene sighed, pulling the hat down over her ears and turning back to her notes with a soft smile. She'd barely highlighted one line when the thundering of footsteps and the clatter of bracelets announced Athena's return.

Except… she wasn't alone.

"Tatie?" Selene blinked as Inas waltzed into the bedroom like she owned it- tiny, dazzling, and dressed like she'd just come from a wedding instead of a weekday afternoon. A silk scarf the color of pomegranates framed her face, gold bangles chiming with every gesture.

"Girls!" She sang, arms thrown open as if she could scoop them both up despite her 4'9 frame. "Look at you two! Like stars- *mashallah!*"

Athena beamed. "Tatie, can you take our picture in these beautiful hats you made?" She thrust her phone toward her aunt, practically vibrating.

Inas drew back as though Athena had offered her a live snake. "I will *not* use a phone. Those things steal your soul!"

Before either niece could protest, she whirled out of the room- tiny sandals slapping down the hall- and returned triumphantly, clutching a Polaroid camera the size of her head.

"*This,*" she declared, dusting it off with great ceremony, "is *real* photography. Hold still- smile like you have good husbands and rich futures!"

*Click- whirr.*

The flash went off, the film hissed out.

Athena and Selene blinked through the dazzle as their aunt fanned the photo in the air like a magic card.

"Perfect," Inas announced. "I will keep this forever. *Or* until one of you becomes famous marriage-and-family therapist," she winked at her oldest niece. "*Then,* I sell it."

The three of them laughed as Inas beckoned them downstairs for a hearty dinner of chicken rfissa and msemmen.

Selene took a look at the Polaroid photo with a soft, genuine smile before meeting her two best friends downstairs.

The art studio was lovely- tall, arched windows, stone walls, real paintings of planets and other celestial bodies seemingly created by previous guests, and a grand easel in the middle of it all, surrounded by small mason jars of paint in every color you can fathom.

But, despite its beauty, the storm clouds cast a dark wash over everything, making the air feel somber, almost *mournful*. The hum of rain against the roof was interrupted only by the occasional boom of thunder- each one louder than the last, like it was chasing them and getting closer and closer and-

Selene let out a shaky, tortured breath as she stood at one side of the large easel, Damien at the other. Neither spoke much, if at all, but both wore black tops and bottoms today, matching both each other and the vibe.

The image that formed between them on the canvas was unintentional but surprisingly cohesive: dark, swelling clouds and thick raindrops.

Selene dipped her brush in silver to draw another drop, but her hand trembled slightly, making the line jagged.

Damien noticed, but said nothing, his own shoulders stiffening with each thunder crack. He forced himself to focus on the easel, but his struggle was palpable, his jaw so tight it looked painful.

Then came the loudest crack yet. A flash of lightning lit up the studio.

Selene flinched, hard, gasping unintentionally.

Her paintbrush slipped from her hand and clattered down, smearing silver over the hardwood.

She took a sharp breath- then another- then crumpled onto the floor, her arms around herself, shoulders shaking.

The sound that escaped her was quiet but unmistakably broken as she grabbed at the hardwood for stability.

Damien froze, lowering his own paintbrush to his side. "Selene…"

She didn't answer at first. Her face was turned toward the window, her thick hair shielding most of it. One tear traced a path down her cheek as her breath shook, quiet little sobs coming out despite herself, her shoulders shaking like they'd been carrying too much and just couldn't anymore.

He took a cautious step closer, the sight of the usually polished woman in shambles making his heart clench. "Hey… you aight?"

She shook her head, still facing away. "I don't know why I'm…" Her voice cracked. "I'm sorry."

"Don't be," Damien said, quieter now, a gravity in his tone as he began to crouch down. "You don't gotta be sorry."

Selene finally looked at him. And when their eyes met- hers glassy with tears, his focused yet open- something shifted.

Maybe it was the storm. Maybe it was the silence. But she felt it with unquestionable truth:

This man wouldn't hurt her with what she was about to say.

She inhaled, slow and shaky, her fingers tightening around her teal knit hat.

"Almost seven years ago," she began, her voice barely above a whisper. "On the 4th of May…"

A heartbeat passed. Another crack of thunder rolled across the sky, making her visibly flinch again.

"I found out my sister died."

## 4 May 2013- Queens, NY

The storm had been roaring all night, and it was still going strong at 5 a.m. Thunder cracked so often it stopped being startling. Rain lashed the windows with an unrelenting rhythm, and lightning lit up the small living room in flashes that made everything feel surreal.

Selene sat cross-legged on the living room floor, her laptop open in front of her, surrounded by notes and open textbooks. Her highlighter squeaked softly across a page as she muttered theories under her breath, trying to will the information into her brain even when she was running on fumes.

Her final exam for AP Psychopathology was on Monday. She had been studying for hours, headphones in one ear, the other left open to the sound of the storm.

That's when they came.

Three knocks- heavy and deliberate.

Familiar in a way that made her stomach twist *violently*.

Before she could move, a bedroom door creaked open.

Inas stepped out in her robe, dark curls wild, eyes already wide with worry. "What going on?"

They looked at each other for one terrible second, dread in their hearts.

Selene rose on shaky legs. Inas moved to her side, and together they approached the door, already feeling sick, already trembling.

Two officers stood on the other side, soaked from the rain. One wore a uniform; the other, a plain black coat with a visible badge.

Both had the same expression: solemn, practiced empathy.

They started speaking, but nothing registered.

All the aunt-niece duo could hear was the broken, agonized *wails* they let out as they collapsed into each other.

◐

"She asked me to come with her on that Disney trip," she said through tears. "I told her no; I told her I needed to study for finals."

She inhaled shakily. "Every day, I wonder what would've happened if I'd just gone with her. If I could've saved her. If she's gone… because of *me.*"

She clinched the knit hat again, her tears soaking it.

She continued, barely able to get the words out. "It was storming. Since then, every time it storms… It's like I'm right back in my old living room. Hearing those *awful* knocks."

For a while, the only sound was rain tapping against the roof.

Damien didn't speak. He just crouched down in front of her, slowly, his always-tired eyes carrying an even heavier weight.

He reached for the dog tags around his neck- the ones he never took off- and gripped them in his fingers like a lifeline.

Then, quietly:

"On that same day…"

Selene looked at him, tears still falling from her large eyes.

His jaw tightened, his eyes flashing with something *tortured.*

"I lost my brother."

## 4 May 2013- Kandahar Province, Afghanistan

Dust clung to every surface, thick in the air and thick in Damien's throat as their convoy rumbled along the ragged road cutting through the valley. The chatter in the Humvee was light but clipped, like everyone felt something off in the air but didn't want to name it.

Xander, 17, sat beside Damien, 18, helmet crooked, smirk the same. "After this mission, I'm beatin' your ass in Spades. You been lucky for *way* too long."

Damien rolled his eyes. "You say that every time, and yet I *embarrass* you every time."

"Man, shut up," Xander laughed, eyes squinting under the Afghan sun. "Annoyin' ass."

Damien grinned- just for a second.

Then the world **cracked.**

The Humvee lifted, tilted, and then *shattered.* Damien was thrown sideways, slammed into something hard, his helmet snapping back. The air left his lungs. He couldn't hear anything for a moment except the high-pitched ringing in his ears. His mouth was full of blood.

He groaned, forcing himself up, disoriented and choking on the smoke. The blast had torn open the side of the vehicle.

Then, he saw Xander.

He lay in the dirt, unmoving, legs twisted unnaturally.

"No… no no no no- *Xan!*"

Damien scrambled toward him, knees buckling under him, palms raw from crawling through debris. He slid into the dirt beside his brother, gripping the front of Xander's vest.

"Stay with me, *stay the fuck with me, man-*"

Damien pressed his forehead to his brother's and sobbed, desperate and feral. "Goddamn it… I promised- I promised you. I *promised.*"

And all Damien could do was scream his brother's name into the burning sky.

◑

The storm had quieted to a soft, distant rumble, but its weight still lingered in the spacious room.

Selene sat still on the hardwood; her fingers still curled tightly around the knit hat in her lap.

Damien inhaled, his breath shaky.

"Storms… they bother me, too. The way the thunder roars… it remind me of the blast."

He unconsciously reached to grip his dog tags.

Selene's tearful gaze fell to them. She'd noticed them, noticed he never took them off, noticed that he gripped them whenever he was uncomfortable or lost in thought or when he was looking at fire- but she hadn't ever thought to read the engraving on them.

Her vision was still a little watery, but she could just make out the words engraved there:

*King, Alexander Malik.*

Her chest ached as more tears stung the back of her eyes. One slid down her cheek as her breath began to shake, her hand twitching on her lap.

And then, almost before she could think, she reached up and pressed that hand- small, warm, and trembling- over his metal tags.

Over his heart.

Damien stiffened, just for a second, not expecting it.

He looked down at her hand, his breath coming in heavier.

Then, quietly, without a word-

He lifted his much larger hand and placed it gently over hers.

For a long time, they stayed like that- crouched in front of each other on a paint-stained floor.

The storm was still loud- thunder was still booming- but they didn't even notice it anymore.

All they noticed was the look in each other's eyes- a look they never thought they'd be able to see in anyone other than themselves.

Then-

Selene blinked, pulling back quickly, like being jolted out of a haze.

"I think it's time for dinner," she said, wiping the last of the tears from her face. "Time really flew today."

Damien exhaled through his nose and nodded. "Yeah."

They stood and walked out then, the canvas behind them still half-painted in storm gray and silver.

# Chapter 14

*Remember the Rain*

## 24 December 2013- Queens, NY

Selene, 18 now, sat in the passenger seat, arms folded tight over her chest, her head pressed lightly against the cold window. Since May, she'd been shaving her head regularly, not having the energy for hair care, nor the stomach to look at the same thick 3c curls that Athena rocked proudly.

The car door swung open with a creak, and Inas, still attempting to appear somewhat put-together with a headwrap and hoops, hopped in with a dramatic *hmph*. A thin plastic bag rattled in her hand.

"I feel lucky today," she said with a grin, tossing the bag into Selene's lap like a gift.

Inside of that bag? At least *seven* freshly bought scratch-off tickets.

Selene gave the bag a dry look. "Tatie… you've been saying that for months."

"*Wa rassi*, today I *mean* it," Inas said, digging through the bag with chubby gold-ringed fingers and snatching one out.

She scratched the silver coating with a key, tongue poking out in focus. "Come on, baby. Come to Ina."

It was a loser, as was the next, and the next. One by one, she scratched them clean, then slapped them against the steering wheel. "This state is *racist* against my luck."

Selene barely cracked a smile- just turned her face back to the window, eyes blank.

Inas glanced at her quietly for a moment. Her silky curls had begun greying at a rapid rate despite her being only 34. "You still not eating enough," she murmured. "You look like feather, *binti.*"

Selene shrugged, lips pressed. Her aunt was right; the thought of eating damn near grossed Selene out these days. It's like her body didn't see the point.

Inas nodded to herself, then shifted in her seat. Her golden eyes were restless, heavy with sleepless bags, like she was trying to think of the best way to word her next sentence.

Finally, she looked at her niece.

"I been reading about stuff. Yoga, meditation, breath stuff. All that hippie white lady stuff, you know?"

She smirked, trying to nudge a reaction out of Selene. "They say it helps with anger and grief. Reconnects you with your body. *Ma ydirch chi lmekna.*"

Selene finally spoke, her voice flat. "You want to do yoga? Tatie, I don't have the energy to *stretch* right now."

Inas' eyes softened. "*Ana bhalek.* Trust me. I ain't tryna turn into no pretzel neither. But they doing a free New Year's class for fresh starts and all that spiritual hippie crap. *Ghir jarrbi m3aya.*"

Selene exhaled silently through her nose. Then:

"You already booked us, didn't you."

"I *did,*" Inas said, proud. "Got us mats and everything. And those tight pants that make *everyone's* booty look good."

Selene rolled her eyes, but a small flicker of something passed over her face. She managed the tiniest of smiles as he imagined her aunt, child-sized and the least limber person on the planet, doing yoga stretches.

"Tatie, you're ridiculous."

"I know." Inas leaned back with a grin. Then, she took her niece's hand in her own. "But I'm all you got."

Selene looked back out the window. "I know."

They sat there for a while, in the kind of silence that *meant* something. Then Inas squeezed Selene's hand, eyes sparkling.

"*Allah yrahmha*, chérie. But you still here. You still breathing."

Selene didn't answer, her eyes hollow. But she didn't let go of her aunt's hand either.

## 8 January 2020- Evervale Lodge

The storm from yesterday hadn't calmed down; in fact, it settled in like an unwelcome guest, thunder booming like it was angry at not only Earth but at everything the planet had ever loved.

Outside, the mountains were smudged with fog and rain; inside, the six lovebirds sat cross-legged on the rug in the living room. The golden envelope at breakfast told them to "spend the week doing whatever they wanted" to celebrate them making it a week in the lodge, and, naturally, they decided to play Monopoly, Uno, and Spades.

And then came the thunder again.

It was a deep, bone-shaking crack that made *everyone* freeze- but Selene jumped *hard.* Her whole body reacted before she could stop it, her eyes closing shut like she was trying to will the thoughts she knew were on their way, out. Damien immediately looked at her, pausing everything he was doing.

He hadn't been able to stop thinking about yesterday evening; not really.

Every time he looked at the yogi, he remembered how her hand felt under his.

Then- another **boom.**

A deep, bone-shaking crack that made Raven grab her purse, stand up, and run across the expansive hardwood floors toward one of the bathrooms.

Damien looked at her protectively, already getting up to follow her, his brows furrowed. "Rae? Baby, you aight?"

"I'm fine," she said hastily. "Don't follow me." She quickly opened the bathroom door and closed it behind her, locking it audibly.

He looked at the door, worried.

Selene looked at it too, brows furrowed, and then whimpered when an even louder thunder crack sounded. She didn't have her knit hat with her today, so she gripped her own knees, trying to count her breaths.

Caleb reached for his wife instinctively, a hand on her back. "Hey- hey, babe, you okay?"

Selene nodded too quickly. "I just... I just need a second, okay?"

She stood, brushing imaginary dust off her leggings, and quietly slipped down the hallway. Damien looked after her, concern written all over his face.

She found a small storage room- windowless, dim, quiet.

*Perfect.*

She stepped inside and closed the door behind herself. There was nothing but her own heartbeat in her ears as she pressed her back against the wall.

She slid down onto the floor and pressed her hands to her knees, grounding herself like she'd been teaching others to do for the past four years. In for four... hold... out for six. Again. Again.

Again.

But her hands still trembled, her thoughts still stomped around like a stampede.

*The crack of thunder.*

*The knocks on the door.*

*The look in the two officers' eyes when-*

**Knock.**

Selene gasped, startling up.

"Y-yes?" she called out, voice soft.

Then, slowly, it creaked open.

Damien.

He didn't speak; just looked at her, strong brows furrowed, deep eyes knowing.

She looked up at him, her voice small.

"Can you just... sit with me? Please?"

Damien nodded just once, no hesitation.

He stepped inside and closed the door behind him.

Then, without a word, he slid down to the floor in front of her, his long legs stretched out, his eyes never leaving hers.

They didn't talk.

But for a reason Selene couldn't quite understand yet-

She could actually breathe normally again.

Raven gripped the sink like a lifeline.

Her chest was tight- so tight it felt like she couldn't *breathe*. She heaved, head shaking like she was refusing what she knew was about to happen.

She squeezed her eyes shut, but the flashbacks came anyway.

*A loud crack of thunder.*

*A narrow, dark hallway.*

*A pair of wide, terrified blue eyes.*

*The heartbroken, devastated way her name was called.*

*The feel of a Jack Daniel's bottle in her palm, and then-*

She gasped and opened her eyes, bracing herself against the mirror. Her reflection didn't look like her. Too pale, too shaken, too vulnerable.

Not Raven Quinn.

She dug into her purse with shaky hands until she found a little orange bottle.

She popped two bars under her tongue like nothing, not even reacting to the bitter taste anymore.

A few minutes passed, full of her breathing and trying to will the flashbacks away. And then-

The panic ebbed. Her breath slowed. Her lids lowered. Her eyes glazed.

She fixed her face in the mirror: little concealer, a touch of liner, lipstick. She ran her fingers through her sleek locks- even blacker than usual, today.

She slipped the bottle back into her purse, turned the lock-

And when she walked out, her signature smirk was back in place.

# Chapter 15

*Such a Winter's Day*

## 25 June 2010- South Boston, MA

The air buzzed with celebration- camera flashes, shouted names, hugs from proud parents and teary-eyed friends. Students in red caps and gowns littered the high school lawn like confetti, clutching their diplomas and looking toward futures that hadn't even begun yet.

Kelly and Kevin were just off to the side of the chaos, fingers laced tightly, their gowns slightly wrinkled from hours of sitting and squeezing. Kelly's long red waves were half-frizzed from the cap she now held at her side, and Kevin's tie was loosened, top button undone.

They were looking at each other with tears sparkling within their eyes as they held hands like they'd fly away otherwise.

"I can't believe we're going to *completely* different colleges," Kelly said, her voice soft as she looked up at him. She was trying hard, *very* hard, not to sob, but it was getting more and more impossible as the realization set in.

The boy she'd spent damn near every day with for thirteen years wouldn't be in the same state as her anymore.

Kevin let out a shaky breath, his sapphire eyes glittering with tears. "Trust me, babe, I wanted to go to Boston U too. You think I *wanna* be that far from you?" He squeezed her hand. "But sadly, I can't exactly resist a full-ride scholarship. Student loans look… terrifying."

Kelly pouted, tugging at his arm like it might keep him closer. "Okay, but... *Central Florida?* That's literally the other end of the country. I can't even *road trip* to you."

Kevin nodded, brushing a strand of hair from her cheek before kissing it tenderly. "I know. I *know* it sucks. But we'll visit each other. Winter breaks, spring breaks, summer... all of that." He offered a small smile. "Plus, haven't you always said you wanted to go to Florida someday?"

She gave a reluctant laugh. "That's true. But I wanted to go there on vacation... *with* you. Not to *visit* you."

He pulled her into his strong arms, his voice low near her ear.

"We'll be okay, Kells. I promise. We've been by each other's side for, like, a *billion* years. *Nothing* can pull us apart, now."

Kelly looked at him like he was everything, her green eyes glowing from the way the sun hit them.

He leaned forward and kissed her forehead like he was making a promise to her.

The young adults hugged, swaying as students ran by in celebration. When they pulled apart, Kelly pressed a kiss to his forehead, then to his nose, then his lips.

"You better not forget about me down there," she whispered, eyes narrowed in that way she always did when she was trying not to cry.

Kevin smiled, brushing his thumb along her jaw.

"I can't *imagine* forgetting you, Kells."

It started, as these things so often do, with Raven sliding a half-full bottle of Don onto the table with a grin that should've come with a warning label. From the overhead speakers, The Mamas and the Papas' "California Dreamin'" played out sardonically.

It wasn't storming anymore, *finally*, but that didn't mean the sky was clear.

"Alright, *lovebirds*," Raven began, her voice syrupy as she swayed a bit from inebriation already. She rocked a corset clinched tight at her waist and a leather miniskirt that revealed her thick thighs.

"Truth or dare. You tap out, you drink. You lie; you drink. You hesitate for more than five seconds… guess what? *Drink.*"

Everyone groaned in unison.

"Raven, come *on*," Laney said in one of Michael's red flannels, massaging her head like it hurt already.

"The hosts have literally *abandoned* us for a week. Well, besides still cooking and cleaning. But still, it's getting *boring*. We need to stir shit *up* in this cabin."

She pointed at Michael. "Truth or dare, Professor?"

Michael adjusted his glasses, rocking a Halo T-shirt today. "Truth."

Raven grinned, her emerald eyes sparkling. "If Laney gave you a hall pass, which one of us would you fuck?"

Michael blinked like someone had just hit him with a flash grenade. He reached for the bottle without a word and took a full shot. Laney raised a brow at him.

"Laaame," Raven groaned, then looked around the group with a mischievous glint in her eyes.

She pointed at Caleb. "Truth or dare, Coach?"

Caleb scratched the back of his neck, his glowing muscles on full display in his white training tank. "Dare, I guess."

"I dare you to strip and do ten push-ups while looking Selene in the eye."

Selene immediately covered her face and shook her head in mortification, her wedding ring sparkling with the crackling fire.

"Nope," Caleb said, already reaching for the bottle. Raven cackled. "Coward!"

Then, Laney. "Truth."

"Would you rather sleep with your ex again or never have sex again for the rest of your life?"

Laney groaned, face already flushing. "Oh my God."

"You've got five seconds."

Laney took a bottle of water and drank, her face beet red.

Then, Selene.

She blinked slowly, nervously. "Truth."

Raven was already smirking. "Who in this room are you most physically attracted to? You know, besides Caleb?"

Selene held Raven's gaze for a heartbeat, her jaw tight, and then calmly reached for the bottle.

Caleb squinted at her. "Seriously?"

Selene raised the shot glass. "Dumb question."

And finally, Damien.

Raven grinned. "Truth or dare, daddy."

Damien smirked in his olive-green Carhartt tee, chin-length locs wavy. "Dare."

"I dare you to kiss someone you *shouldn't* kiss."

He chuckled low, then raised his hands in surrender. "You tryna trap me and kill me. Pour it."

The bottle quickly emptied as the game went on. Raven held it up by the neck like a trophy, squinting at it as she swayed in place, utterly loose. "Moment of silence for our fallen soldier."

Michael, already plastered, raised an eyebrow, his face beet red. "One last dare before we call it. I dare you to spin that empty-ass bottle... and…"

He leaned forward, something *wicked* in his eyes.

"And *kiss* whoever it lands on."

Raven grinned slowly, as if he'd just said something *wonderful.*

"You always *did* know how to end a party."

Everyone groaned in protest, except for Selene, who just looked at Caleb sideways.

Raven placed the bottle back on the hardwood floor and gave it a dramatic spin. It clinked as it twirled, a perfect, slow, teasing circle. A hush fell over the group. Damien leaned forward slightly, brow furrowed.

And then… click.

It landed on-

Caleb.

The air *changed.*

Before Caleb could open his mouth, Raven leaned across the floor, swaying slightly, and kissed the handsome personal trainer like it was the most natural thing in the world, her black-painted lips parting, and then locking with his.

It wasn't a peck. Wasn't innocent.

It was so deep that someone *gasped.*

Caleb froze, his ocean eyes wide in complete shock, his strong arms limp at his sides.

But for one second- one tipsy second-

He kissed her back- his lips parting and then enveloping hers, the warmth of them pulling him in.

Selene stood so fast, the pouf she'd been sitting on screeched back.

She didn't say a word; just turned and walked out of the living room and up the stairs, eyes focused on nothing but getting out of the room.

Caleb broke the kiss with an audible smack.

"Selene!"

He shot up and jogged behind her, guilt rising fast as he bumped into damn near every piece of furniture trying to jog upstairs and get to his wife.

Damien, meanwhile, was stone still, his eyes locked on Raven like she was something dangerous.

"What the fuck was that?"

Raven blinked slowly, like she wasn't fully present. "A kiss."

Michael coughed awkwardly. "I didn't mean-"

"You kissed Caleb. In front of me. In front of *Selene,*" Damien snapped.

"For a *dare,*" she said, her posture defensive.

Damien stood now, slow, deliberate, jaw tight.

Raven didn't move; just stared back at him like he was being irrational.

"Don't start," she said, voice still smooth. "It was a *game.*"

Damien shook his head, breath heavy now.

"Nah. That was a *choice.*"

Caleb found Selene in their bedroom, sitting on the edge of the bed, her back to the door, her eyes fixed on the window of their suite. Her curls were down now, as if having them tied up added to her pain.

"Selene," he started, stepping in, voice soft. "I'm… I'm sorry."

She didn't turn.

"I'm already on edge, Caleb," she said finally, still facing the window. "You know that. You *know* I am. You still haven't told me what happened with Laney, and now you're out here… doing things like *this?*" Her voice cracked on the last word.

Caleb closed the door behind him, leaning against it.

"I know, Selene. I *know*. And I *promise* I'll tell you soon, but… You gotta understand some things are hard to talk about. They're just… *hard.*"

That's when she turned around and looked at him. *Really* looked at him.

"Caleb," she began, voice low and serious. "I opened up to you about Thena's death. About how immensely guilty I felt. *Still* feel. And when I told you, it had only been *four* years, Caleb. It was still somewhat *fresh.*"

He swallowed, jaw tight. He could hardly bear to look at her, understanding what she meant immediately.

Her voice cracked like she had lost hope in something. "But you can't tell me about something that happened *seven years ago?*"

Caleb's mouth opened, getting ready to speak-

Then, it closed, and his brows furrowed.

"Why do you feel so *entitled* to my past?"

His tone was so sharp, it sliced through the suite.

Selene gasped like she'd been struck.

He looked dead in her eyes then, his expression one of pure defensiveness; one she'd never seen on his face before.

"Seven years ago is what? *Four* years before I even *met* you? Yet you think you have the right to know about shit that doesn't even *concern* you?"

Selene's fists tightened at her sides. Her heart rate picked up. She got up and started stepping closer to him, her eyes never leaving his, dwarfed by his frame but still confident.

"Caleb, I am your *wife*. Legally, we are *one*. How does that even *work* if we don't *know* each other?"

Caleb scoffed. "You're so fucking naïve, Selene. You really think most married people know everything about each other? I promise you, even your *parents* kept secrets."

Selene flinched like she'd been *stabbed*.

He closed his eyes then, taking a deep breath.

"Look… I'm sorry. I didn't mean to say it like that. But my family… that shit is something I thought I left behind for good. You don't need to know that guy, because I'm *not* that guy. Haven't been for seven years."

He stepped forward then, wrapping her trembling frame into his arms and kissing her head. "I love you, okay? *That's* all you should care about."

She stayed in his arms, but her eyes, still glassy, never closed.

Laney had already pulled Michael and his half-eaten popcorn into their suite upstairs and shut the door, leaving Damien and Raven alone in the living room.

The usually chatty couple had been silent for minutes, ones that seemed to stretch and stretch.

The fire in the hearth had died down to a flicker, and Raven was standing near it, arms crossed, looking… unlike herself. Her usually perfect black hair was tangled; her cheeks flushed slightly from the Don. Even the way she *stood-* usually so confident, so upright- was subdued, like she was trying to hide herself.

Finally, she took a deep breath and looked at her boyfriend of two years.

"I'm sorry. I mean it, King. I shouldn't have done that."

Damien stayed silent for a heartbeat, then shifted his weight on the couch, jaw clicking. His shirt was wrinkled, his locs wild around his face.

Raven let out a bitter little laugh then, her head shaking almost in disbelief at her own state. "I don't know what's *wrong* with me. Every time things start to feel too… *lovey-dovey*, I… I freak out. I do something stupid. I… I ruin it."

Her voice cracked, just barely.

"What happened to me… it *broke* something in me, King. I can't fix it."

Damien's voice came low and deep. "Rae… I been through the same thing. You know that, right? The *exact same thing*. But you don't see *me* out here doin' shit like that."

Raven tensed, her head dropping slightly.

"King…" she started, her usually loud voice barely above a whisper.

"I didn't tell you… everything. *Everything* that happened that night."

That caught him. His eyes sharpened as he took her in; her tense jaw, her frozen stance, her shifting eyes like she was trying to figure out how to phrase her next words.

He knew it then- his girlfriend was even more broken than he thought.

"It was…" She exhaled hard and looked away, jaw tight.

"It was *awful.*"

Damien's expression softened immediately.

"What happened, Rae?"

Silence stretched. The flicker of the fire danced in her emerald eyes. For a moment, she looked like she might say it-

But then, she just shook her head.

"I want to tell you, but… It's just too painful. Please don't think I'm hiding things from you; it's just… talking about it always brings it right back up, and I get…" She sighed. "I *will* tell you, just not tonight. Okay?"

Damien nodded slowly, concern still written all over his face as he studied his once-fearless girlfriend.

"Aight. Not tonight."

But his eyes never left her.

# Chapter 16

*Found in Winter Flowers*

## New Year's Day 2016- Brooklyn, NY

The studio smelled faintly of lavender and eucalyptus, steam still clinging to the windows from the class that had just finished. Outside, Brooklyn hummed with the muted quiet of New Year's Day- streets littered with confetti and discarded champagne bottles- but inside, the wellness center pulsed with warm light and calm.

Selene, 20 now, stood at the front of the small room, barefoot on her lavender mat. Her palms were damp with nerves, but she rubbed them together like she was kindling fire, grounding herself. She looked out at the dozen or so faces- women in leggings, an older man in loose sweats, a young couple who still looked hungover.

All eyes were on her.

Her voice came out softer than she intended. "Welcome, everyone. Happy New Year. Thank you for being here."

She'd decided that this was the year she would let her curls grow back, and her head held the tiniest *TWA*. She usually wore baggy clothes, but decided to wear a cute, form-fitting set today. From speakers, Vallis Alps' "Young" played out softly. She'd hoped soothing music like that would calm her on her first day teaching.

"Yoga saved me," she admitted, surprising herself with the honesty spilling out of her.

"I started exactly two years ago, to this day. I was… in a very dark place. And it showed me how to *breathe* again. So, if today is your first day, know that you don't have to be perfect. You just have to be *here.*"

Something loosened in her chest as she began leading them through cat-cow stretches, her voice warming with each cue.

She thought of Athena- the mystical young teen who used to read tarot to her, who once told her that "the body is the spirit's oldest friend." Selene's throat tightened, but she pushed through, guiding the class into warrior pose. Her voice steadied: "Strong legs, soft heart."

By the time they were lying in savasana, the room felt different. The couple had stopped fidgeting. The older man's chest rose and fell in an even tide. Someone even sighed, the sound of release.

Selene lowered her voice almost to a whisper. "Set an intention for your year. Even if it's just to remember to breathe."

For a moment, she closed her eyes, too. Her own intention formed like a whisper in her mind:

*Keep going. You **have** to keep going. For her.*

## 10 January 2020- Evervale Lodge

Selene was back in the lodge's living room.

The fire still crackled. The empty bottle still sat on the rug. Raven was still laughing, drunk and bold, still spinning that golden glass bottle like fate had a sense of humor.

And it still landed on Caleb.

But this time… they didn't just kiss.

Raven crawled into his lap- slow, serpentine- and French-kissed him like she already owned him- like he was something she'd taken once before and was simply reclaiming. Her fingers ran through his golden locks, her hips rolled against his groin, and Caleb?

He *let* her.

Worse- he pulled her closer, kissing down her neck, making her moan in a way that made Selene's gut twist.

But she couldn't move. Couldn't speak.

It was like her body had morphed into stiff wax.

"I wouldn't take it personally," Raven said, voice sickeningly bright, breaking the kiss with a wet smack to twist her head toward Selene.

"You know what I do. I take what's yours and then keep on living like nothing even happened."

Selene tried to speak, but her mouth wouldn't open. Tears kept streaking down her cheeks.

Caleb looked over Raven's shoulder, right into Selene's face, those usually vivid aquamarine eyes *blank*.

"You should've seen this coming, Selene. You know who I *really* am. You know our marriage was built on a lie."

Selene wanted to run, but her body was paralyzed. It was like her feet were bolted to the ground.

And then, suddenly, jarringly-

Raven's hands were covered in blood.

It dripped down her fingers, slick and wet, onto Caleb's shoulders.

Caleb's eyes began to bleed too, slow crimson streams trailing down his cheeks like tears.

A sticky, metallic flood seeped up through the floorboards-

-where Athena's lavender knit hat now lay, soaked through.

And then-

***"Thena!"***

Selene jolted awake with a choked gasp, her silky black slip clinging to her damp skin.

She felt a warm wetness beneath her.

*Blood.*

She turned her head to the suite window. The Wolf Moon hung bright and undeniable.

She always bled upon full moons, but she was so stressed that she'd forgotten to put on her period undies before bed.

She looked down beside her. Caleb was sleeping peacefully, like he had no real worries at all.

She sighed shakily as she carefully got out of bed to clean up.

It was just a nightmare. She *knew* it was just a nightmare.

So why did she feel like things in the lodge would never be the same?

# Chapter 17

*An Ache I Still Remember*

## 17 August 2012- University of Central Florida

The central Florida heat was a different breed. Sticky, oppressive, *personal.*

Kelly, now 20, fanned herself lazily with a wrinkled pamphlet from the university office as she sprawled across Kevin's tiny twin XL bed- barely big enough for one person, let alone two. From someone's dorm within the hall, Gotye's "Somebody That I Used to Know" boomed.

"I cannot *believe* you let me transfer here," she groaned, kicking off one sandal with her toe. "This dorm is literally the size of a shoebox."

Kevin chuckled from the kitchenette, where he was trying- and failing- to figure out the microwave. "Yeah, but it's *our* shoebox."

Kelly smiled despite herself. He always had a way of softening the blow.

Then came a knock.

Kevin looked up. "Oh- hold on," he said, heading for the dorm door. Kelly sat up, pulling her curls into a quick ponytail just as he opened it.

Standing on the other side was a girl- beautiful, olive-toned, with glossy black hair tied into a messy bun. She wore a fitted tank and cutoff shorts, a Tupperware container cradled in her arms like a newborn.

"Hey!" she chirped, her brown eyes twinkling. "I made too much arroz con pollo last night. I know it's your favorite, so…" She held it out with a bashful grin, her posture… interestingly comfortable.

Kevin's face lit up immediately. "Yo, Gabi! You're the best- seriously." He took the container from her with a grateful nod. "Oh- uh, Gabs, this is Kelly, my girlfriend. Kelly, this is Gabriela- my neighbor and probably my closest friend here."

Kelly stood and smiled, polite but cool. "Nice to meet you."

Gabriela's breath caught, just slightly enough for Kelly to notice, but she smiled. "Oh my gosh, you too! Wow, you came all the way down here? That's *love.*"

"Mhm." Kelly's smile didn't waver, but her green eyes narrowed just the slightest bit after she noticed the young woman's hesitation.

"*Sure* is."

Gabriela didn't overstay; she waved and disappeared as quickly as she'd come- but the silence that followed her exit was *heavy.*

Kevin smiled widely, his cobalt eyes sparkling as he opened the Tupperware and already began eating it like it was the first good meal he'd had.

Kelly studied him, eyes narrowed, heart thudding.

She'd known Kevin for fourteen years now- as a sun-bleached little boy with hair like summer wheat. She watched him grow through every season of childhood: the earnest "big kid," the awkward preteen, the restless teenager, and now this handsome young man stepping into the wide-open country of adulthood.

She knew when something was off with him.

And right now?

Something was *off* with him.

○

The six lovebirds went down to the dining room at 9 a.m. like always, expecting the feast and golden envelope that had welcomed them for over a week now.

But...

There was no breakfast.

Just... silence.

Well... and something that sent chills down each of their spines.

A single envelope.

But this time, it wasn't gold.

It was *black*.

So black, so void of light, that it looked like the color of closed doors and locked hearts.

"Oh, *fuck* no," Raven said, rubbing her temples from the massive hangover that seemed to pulse like a heartbeat beneath her skull. "No breakfast, and *this* shit? I knew it was gonna be cult vibes eventually, but I thought they'd wait till at least *February* to show their ass."

Caleb, still a bit tense after the argument he'd had with Selene the night before, let out a frustrated sigh. "I almost don't even wanna open that."

Michael, trying to be his usual easygoing self, let out a laugh, but it came out slightly shaky. "What if they're just trying to scare us, and really it says, 'make your own breakfast this morning with your partner' or some shit?"

Laney groaned. "Honestly, that would piss me off even *more* than something creepy would. I really hope I didn't take being pampered for granted."

It was quiet for a few heartbeats, then Selene, ever the gentle leader, stepped toward it.

She picked it up delicately with her gold-ringed fingers, her brows already furrowed. The letter inside was just as black as the envelope, the writing in silver ink- the exact same handwriting as always.

Slowly, nervously, she read aloud:

"Lovebirds- we cannot continue the retreat as normal because we do not believe you've fulfilled the goals you should have by this time. It's okay; we'll make it easier for you. At noon sharp, you will partner up for specific activities. Not with your actual partner, though; with the partner you were given on the 7th. You will also be going to the same places you went to before. We believe this will lead you to your personal goals much faster."

The 'i' in 'Lovebirds' was dotted with a bird motif this time.

There was a heartbeat of silence.

Then:

"…You've got to be fucking kidding me," Caleb said flatly.

Laney pressed a hand to her temple. "What type of cryptic bullshit are they *on?*"

Michael groaned, rocking a bright yellow flannel that *should* have matched the vibe. "We barely survived it last time."

Damien didn't say anything. He was already looking at Selene, who still hadn't moved.

Then, slowly, she looked up at him.

And for a second, the whole room blurred out of focus-

For all they could remember was the storm.

# Chapter 18

*Black and Gold*

**New Year's Day 2013- South Allentown, PA**

Caleb stood in front of the motel mirror, shirtless, chest rising and falling like something barely caged. His reflection stared back at him with dead, bitter eyes.

His jaw and fists tightened at once.

And then-

**Crash.**

His fist slammed into the mirror, cracking it straight down the center. Tiny shards clattered into the rust-stained sink below, a few catching the flickering light like broken stars.

Immediately, he got a flashback of the goddamn broken glass from July, and he hit himself on the head angrily.

"Look at you," he muttered under his breath, voice ragged as he stared at his jumbled reflection in the cracked mirror.

"Fucking useless piece of *nothing.*"

His body trembled- not from the pain, but from *rage*; the kind that calcifies.

He sat on the edge of the sagging bed, his bloodied hand resting on his knee, and grabbed his phone.

He unlocked it with a swipe of his thumb and opened the browser, clumsy and slow. The signal was weak, the screen grainy, but it didn't matter.

He typed in:

**Gyms in NYC.**

The search spun, and a list popped up- a long list that seemed to scream *possibility*.

Caleb stared at it as if it were scripture.

If he couldn't change himself? He could at least change his location. He could at least change how he looked. He could at least change how much weight he could lift and how hard he could push himself.

He could at least change the guy his own family didn't want.

O

Caleb and Laney stepped into the ballroom like two kids summoned to the principal's office, eyes avoiding one another's.

The air there felt *colder* somehow, much different from the beautiful, lively place where the group had done trust exercises prompted by golden envelopes.

On the glossy grand piano sat a *black* envelope, though, like the one from breakfast.

It looked like it had secrets pressed into every fiber of the paper.

Caleb let out a deep, annoyed sigh, his sea glass eyes looking tired already. "Well, I guess it's time to see what the cult leaders want, now."

Laney held her belly, jaw tight, leaning against the piano like she was trying *hard* to appear casual. Even her outfit- a baggy hoodie and sweats- played its part.

Caleb picked the envelope up and ripped it open with his own feigned casualness.

Laney watched as his eyes scanned the words, her heart thudding faster for a reason she couldn't yet place.

He read aloud, voice ever so slightly shaky:

"We think it may be time to address the elephant in the room. Go inside the hidden door beside the window if you want privacy to do so."

They both looked toward the window.

And there it was- a narrow wooden door, blending almost *perfectly* into the molding of the wall.

Neither of them had noticed it before.

Laney inhaled sharply through her nose. "Fucking creeps. I *knew* they had cameras. Now they wanna include *us* in their weird therapy bullshit."

Caleb looked at her, his mouth tight.

"Laney… creepy therapy bullshit or not…keeping it in is poisoning *both* of us. I think… I think it's time."

Laney's breath caught as she looked toward the secret confessional.

## New Year's Day 2013- West Philadelphia, PA

The knock was already too loud.

Laney didn't even flinch. She knew that knock- had known it her whole miserable life.

When she opened the door, Deborah stood there shaking like a woman possessed.

Her leathery face was twisted with something *far* worse than anger- a sickened, horrified *revulsion* that made her look ten years older in seconds. In her trembling hand, she clutched Caleb's phone like it was evidence from a crime scene.

"This…" Deborah's voice cracked, barely human. *"This* is how you repay me, Delaney?"

She shoved the phone forward, inches from Laney's face, her hand shaking so violently the screen kept catching the light.

"After everything I've done for you two… you *shit all over my name?* You turn my own children into… into *this?"*

Laney stared at her mother, unflinching.

Then, slowly, a cold little smile curved her lips.

"After all you've 'done' for us?" she echoed, stepping closer. "Like leaving us alone for days? Like letting any and *everybody* into our space?"

She leaned in until their noses nearly brushed, voice dropping into something poisonous and sweet.

"We were just acting like our mother's ch-"

The slap cracked across Laney's face with brutal force.

Laney stumbled back, cheek blooming red, but Deborah looked even more devastated- like she'd just slapped *herself.* Her hand hovered mid-air, trembling, eyes wide with pure horror. For a moment, she looked like she might throw up.

"If I didn't care about our name…" her voice was low, feral, barely above a whisper.

"If I didn't care about what people would say about *me…*"

She stepped forward, close enough that Laney could smell the menthols on her breath.

"Oh, your ass would be *ruined.*"

Then, Deborah turned and stormed down the hallway, boots thudding like gunshots.

# Chapter 19

*I Won't Ever Be Repeated*

## 4 May 2013- University of Central Florida

Kelly, 21 now, slid her key into the lock. Her coworker wanted to pick up a shift at the bar, so she was able to come home early. Although it was storming, she figured she'd surprise Kevin with a late-night snack from the Cuban spot down the street- his favorite. She smiled, thinking about how happy she was living with him full-time despite the issues they'd been having lately.

Namely, her insecurity around his "friend" Gabriela and his refusal to admit they were anything more than that.

They'd gotten into more arguments over it than they ever had over anything. But eventually, she'd decided to trust the boy she'd known for three-fourths of her life.

When she stepped inside the tiny apartment, it smelled like pine cleaner and microwaved takeout- normal enough.

But-

Something felt off. The air wasn't *right*.

She stepped in slowly, setting the brown paper bag on the counter. The bedroom door was mostly closed, but not latched-

And there it was.

Noises.

Muffled, rhythmic, *awful* noises coming from the narrow, dark hallway.

Her stomach *plummeted*. Somehow, despite never having been in a situation like this, her heart knew immediately that it was in danger.

She didn't speak; didn't call his name.

Just walked down the hallway-

Pushed the door of the bedroom they'd been sharing for nine months open-

*And there they were.*

Kevin and Gabriela, tangled in their sheets like they belonged to each other.

Gabriela was riding him sensually, a light sheen of sweat on her bare olive-toned back.

Kevin's hands- *her* Kevin's hands- gripped this other woman's hips as they moved together on their sheets, panting loudly like they were entitled to make the room hold their breath.

It took them a second to notice her.

Then-

Gabriela screamed. Kevin *scrambled*.

"Kells-!" he called out, the devastation audible in his tone.

But Kelly didn't hear him. She didn't even *see* him.

All she saw was red.

She let out a sound that didn't sound human-

And then she *lost* it.

She threw the lamp first. The picture frame, next.

Screaming, sobbing, breaking things just to hear the sound of something else shattering besides her own chest.

Kevin tried to reach her, those blue eyes she'd loved for almost fifteen years now looking utterly *terrified* as they filled with tears.

"Kelly, *please-!*"

*"Don't fucking touch me!!"* she shrieked, her voice cracking so hard it didn't even sound like English.

And, then, without even thinking-

She grabbed the half-drunk Jack Daniel's bottle from the dresser. It slipped a bit from her sweaty palm, but she held it dear.

And then, in the haze of betrayal, and rage-

She made a decision that would cost her forever.

O

Raven rolled her eyes so hard it looked like it might be permanent. "Oh, of *course* it's black," she muttered, already sauntering toward the ominous black envelope on a lavender yoga mat. "Chances they're gonna ask us to write our wills?" She said, looking back at the curly-haired programmer with a smirk.

Michael sighed so hard it could've stirred dust, having changed into a black hoodie and sweats to better match the now-creepy vibe of the lodge. "I think it's even *more* likely they're gonna tell us to do a sun salutation while confessing our deepest sins."

Raven snorted. "That *definitely* seems more their speed."

She crouched down, picked the envelope up, hummed curiously at the surprising weight of it, and then ripped it open like she couldn't be assed for theatrics.

And then…

She *froze.*

Michael leaned over her shoulder, glasses-covered eyes scanning the letter with a focused squint as his heart rate picked up ever so slightly.

Then, his jaw hung open, every emotion known to man swirling within him at once.

"Oh *shit.*"

In ink so silver that it sparkled with the lights overhead:

*Answer these three questions below:*

1.	*What is the date your life changed?*
2.	*What is a symbol of that date?*
3.	*When you close your eyes and think of that date, what is the first thing you see?*

*When you are finished, head into the gaming room. Not only will you get an hour of Wi-Fi… you'll receive your own private rooms with Smart TVs to use it in HD.*

Raven blinked. "No fucking *way.*"

Michael raised his arms like he was thanking the lord himself. "Thank you! Thank you, creepy invisible retreat gods! I knew you wouldn't steer us astray! *I KNEW YOU WOULD DO RIGHT BY US!*"

He looked at Raven with a look of utter relief, tears damn near filling his eyes. "I don't think I can *begin* to explain to you how fucking *miserable* I've been without internet. I've been trying to hide it from Laney, but God damn, it's been *rough*. There's only so many games you can play and cuddles you can do before the boredom begins eating you from the inside."

He looked like an addict who was about to get his fix, his entire body jittering with anticipation for what he could do on that smart TV.

Raven cackled. "You're telling *me?* I'm a literal *influencer*. My whole *life* is online. Being here has made me feel like I'm not even *me* anymore."

"Exactly!" Michael yelled, eyes wild. "Humans weren't meant to live like this. I'm convinced!"

Then, without even a sliver of hesitation, he went over to a wooden bench where two sheets of paper, already typed with the three questions, and two pens lay.

He sighed. "I dunno what they're gonna do with our responses, but it cannot *possibly* be worse than spending another day without connection to the outside world."

Raven snorted in agreement as she sauntered over and plopped down right beside him, studying the questions on her own sheet.

Michael sat down on the bench and wrote, without even thinking for five seconds about it:

1.      *January 1st, 2014.*
2.      *Wedding dress.*
3.      *Her.*

The day Laney became his wife, of course. I mean, that *had* to be what they were looking for, right?

As Raven looked over the same questions, she felt a *lot* less certainty than Michael did.

Her jaw had locked tight. Her heart rate had picked up so much that she wondered if it was visible beneath her skin.

For a while, she just stood, unmoving, going over the three questions like they were about to unearth her longest-buried secrets.

Then, without a word, she sat beside him, picked up the other pen, and wrote slowly, tentatively, on the other sheet of paper:

1.      *May 4th, 2013.*
2.      *Jack Daniels.*
3.      *The two of them.*

### Summer 2013- Miami, FL

It was almost funny, in a sick kind of way.

Kelly O'Connor had spent her whole life dreaming of fairytales- of happy endings and promises kept. Of being loved by the blue-eyed boy from the sandbox forever and ever.

But forever had walked out the second she opened that bedroom door and saw that same boy tangled up with someone else. In *her* bed.

So, she figured if *he* could treat her like she never existed, she could treat herself the same.

She ditched her car somewhere she didn't even remember, flew to Miami, and took the first shitty job she could find- some grungy hookah bar that barely paid enough for the roach-infested apartment she now shared with four other girls who all had dreams bigger than their paychecks.

She stood in front of the cracked, blurry mirror and stared at her reflection as Capital Cities' "Kangaroo Court" played in the background.

There she was.

Curly red hair. Freckled skin. Some cutesy pink outfit.

She felt nothing but *disgust*.

Because the girl in the glass? *That* was the girl who believed in forever.

*That* was the girl who thought the boy from the sandbox actually *loved* her.

Her hair pissed her off the most. Kevin used to fawn over her fiery curls. He'd say she looked magical, like she wasn't even from Earth.

So, she grabbed the black dye box she'd just bought from CVS and went to *war*.

The curls went black first- then flat. Burnt into submission with the highest heat setting on her seven-dollar flat iron.

Then came the makeup. All the pinks, the peaches, the sweet blushes and glosses- trashed. She traded them in for thick, dark eyeliner that made her emerald eyes look *unreal*, and foundation that erased every last freckle.

And the clothes? Gone were the trendy little sundresses and cute high-waisted shorts. She replaced them with leather, fishnets, corsets, and boots with platforms that could crush a man's head.

And the best part about it all?

People *noticed*.

She started posting on Tumblr, just for fun at first. But the photos- the poses in alleys, the makeup, the energy- they *hit*. People loved her. Called her a 'dark angel', an 'alt goddess', a '90s vampire queen with curves.' Before long, she started getting brand deals and sponsorships, earning enough money to move to a luxury place and forget her old life even existed.

Forget *Kelly O'Connor* ever existed.

She smiled at the thought of that stupid girl fading into oblivion.

The next time she logged in, she changed her display name without hesitation:

**Raven Quinn.**

# Chapter 20

*The People You Love*

## 15 October 2016- Southwest Atlanta, GA

It was Damien's 22nd birthday, but he wasn't in the mood for parties. He'd served for 3 more years after Xan's death, not wanting to be even more of a failure than he already was by leaving. Eventually, he was honorably discharged, and now just wanted to exist without crumbling completely.

He was mid-combo on the gym punching bag, punching to the beat of J Cole's "She Knows", when his phone buzzed in his joggers' pocket.

He had every intention to ignore it, but something told him he should pick up.

"Yeah," he grunted, wiping his face with the back of his hand. He'd loc'd his hair, not in the mood to get haircuts, and the baby locs stuck up like cropped cords.

"Damien King?" came a clipped voice- some white man, businesslike. "We were given your name and contact info. You came heavily recommended, so we'd like to have you on our private security team."

Damien exhaled hard, rolling his neck as well as his eyes. "Private security? Like… babysitting celebs?"

*"Protect,"* the voice corrected smoothly. "It's a great opportunity. Can get you into big rooms with big names."

Damien's first instinct was *hell no*. He didn't do parties. Didn't do glitz, or glam, or makeup-caked girls who'd probably call him rude for not smiling.

But the word 'protect' stuck with him.

He thought of Xander's face again- baby-faced even with a shaven head and tattoos. Grinning under the Afghan sun, loose and confident, because he knew his big brother would protect him.

Damien didn't protect shit.

He let out a long, heavy breath.

"Yeah. Aight."

○

Damien followed behind Selene as she entered the art studio with soft steps, quiet, his eyes already skimming the space.

Their painting from the 7th was still there- dark, sad clouds and silver raindrops.

On the main table sat a black envelope, so dark it seemed to absorb the light around it.

He scoffed immediately. "'*Course* there's another one."

Selene lifted it, brow raised. She smiled a bit to herself when she realized she and Damien were matching in all-black again.

"I swear to God, if this one says 'paint your deepest trauma," she muttered, tearing the flap. She didn't notice how much quicker she'd begun breathing.

Damien smirked. "Shit, wouldn't put it past 'em."

She pulled out the letter, read it, and then blinked. Once, twice, three times.

He tilted his head. "What's it say?"

Selene looked up at him, a little amused, a little incredulous. She opened the envelope and read aloud:

"There is a lone bookshelf on the second floor, a few feet from your master suites. Behind it is a hidden room. Go in there for your task."

Selene blinked and turned the envelope upside down.

A perfectly golden key fell out with a little *cling*. It glimmered beneath the dim light- heavy, old-fashioned, the kind you'd find in a haunted manor or a secret garden.

Damien blinked at the shiny object. "The fuck? We 'boutta die or somethin'?"

Selene bit her plush bottom lip, her bronze eyes shifting. "Possibly."

He looked at the yoga instructor then, long and quiet.

Despite how much he didn't trust her just nine days ago, something within him felt… *curious.*

"You wanna do this?"

She hesitated- but only for a second.

She looked in his eyes, then down at the key, then back at him again.

"I *am* kinda curious about this 'hidden room."

Without another word, they walked out of the studio, up the stairs, and past their suites. Selene led, her steps graceful and sure.

Damien inwardly chastised himself for even doing this, not knowing what the hell these hosts could possibly want from the two of them, but his curiosity was stronger than his suspicion.

Eventually, Selene stopped in front of a narrow bookshelf.

She reached into the pocket of her yoga pants and pulled out the key. Her fingers hesitated for a second at the lock- hidden between two, apparently, fake books on the bottom.

Then- **click.**

The bookshelf shifted with a soft groan, revealing a narrow spiraling staircase wrapped in shadow and warm wood.

They both just stared.

"The hell is *this?*" Damien said, his voice low, more awed than suspicious. "This shit was just… *hidin'* here?"

Selene gave a quiet scoff. "This whole *place* is insane. Why not a secret tower room, too?"

He glanced at her, a small smirk on his firm yet soft lips. "You scared?"

"Only of what's *not* behind this door," she muttered before starting inside.

They climbed the stairs together, the spiral swirling like a secret. With each step, the air felt different- denser, closer.

At the top was a round, windowless room that looked like something out of a dream: dim and warm, all glowing gold lamp light and plush wine-red textures. There were no windows, seemingly no connection to the outside world- nothing but a couch, a thick circular rug, and a low table.

And on that table- a sand timer and *another* black envelope.

They looked at each other for three good seconds, hearing nothing outside of the room.

They realized pretty quickly that it was soundproof.

Eventually, Selene sighed, picked up the envelope, broke the seal, and read the handwritten words.

Her brows pulled together slowly. Her lips parted.

Damien blinked. "What does it say?"

She swallowed and then gave a small, incredulous smile.

"Talk until the timer runs out."

For a few heartbeats, they just stared at each other, equally dumbfounded.

Finally, Selene giggled. "They dragged us up to a secret tower… to *talk?*"

Damien laughed too, shaking his head. "This *gotta* be the most senseless cult I ever joined."

Selene tilted her head at the inviting couch pushed against the curve of the wall.

"Well. If we're *stuck* here…"

Damien smirked, following her gaze. "That couch *do* look comfy as hell."

They moved over together, sitting with more space between them than necessary. Selene flipped the timer, and the golden sand began to fall slowly, grain by grain.

After a few seconds, she spoke, her voice so soft it sounded like she was telling a secret.

"Athena was… a *woo-woo* kind of girl. Always with her head in the stars. Astrology charts, tarot cards, crystals. She made the world feel… bigger. *Softer.* She especially loved the moon- talked about how it connected everyone. That's… that's the reason I look at it so much."

Damien's throat worked.

He leaned back into the couch, staring at the flicker of a nearby lamp.

"Xan was like that, too. Poetic. Dramatic as hell, but in the best way. He *loved* fire." His lips curved slightly, bittersweet. "Couldn't pass a candle without stoppin' to stare at it. Guess that's why I'm always lookin' at fire now. Make me feel like he still around."

Selene sniffed, her nose red from tears brimming behind her eyes. "Sounds like they would've gotten along."

"Yeah," Damien said, voice low. "Probably up there, laughin' at us right now."

That earned a laugh out of Selene- quiet, but real.

Slowly, the conversation moved from their siblings to how their parents met.

Selene told him about Lashawn, who was a Howard student studying midwifery and African American studies, carrying the quiet pain of having been neglected by the hospital staff during her birth in favor of the white babies, leaving her with lifelong speech and motor issues. How she worked on her motor issues by cutting shapes into fruit.

Then, she told him about Youssef, an exchange student from Morocco who barely spoke English. How he and her mother had met in a café and somehow fell in love, language barrier and all. How his family back home had disowned him for his choice, except for his little sister, her Tatie Inas.

Damien had gone still while she spoke, his dark eyes uncharacteristically soft. "That's beautiful. Strong as hell."

Selene smiled, trying to hide that she was tearing up.

He leaned back, the words slow to come. "Mine's not as international, but… It's beautiful in its own way."

He told her about Andre, the activist, and Tonya, home from the army after losing her brother Maurice to police brutality. How grief and fury had led them to each other. How his mom had *fire* in her, and his dad had needed that fire after a childhood of abuse by his officer stepfather and neglect by his mother. How, together, they built a home that was fierce, protective, unbreakable.

And when he said Xan's name, his voice cracked.

Is Selene noticed. Her hand twitched against her lap, as if it wanted to reach for his.

The sand had fallen completely long ago, but they didn't even notice.

They leaned back, still talking, the conversation shifting from their families to embarrassing shit they did that kept them up at night.

After an hour, Selene's eyes were still sparkling from leftover laughter, her cheeks flushed with warmth. She tilted her head, studying him with open curiosity.

"You and Raven seem *so* in love," she said softly. "You must think she's your soulmate."

Damien went quiet for a long moment, staring into the distance.

The easy smile on his face slowly faded, replaced by something deeper, almost *pained.* He rubbed a hand over his locs, exhaling slowly.

"Rae… she came in *hot,*"he said, voice low and rough. "She was a *storm,* man. We burn bright together. Real intense. But *before* her…"

His jaw tightened, bracing for the words.

"There was Jasmine."

The air itself felt heavier. Selene blinked, something unexpected stirring in her chest.

"Jasmine Chandrika Campbell," he continued, voice quieter now, like the name itself was sacred. "She was my first love. First *everything.* We met when we was five years old, man. *Five.* I knew from the moment I saw her that she was it for me. Ain't *nobody* else existed after that. She was smart, funny, gorgeous as hell… she got me on a level nobody else *ever* has. I was completely *gone* for her. Soulmate type shit. I used to think God made her just for me."

He let out a quiet, broken chuckle, but there was no real humor in it.

"Then she left me for another dude when she went to college. Just… walked away. Broke my heart so bad I ain't think I was *ever* gon' recover."

Selene exhaled slowly, sadness filling her chest from the raw pain still lingering in his eyes. She could tell- even now, years later, with someone entirely new on his arm- a part of him would *still* be with Jasmine if it were up to him.

After a few seconds of heavy silence, she spoke gently.

"I've never experienced that kind of heartbreak," she admitted. "Before Caleb… I didn't really *date* anyone. I was too busy raising Thena after our parents died, and then… *grieving* her. Romance felt like a luxury I couldn't afford."

Damien looked at her then, his dark eyes softening with understanding. "Damn. That's heavy."

Selene gave a small, sad smile. "It was. Still is."

They sat in the quiet for a long moment, the weight of their shared pain settling between them like a third presence in the room. The fire crackled softly. The mountain wind whispered against the tall windows.

Finally, Damien broke the silence, voice low.

"You know… You ain't who I thought you'd be."

Selene met his gaze, curious. "What'd you think I'd be?"

He paused, thinking carefully as he looked her up and down. "Like… glass. Polished, clean… but *fragile*. Like one wrong move and you'd break."

She waited a heartbeat. "And now?"

He looked right into her eyes, his own deep and focused.

"You still glass," he said slowly, "but the kind that'll cut somebody before it let itself be broken."

Selene blinked, a faint gasp escaping her. She didn't expect that.

He smirked, looking down. "Truth is… I ain't like you at first. Ain't trust whatever could be under all that polish."

Selene smiled faintly. "Funny. I didn't like *you*, either."

Damien gasped in mock offense. "Impossible."

She let out a little laugh. "I saw someone… cold. Arrogant, even."

Damien just smiled softly, fingers unconsciously toying with his tags.

Selene tilted her head, her voice gentle but certain.

"But now? I think you're full of love, Damien King. You just don't know where to put it."

They stayed quiet for a long moment, letting the truth of their words settle between them in the incredibly intimate room.

Finally, Damien stood and offered his hand. "Come on. Let's get out of here before the bookcase locks us in here and we die for real."

Selene took his hand, chuckling faintly. "Lead the way."

# Chapter 21

*Fated Not to be Tamed*

**21 June 2017- Manhattan, NY**

The Harlem sidewalks were still warm from the summer solstice sun, gold light stretching across pavement like melted honey. The air smelled of roasted peanuts and hot pretzels, city heat clinging to every step.

Inas moved like she always did- with purpose and a little flair- her scarf tied high on her head like a crown, her gold hoops glinting like even *they* had somewhere important to be.

Selene, 21 now, trailed just behind, her arms crossed, tote bag swinging lazily off one shoulder. "Tatie," she said, her thick curls, now a shapely afro, fluttering, "You really think you're gonna win this time?"

Inas didn't even slow her stride.

*"Choufi,* hope is for tired women. *Azma* will take you places," she replied, slipping into the corner bodega with a flick of her small hand like she owned the place.

The bell jingled above them as the fluorescent lights buzzed to life. Inas walked straight to the counter and laid her hand flat, as she always did, as if it were a ritual older than life.

"Ramy, *yallah.* My usual."

The cashier- a wiry Arab guy with sleepy eyes and a gentle smirk- already had her tickets ready.

"Two Quick Picks and one golden scratch," he said with a thick accent, handing them over like they were royal.

Selene leaned on the counter, sipping what was left of her chai latte. "You come here for tickets *that* often?"

Inas shrugged. "This is your mama's hometown. If her spirit touched this place, we will *definitely* get lucky eventually."

Selene giggled and shook her head, but her eyes focused on the tickets.

Inas wasted no time and began scratching with intent, like the numbers would reveal themselves out of respect. And…

Nothing.

Still, she folded the ticket and tucked it into her scarf like it had secrets worth saving.

"Almost," she said, already turning toward the door. "Next time, *Inshallah.*"

Selene followed, her eyes squinting in the light. "You've done this every week for *four years,* Tatie."

"And I will keep doing it every week for the next *twenty* if I have to," Inas said. "*Li fat ma mat.* What's passed isn't dead. It just hasn't finished becoming."

They walked in rhythm now, back into the golden Harlem dusk.

Inas looped her plump arm around her niece's, giving her a teasing, mischievous look that made Selene feel pre-embarrassed.

"Now, talk to me about that hot *trainer* you're seeing later."

Selene snorted from her aunt's antics, but even she couldn't hide her excitement.

The group descended into the kitchen, groggy-eyed and half-prepared to see another black envelope and do another weird task.

But then, stopped in their tracks.

The dining table was already set- baskets of flaky, buttery croissants, steamy, soft scrambled eggs with scallions and cheese, glazed turkey bacon, golden hash browns crisped to perfection, and even carafes of freshly squeezed orange juice and strong Maghrebi mint tea. There was fruit, too, arranged like art- strawberry hearts, cantaloupe stars, flower pineapples.

And there it was, sitting right in the middle of the table like a crown:

A golden envelope.

Caleb was the first to exhale, wearing a grey thermal this morning. "Oh, my God. I never thought I'd be this excited to see gold paper again."

Raven raised her coffee like a glass of champagne, her wine-red bodycon dress hugging her like it adored her. "Cheers to creepy group exercises, instead of creepy... whatever the fuck yesterday was."

"Guess we succeeded in our 'tasks'," Selene said with a giggle, but by accident, she glanced at Damien.

He was already looking at her.

Then, his jaw tightened as he reached for the envelope, opened it, and read:

"We're sorry for leaving you hanging, lovebirds, but don't worry; we'll make it up to you. The next two weeks will be full of the most fun you can possibly have at a mountain lodge."

Selene had almost canceled.

She wasn't sure why. Maybe it was the dark clouds above signaling rain, or maybe it was that she wasn't entirely sure she believed in strength training. Or maybe it was that something inside her still didn't believe she deserved to be strong in the first place.

Not after everything.

But here she was, doing an effortless front split on the mat like she could do so in her sleep, eyeing the man himself.

And, God, what a man he was.

Tall. Broad. Gold-toned hair that seemed to sparkle. A jawline that could cut glass. Muscles that screamed, *'I can carry you* **and** *everything you love.'* And those *eyes-* the most *unique* color she'd ever seen- not quite blue, not quite green, but something heartbreakingly in-between.

The kind of eyes that Thena would've gone on and on about.

When those eyes met hers across the gym, she immediately looked away, cheeks flushed visibly.

He walked over a few minutes later, clipboard in hand.

"Selene?"

She nodded, brushing a coil behind her ear. "That's me."

He offered his hand.

"Caleb. I'll be working with you."

His palm was large and warm, but she couldn't help but notice a long bruise along his knuckles.

Still, when she took his hand in hers, it was like she forgot every pose she'd ever learned.

"You've done yoga for a while, right?" he asked as they moved to the mats. He had a calmness about him that further intrigued her.

She nodded. "Been teaching at this center for a year and a half, now."

"Cool," he said. "That means your flexibility's probably amazing. We'll focus on strength and stability. Build from your foundation."

Something about the way he said *foundation* felt heavier than it should've.

"You ever trained before?" he asked, already setting out kettlebells.

"Not like this," Selene admitted bashfully, her dimples deepening. "I'm more used to... *listening* to my body, not challenging it."

He nodded like he understood her completely. "We'll do both. No pressure. Just let me know if anything doesn't feel right."

Selene exhaled slowly, watching him move—controlled, grounded, patient. He didn't rush her through anything, didn't bark orders. He asked questions. Checked in. Met her where she was.

By the end of the session, her arms were shaking from a new kind of burn, and her breath came out in surprised laughter.

"You okay?" he asked, grinning, those eyes that captivated her the moment she saw them, twinkling under the gym lights.

She couldn't help but gaze into them, a soft smile on her lips.

"I think... I think I might be."

The backdoor was unlocked for snowy fun, as was the indoor pool room, jacuzzi room, game room, and they'd even learned that there was a whole ass *auditorium*.

Who had the most fun, though, were Damien and Selene.

They threw snowballs at each other like kids desperate to win a competition; splashed at each other in the pool, laughing so loudly that it echoed; sang along to "Fly in the Freedom" as they battled to find emeralds in *Sonic Adventure 2 Battle*, then talked softly about how they used to play the game with their siblings. By the 23rd, they had inside jokes and noticed when the other wasn't in the room. Damien had even begun calling Selene "moon girl", which made her breath catch- no one but Athena had ever called her that, and she never even told him she had.

Raven noticed it all.

That night, she stretched out across the bed, sheets tangled around her waist, her dark, freshly dyed hair spilling over Damien's chest. Their breathing was still slowing, the faint sheen of sweat over their naked bodies cooling from the open balcony doors. She toyed lazily with his dog tags, watching them glint against his delicious mahogany-brown skin.

"So…" she said at last, voice light but edged with curiosity.

"You and the girl you said was weird and untrustworthy…"

Damien snorted, tilting his head on the pillow, one brow raised. "What you gettin' at, boo?"

"Don't play dumb." She smirked, propping herself on an elbow to look at him properly, eyes extra focused, a hint of something in them that he hadn't really seen in them before.

"I see the way y'all are. Laughing, scheming, catching each other at the bottom of waterslides…"

Damien let out a sigh, looking up at the large wooden ceiling fan above them, eyes attempting to catch each fleeing blade.

"Turns out we got more in common than I thought."

Raven narrowed her eyes.

"You're not leaving me for someone else's wife at a couple's retreat, are you?"

Damien gave her a look. "It ain't like you to ask stupid shit."

Raven laughed, dropping back down. "Just checking."

For a while, the only sound was her slow breathing, easing into sleep. Damien smoothed a hand down her smooth back, steady and protective, but his eyes stayed fixed on the ceiling.

Eventually, they shifted, catching on the window.

The tiny waning crescent hung high over the mountains. His chest rose and fell slowly as he stared at it, remembering Selene's soft voice in the tower room when she talked about Athena loving it, about that being the reason she herself loved it so much.

He wondered if she was awake right then, looking at the same moon.

Quickly, he tore his eyes away from it and kissed Raven's forehead like a reminder.

☾

In the suite just next door, Caleb snored, sleep overtaking him completely in the impossibly plush bed.

Selene, though? She couldn't sleep at all.

Her eyes were not focused on the window as they usually were, but on the mantle- on the flames flickering and popping within the stone, dancing as if each particle had a mind of its own.

She smiled, remembering her long conversation with Damien in the tower room, how low and soft his voice got near the end.

Remembering how his deep-set eyes seemed to look into her *soul* when he told her she was glass that could cut.

She did a little breathing exercise in bed, trying to calm her quickly-beating heart.

She grabbed her teal hat and kissed it like a reminder.

# Chapter 22

*Stars, When You Shine*

## Halloween 2017- The Fox Theatre

The air smelled like expensive perfume and ambition. Chandeliers sparkled overhead like stars too proud to live in the sky, and every guest moved like they knew they belonged- or were faking it so well no one could tell. Swae Lee's "Unforgettable" boomed overhead.

Damien, now 23, stood off to the side of the velvet entryway, his arms crossed, black suit tailored to his now even broader frame, earpiece tucked in. He was all sharp lines and calmness, except for the way his dark eyes scanned every guest that walked in, professional and intimidating. He'd been a guard for a year now, and he'd already been in rooms with the greatest, the most beautiful. Nothing could make him stir anymore.

And then, *she* arrived.

The crowd murmured and cameras clicked as Raven Quinn, 25, walked in, owning the marble floor like it owed her money. She wore a black velvet gown that hugged her hourglass curves, with a thigh-high slit and plunging neckline that made subtlety beg for mercy. Her jet-black hair was sleek and glossy, falling like ink down her back. Her lips were painted wine-dark, and around her neck hung a silver choker that glinted under the lights.

Damien didn't know who she was until he did.

She walked straight toward him, her hips swaying with each step like flowing water.

"You my bodyguard tonight?"

Damien looked her up and down once, slow. Not disrespectful- just taking in the threat level.

The problem was, the only threat she posed to anyone was to his self-control.

"Yeah," he said, voice much lower than he intended it to be. "Apparently, someone out here thinks you important enough to need protectin'."

Raven tilted her head, her otherworldly green eyes glittering. He wasn't the type of guy to be nervous- the Army beat that the fuck out of him- but something about this woman's eyes froze him in place.

She smirked softly. "You don't follow influencers, huh?"

His dark eyes bore into hers. "Ion' follow nobody. I lead."

That made her laugh- the *real* kind, not the Instagram kind. "Alright, Mr. Alpha Male. I'm Raven."

She reached her hand out, jet-black acrylics sharp as knives, an ouroboros tattoo on the back of her hand captioned *Trust No One.*

Damien looked at her hand, and then took it into his own, his watch glinting. "Damien".

There was a heartbeat of silence as the two powerhouses looked at one another. Everyone around them couldn't help but stop and stare.

Raven stepped just a little closer.

"You got that *look.*"

Damien's eyes looked her up and down. He knew he was being paid to protect her, but he couldn't deny how *decadent* she was.

"What look's that?"

She looked him up and down in return, taking in his impressive frame. "Like you've seen some shit."

He smirked, eyes flickering down at the slit in her dress, then back up like he wasn't fazed. "That obvious?"

"Only to someone who's got the same look."

And in that moment, under all that silk and gold, an electric current passed between them.

## 24 January 2020- Evervale Lodge

The golden envelope had been taped to the inside of the breakfast bar. This time, it shimmered a little more than usual- as if the hosts *knew* they were about to deliver.

*"Tonight's your last treat of the two weeks, lovebirds. So, dress hot as hell. The ballroom opens at 10 p.m. Trust us - you'll know what to do once you get there."*

They did, indeed.

By 9:45, the entire group had *transformed*. Leather, glitter, slick-back hair, red-bottoms, redder lips. The ballroom had been drenched in darkness, lit only by moody purples and flashing strobes. A version of Nina Simone's "Feeling Good" with enhanced bass and a deliciously sultry beat played from speakers overhead.

There was no golden envelope this time; just what looked like thousands of open bottles in a large free-standing bar and pure suggestion.

It... didn't take long for them to all get plastered.

Michael and Laney disappeared to a velvet couch in the corner after two cocktails (and mocktails) too many. Raven was on the dance floor nearly the whole time- somehow managing to grind on Damien *and* Caleb in the same song. Selene had laughed and shaken her head, but that was before the tequila started talking.

Damien had been sitting on the barstool, just enjoying the strobes and bass with drinks, when she walked over.

His jaw was already slack from the Bacardi, but now it hung *fully* open.

Selene wore a tiny strapless black minidress that hugged her impossibly graceful curves, gold arm cuffs, and stilettos that seemed to sculpt her golden legs. Along her forearms were tattoos that she'd kept hidden until now: the triple-moon symbol, a pentagram, a sword surrounded by a wreath, and a heart with *'T&M Forever'* inside it. Her hair was straightened, flowing down her curved back like thick satin.

"You look..." he started, but didn't finish.

Selene raised a freshly threaded brow and took a slow sip of whatever cocktail Raven had shoved into her hand. "You dancing or nah?"

Damien blinked, smirking slowly. "You tryna challenge me, moon girl?"

"I'm just saying," she said, stepping closer, her voice a little softer now.

"I *know* you got rhythm, fire boy."

That was all it took.

He followed her to the floor like a moth that already knew the flame would take him and didn't even care. He was already intoxicated by the scent of her caramel-pistachio body cream before they even started dancing.

It started with space; the kind of teasing distance that still let air pass between them, that said *'this is a dance between friends.'*

But then the music dropped, and Selene rolled her hips, and Damien instinctively moved with her. She turned around, her back to his chest, and his hands found her waist before either of them could think twice. Even with the alcohol coursing through her veins, her body *shivered* at the feel of his heat.

They were close now.

*Too* close.

But it was dark, and no one could really see them, and the others were busy doing a group dance, and...

Selene continued rolling against him, hips loose, lost in the music, in his scent: cocoa butter and something uniquely *him*. She looked back at him over her shoulder, and her breath caught in her throat.

Damien was looking at her like she was fire itself.

Her full, berry-painted lips curved just slightly, making his jaw tighten as one of his hands instinctively fisted her dress, making heat pool within her.

As the strobe lights painted the room in flashes, the two of them continued moving like one organism; her hips brushing his, his lips dipping low, brushing the shell of her ear ever so slightly- ever so *dangerously*. Her eyes, already low-lidded from the tequila, fluttered shut, and then-

Somebody's booming, plastered laugh broke somewhere nearby, and reality surged as the grief twins scrambled to find the people they came to this lodge with.

The music was too loud for conversation, the bass rattling the plastic cups, but Selene, 22 now, hardly noticed.

Her vampire cape kept snagging on people's costumes as they pushed past her, but all she could think about was the way Caleb, almost 24, stood beside her, a whole foot taller than she, his werewolf mask pushed up so she could see his grin- one that made her both nervous and comforted.

They had said they'd come as friends. Nothing more. Just a party they could crash and celebrate his upcoming birthday.

And yet, when his arm brushed hers as someone jostled them closer together, her breath caught as if she'd been sprinting. His body heat was almost dizzying, and she couldn't stop staring into his sparkling sea-glass eyes.

He bent down, voice low and rough in her ear. "Want to step outside? It's too packed in here."

She nodded, almost too quickly.

The autumn air hit cool and sharp when they slipped onto the porch. For a moment, neither spoke.

"I'm glad you came tonight," Caleb finally said, leaning against the railing, his eyes catching the glow of the jack-o-lantern at their feet. "I usually *hate* parties."

She laughed softly, nervously. "You invited me to a party when you don't even *like* them?"

He studied her.

"I knew I'd like it with *you.*"

Something in her chest flipped.

She had imagined this moment a hundred ways, and still her heart was racing too hard to think straight. He was her trainer, technically, and this was *not* supposed to happen. But she wanted it.

She wanted *him.*

Before she could overthink, Caleb stepped closer. His voice dropped to a whisper. "Can I-?"

Selene nodded before he finished.

The kiss was tentative at first- warm and soft- and she felt her pulse spark like firecrackers.

When they pulled apart, she blinked up at him, breathless. She blinked, stars in her eyes.

"That was my first kiss."

Caleb smiled, though his shoulders tensed up just a bit.

"That was… my first, too."

●

The fire in the stone mantle was down to embers. Most of the group had passed out in their beds, drunk as hell.

Selene, however, was wide awake.

She stood alone in the glow of the flames in the living room, swaying slightly in that black mini-dress, her hair now frizzy in an enchanting way. Her eyes were soft, dazed, still high on the buzz of music and liquor. She spun slowly in place, arms lifting over her head like the night hadn't ended, like the party was still living inside her.

Damien stopped in the middle of the staircase.

She didn't see him right away. He didn't say anything; just watched.

Her glow was *unreal,* her body shimmering with sweat and glitter. She looked like she adored being *alive.*

She turned and finally caught him looking. She smiled, slowly and loosely, her cheeks flushed.

"Hey."

"Hey."

She padded toward him barefoot, her anklet sparkling. Her stiletto pumps were thrown wherever.

"You tired?"

He hesitated. "Not really."

"Me neither."

They stood there for a heartbeat too long.

Then she tilted her head, her eyes still dreamy, still low. "You wanna finish that painting we started?"

Damien tilted his head. "At 3 a.m.?"

Selene shrugged playfully. "Perfect timing. Tipsy enough to be brave. Drunk enough not to care if it sucks."

She smiled at him, almost mischievous.

He didn't even need to say yes.

When they got to the tall wooden double doors, she took a tiny remote from out of a pocket stitched into her dress and unlocked the door with a single press of a button.

Damien quirked a brow. "You just…*had* that?"

Selene giggled, stumbling a bit in tipsiness as she stepped inside. "I don't sleep, remember? You find a *lot* of things when you explore."

He rolled his eyes. "You such a god damn weirdo. I *know* Caleb wonder what the hell he got himself into sometimes."

"Shush it!" Selene giggled out, swatting his arm before opening the doors.

The art studio was dark and quiet tonight. The tall, arched windows did not spill any moonlight as the moon had just begun its new phase, but the stars twinkled so intensely that they were visible beyond the glass.

Their canvas stood in the corner- the same sad storm.

Selene practically skipped over to the easel and used a small clicker to turn the lamp on, which painted the entire studio in a surreal kind of gold.

Damien raised his brow, removing his jacket and revealing a well-fitted black dress shirt, unbuttoned just enough to show off his dog tags.

Selene didn't even bother with brushes; she just dipped her fingers into thick yellow paint and painted a circle peeking out behind a dark cloud.

A sun.

"Now, it's *happy,*" she said, her low-lidded eyes sparkling.

Damien chuckled, stepping beside her, eyes lingering on hers. "And what we doin' with the rain? Turnin' it into stars?"

Selene gasped like he said something beautiful. "*Yesss.*"

He chuckled again, looking at her a heartbeat too long as they both dipped their fingers in silver and attempted to turn the raindrops into shining stars, stifling giggles.

Then, Selene paused.

Put on the most mischievous little smile.

And drew a line up his forearm.

Damien froze in place.

Looked at the mark on his arm, then back at her.

"Oh, *hell* nah."

She stifled a giggle, her cheeks puffing up.

He quickly dipped his fingers in sky-blue and drew a circle on her cheek.

Selene gasped. "You're gonna start a war," she warned, biting her lip.

He smirked, eyes oddly intense despite the alcohol flowing through his veins. "Start*ed*. Past tense."

She then dipped her finger in red and lunged at him, laughing breathlessly. He dodged, barely, both of them laughing now, spinning around the table like kids on a sugar high. She shrieked as he grabbed a fistful of yellow, clapped his hands together, and painted her bare shoulders.

She went for his jaw, then missed. He caught her waist, yanking her to himself unintentionally in the inertia.

Then… they stopped.

Their bodies were close, *way* too close. Her strapless dress had moved lower, exposing the full swell of her cleavage.

His chest rose and fell with more and more speed.

She was breathing just hard, and not from running.

Damien looked down at her, eyes glued to her plush lips.

Selene looked up at him, knees weak from his hypnotized stare.

And then-

He kissed her like he'd lost control.

She moaned, fingers immediately clawing into his locs, painting them like they were her own canvas.

He backed her into the table, his palms sliding paint up her thighs, bunching the fabric of her dress up.

He hissed when he realized she wore nothing underneath it.

"Damien," she whispered shakily between kisses. "What are we doing…"

He pulled back just enough to look at her, his eyes heat-dazed. "Tell me to stop," he breathed out, hands still on her waist. "Selene, say stop."

She didn't.

She jumped up and kissed him instead, and he immediately lifted her up in his arms. Her legs wrapped around his waist as he sat her down hard onto the table, making brushes clatter to the floor and a jar of water spill behind them.

They didn't even notice.

Selene spread her legs and pulled him in, bare heels digging into the backs of his thighs as their lips smacked audibly, echoing inside the spacious room.

His lips left hers to trail down her neck, biting the side of it like a claim, his tongue tracing a clean stripe from her throat to her ear. Her eyes rolled back from the intoxicating sensation, even as her hands fought about whether to push him away or pull him in.

His large hand found the top edge of her dress and practically yanked it down, making her gasp as her bare, perky breasts bounced out. He groaned and kissed and sucked at her skin. "Jesus… *Damien,*" she crooned breathlessly.

Need defeated guilt after that, and she shoved his dress shirt off him, her small hands hungrily exploring his bare shoulders, arms, and torso before pushing his slacks down, along with his boxer briefs, baring him entirely.

But suddenly-

A pang slashed through Damien's heart.

Raven's face, gorgeous and trusting despite her past, flashed in his mind. His thoughts were *loud.*

*'Rae… nah… What the fuck am I doing? I can't-'*

And then, Selene reached down, wrapping her hand- her left hand- around him, making him groan and forget every circumstance that had led him here.

Without even thinking, he pushed her flat onto the table, making even more brushes clatter down. She let out a startled gasp that melted into a strangled moan as he pushed between her legs.

His jaw clenched tight as he felt her snug heat. "Fuck, Selene…"

Her blood-red manicured nails scraped down his strong back, leaving imprints as well as paint streaks as she rocked her hips up, her breath coming out in soft, open sounds that made him lose rhythm. She couldn't, *couldn't* think anymore.

There was nothing but the sound of their pleasure, the wood groaning as if even *it* knew what was happening atop it was wrong, and Damien's- Xander's- dog tags clinking against Selene's skin with every traitorous rut of his hips.

She clutched those tags. He *growled* from the motion.

Without even thinking, he bit her bottom lip hard, making her yelp out a moan as blood dribbled out. He licked it, tending to the wound, and she sucked his tongue into her mouth wantonly, making him groan aloud.

Before he could help it, his hips moved faster, harder, pleasure rising so fast that it terrified him, his hands gripping her hips hard enough to bruise, another paint jar crashing onto the ground, splattering crimson like a crime scene.

Selene was chanting his name now, breathless, every part of her tightening around him, pulling him in her, *with* her as he bit into her shoulder to keep some kind of control, uselessly, as it was fading away *fast* in real time.

And then, every color surrounding them faded to white.

# Chapter 23

*Dying Like a Shooting Star*

**New Year's Eve 2017- Manhattan, NY**

The countdown echoed around them like a heartbeat.

*Ten... nine... eight...*

The rooftop party was packed, but Selene hardly noticed the crowd. There were glittering lights wrapped around the balcony railings, people dancing like there was no tomorrow, Coldplay's "Hymn for the Weekend" booming through the large stereo speakers-

But her focus was on the man standing next to her, his thumb tracing slow circles on the back of her hand.

*Seven... six...*

Caleb stood just a little too close, wearing a dark button-up with the sleeves rolled to his elbows and a subtle nervous energy behind his smile.

He looked different tonight- not because of his outfit, or the twinkle lights casting soft gold across his features, but because of the look in his eyes- intense and certain, like he was looking at something he'd been waiting years for.

The look made her heart pitter-patter in her chest.

*Five... four...*

"Selene," he murmured, leaning closer so only she could hear. "There's something I've been wanting to ask you..."

*Three...*

She blinked up at him, eyes wide, berry-glossed lips parted in surprise. "Now?" she whispered.

*Two…*

His fingers curled gently around her wrist, teeth biting his lip just so. "Yeah. Now."

*One…*

"HAPPY NEW YEAR!!!" erupted around them. Fireworks exploded in the distance. Strangers kissed and clinked glasses and whooped into the night air- but Selene heard none of it.

Because Caleb was holding her hand like it was precious. Like *she* was precious.

And then-

He dropped to one knee.

Selene gasped, loud enough for the entire city to hear.

Caleb held out a gold ring with a tiny but real diamond; it sparkled like the clearest water on the starriest night.

"Selene Fatima Amrani… will you marry me?"

Selene froze, trembling, eyes sparkling with the fireworks booming above her.

"M-*marry*? Caleb, we're not even *official!*"

Caleb smiled, bashful. "I know, Selene. But I've known you for six months, and God, I haven't felt this way in *years*. I genuinely want to spend the rest of my life with you."

And right there, as the city rang in a new year and confetti rained from above-

Caleb got up from the ground and kissed her. It was full and passionate, as if he were trying to fuse with her.

He pulled away, his ocean eyes twinkling with the fireworks. One of them just happened to explode into something that resembled a heart.

He looked down at the woman he desperately wanted to make his fiancée. "So… what do you say?"

Selene smiled, her eyes filling with tears.

"Of course. Of *course,* you crazy motherfucker."

The two laughed and kissed as cheers and fireworks continued exploding around them.

### 25 January 2020- Evervale Lodge

Selene stirred, her thick lashes fluttering open on a soft rug, a drop cloth draped over her body. She didn't know where she was- only that she felt a divine mixture of ache and warmth.

A tiny smile graced her lips as she snuggled into the body heat behind her.

*…And then it hit her who that body heat belonged to.*

Damien's thick arm was heavy against her waist, each line of his body melding into each curve of hers as he snored softly like he had no worries.

*They were both naked.*

Her breath caught in her throat as she turned to look at his face- beautiful and oblivious, his jaw slack in pure comfort like he wasn't sleeping on a rug on a paint-covered ground.

He moved slightly, murmuring something low and sleepy. Then he blinked his eyes open, his gaze heavy and fogged, until it landed on her.

They stared at each other for a second too long.

Then it *slammed* into them both.

Selene sat up fast, holding the drop cloth over her still-sensitive breasts, panting in disbelief.

Damien rubbed his face, brows furrowed in utter torture.

"Shit. *Shit*, Selene-"

"I know," she said quickly, pushing her fluffy, paint-splattered curls out of her rapidly paling face. "I know."

The silence that followed was choking. The air wasn't warm and electric like it was a couple of hours ago.

It was heavy with the names of the people they hadn't said all night.

Selene stood fast, holding the drop cloth over her body, guilt *loud* in her gold-flecked eyes.

"Okay. We *have* to be smart about this."

Damien slapped both hands over his face, dreads wild and paint-stained. "The fuck is *wrong* with me?" he grunted below his breath before reaching for his boxer-briefs.

Her eyes softened at his panic, but her voice remained firm as she held the drop cloth tighter. "There is *no* time for freaking out. We have to be smart. Go shower. Tell Raven you passed out in the living room. She should still be asleep."

He got up then, jaw tight, pulling his grey boxer-briefs over his strong thighs. Selene looked away with a blush as it *fully* set in what they'd done hours before.

Quickly, he pulled up his slacks before turning to her with a pained look in his eyes. "What *you* gonna do?"

Her mouth tightened. "I'm gonna go cook breakfast. Now, go, go," she said in a rushed tone, waving a hand.

He nodded, jaw tight, and slipped out the double doors.

And Selene, still aching in all the places that told the truth, bent down to pick up the paintbrushes they'd abandoned in the storm they made.

## New Year's Eve 2017- Atlanta, GA

They weren't official; weren't anything with a name. But for the past two months, they'd been everywhere together- him on security, her being the show.

To the public, they were bodyguard and internet celebrity. In private, though, they were a different story- sharing secrets, pains, hotel beds.

Just last week, they'd opened up about the people who broke them and changed them forever. Kevin, the blue-eyed boy from the sandbox. Jasmine, the radiant girl from the Smith Elementary kindergarten class.

"You remember what I said about not catching feelings for your bodyguard?" Raven teased, looking ravishing in a black mini-dress and matching stilettos. Her hair was especially dark today, flowing down her back like an inky waterfall.

He stepped closer, blazer hugging his strong form. "Yeah. I remember you said it right *after* you caught 'em."

Raven narrowed her eyes, trying not to grin. "Cocky."

"Not cocky," Damien said, eyes tracing her face like it was the first time all over again. *"Real."*

Ten seconds to midnight.

She looked at him- really looked.

His dreads- stopping at his ears, now, which glinted with tiny hoops. His brows- thick and impossibly dark. His nose- so, so handsomely shaped, and his lips- those *lips*- just utterly kissable.

The more she studied him, the more her smile faded into something raw. "King…" she started, but his hand caught hers.

"Rae," he said, low. "We can stop playin'."

Tears started to sting her verdant eyes. "But I never… I never wanted to love again. Not after Kev. Not after-"

*Three. Two. One.*

Fireworks exploded over the skyline just as Damien pulled her into a deep, passionate, claiming kiss, like he was sealing a covenant with their lips alone.

When they pulled apart, her lips were redder than before, and her eyes were hazy.

Damien held her impossibly smooth cheeks in his large hands, his dark eyes looking in between hers.

"I know you been hurt," he began, voice shockingly soft. "I been hurt, too. Shit, after Jas, I swore I'd only fuck and run for the rest of my life. I can't be too sure you won't hurt me like she did. But you know what I *am* sure about?"

She looked up at him, her beautiful eyes shimmering with rare, vulnerable tears.

He continued, his dark eyes the softest she'd ever seen them. "I'm sure that long as I call you mine? I ain't hurtin' *you.*"

Steam filled the luxurious ensuite bathroom like a thick fog, swirling around Damien's tense frame as he took deep, labored breaths.

He stood under the large rainfall showerhead, the water *way* too hot. He'd put it on that temperature on purpose, knowing he deserved to feel *some* kind of pain for his actions.

He braced his hands against the stone-

-hands that were still inked with Raven's name.

He felt like he was trying to scrub sin off his skin, but guilt wasn't water-soluble.

Every scrub took a streak of paint off. Every streak of paint brought back memories- ridiculously vivid despite how drunk he was at the time.

*Selene gasping in his mouth.*

*Squeezing him with her legs.*

*Throwing her head back like she'd never imagined anything feeling so good.*

*The sound she made when he-*

He shook his head, dragging his hands down his face as swirls of yellow, red, blue, and silver circled the drain.

His locs stuck to his shoulders- locs that Raven loved like her own.

Locs that didn't deserve to be in her hands ever again.

"Fuck," he hissed below his breath, jaw tight. He felt tears sting the backs of his eyes.

He'd really done it. He'd done exactly what he promised Raven he never would.

The *second* major promise he'd broken in his life.

Nauseated with guilt, he turned off the water, standing in the silence for a heartbeat longer.

Simply being *naked* triggered memories, so he quickly grabbed one of the fluffy charcoal-colored towels from the wall rack and wrapped it around his waist. Steam swirled around him like the ghosts of last night.

And then-

"Babe?"

He nearly jumped, his heart rate picking up instantly.

He turned, gulping, to see Raven in the doorway, blinking at him from beneath her tousled black waves, wearing one of his old Army shirts and nothing else.

The sight of her in that shirt made him want to break down right then and there.

Her eyeliner was a bit smudged- but her eyes were the opposite as she stepped further into the bathroom.

"What the hell are you doing showering *this* early?" she asked, her voice rough with sleep and something else. "You always shower *after* breakfast."

Damien's throat tightened, his heart suddenly beating so hard that he could've sworn she could hear it.

"Passed out in the living room," he said too fast. "Felt nasty when I woke up."

To say the least.

Raven's eyes narrowed just slightly. Not angry, but *curious*.

Somehow, that was *so* much worse.

"Huh," she said. "You didn't come up at *all* last night? Like you just… *slept* down there?"

"Yeah," he muttered, turning back toward the sink like he was busy drying off, even though he didn't have a towel in his hand. "Too drunk to even make it up the stairs thanks to your mystery cocktails."

"Hmm."

Just that sound. That 'Raven' *hmm*, like her gut knew something her brain hadn't figured out yet.

He didn't dare meet her eyes. He grabbed a towel from the rack and put 100% of his focus on patting his chest dry, on not shaking.

Then-

"Do you smell that?" Raven's head tilted, nostrils flaring like a bloodhound. "It's kinda early for breakfast, no? We usually don't smell it till like 8."

Damien froze, grateful as hell for the change of subject, even though the new subject wasn't exactly comforting either.

"Yeah," he said, clearing his throat. "Must be Selene. You know how weird she is, getting up early to do weird shit in the kitchen."

He stammered a bit on her name.

He cringed at how extremely hard he was trying to act normally. He just *knew* the black-haired stunner could see right through him.

But to his shock, she grinned a little, distracted by the scent. "God, she's really trying to make us fat."

Damien forced a laugh as he pulled on a shirt.

"Guess so."

Selene moved as if on a *mission*. Plates clinked softly as she set them out with expert precision- forks on the left, knives and spoons on the right, napkins folded like origami.

The table was stunning- a warm, glowing feast of cheesy Gouda grits, crispy salmon patties, cinnamon-slicked French toast with spiced honey butter, the fluffiest eggs you've ever seen, rosemary sausage links, perfectly-cut star fruit, Maghrebi mint tea, and warm blueberry biscuits baked damn near to perfection.

Because how *else* do you make it up to a group when you just did something that would tear them clean apart?

She adjusted the biscuits just because, Marina's "Valley of the Dolls" playing out of her phone like an echo of her soul.

Footsteps sounded from down the hall. Then Caleb's ever-charming voice rang out:

"Damn, babe."

He walked straight up to her and wrapped his muscular arms around her waist from behind, pressing a loving kiss into the crook of her neck.

Selene tensed but forced herself to smile.

She couldn't help but remember the way Damien had bitten that exact same spot hours before.

Caleb beamed at her, totally unaware. "Only *you'd* get up early to cook," he said. "Better hope the hosts won't be pissed you took their job."

Selene chuckled tightly, hands fidgeting with the biscuits again. "Guess I beat them to it."

Just then, he pulled back slightly and tilted his head, his eyes narrowing in a way that made her heart drop.

"Wait… babe…" He reached out and rubbed at a silver smear near her collarbone.

"Why are you covered in… paint?"

She could've died right then. She thought she'd gotten it all before she started cooking.

Damien, newly arrived and halfway into a chair, tensed so hard his jaw twitched. As if his… recent actions weren't bad enough, he *also* had a harrowing hangover.

Selene then let out a laugh so quick it almost sounded real. "I was *so* drunk last night, I decided to paint something in the art studio. Then of course, I passed out there."

It wasn't a lie. Not *technically*.

Caleb gave her a look. "You… painted and… passed out?"

"Weird shit happens when you drunk, man," Damien managed to mutter out, but his eye twitched despite himself.

Raven narrowed her eyes at him. "I know my cocktails are strong as fuck, but damn, both of y'all are acting like I gave you moonshine."

Selene could hardly even crack a half-smile.

Michael and Laney shuffled in then, both looking like they'd just barely survived the club night, and the tension faded.

They all took their seats, enjoying the decadent meal-

And two of the six lovebirds didn't even so much as *glance* at one another.

# Chapter 24

*S'envoler*

## 4 May 2018- Brooklyn, NY

The knock came like *thunder.*

Selene jumped, nearly dropping the spatula she was using to flip msemmen. "What the hell-?"

Caleb was halfway off the couch, one sock on, remote still in his hand, exhausted from having gymmed all week. "Did someone crash a car into the building?"

Another series of bangs shook the door.

Selene rushed over, heart thudding.

She yanked it open.

"Tatie…?"

Inas stood there in a flurry of grey waves and breathlessness, one hand pressed dramatically to her chest, the other clutching a wrinkled piece of paper.

Her eyes were wild as tears streaked her cheeks. "*Binti...* I *won.*"

Selene blinked, not processing her aunt's words at all.

"What?"

Inas shoved the paper into her hands like she'd lost all motor control. "The numbers. They finally came. *Ya Latiif!*"

Selene stared at the ticket, then back at her aunt, her already large eyes as wide as they could get.

Her voice cracked. "Are you serious?"

Inas's hands trembled. "I thought it was a mistake. I checked it *seven* times."

She started to laugh, but it cracked in the middle and turned into a choked sob.

"On a gagné, ma chérie. On peut enfin faire ce qu'on rêve de faire depuis cinq ans."

Selene's throat tightened, tears spilling down her cheeks, her breathing coming in quick and labored. She pulled Inas into a huge hug.

"Et c'est le jour de l'anniversaire de sa mort, Tatie. Elle veut qu'on le fasse, elle le veut."

Inas squeezed her tight.

Then-

"I'm paying for your wedding as well," she said, her voice shaking. "I don't care what you say. I don't care if you want it simple. I don't care if you want to elope. I'm doing it. You deserve everything. You and that big tree of a man."

Behind them, Caleb finally stepped into the doorway, confused and a little scared by all the commotion he'd heard.

"Is… is everything okay?"

Inas turned to him with tear-filled golden eyes and pointed like he'd been caught red-handed.

"*You*," she said, bass in her voice. "You're getting married properly. None of this backyard nonsense you wanted to do. We gonna have lamb, and lights, and a DJ who doesn't play *one* damn Ed Sheeran song."

Selene giggled, tears still flowing down.

Caleb blinked. "Okay?"

Inas grabbed them both then, sobbing aloud as the loveliest spirit flowed by.

$$\math)$$

As if the 'invisible' hosts knew *just* how to make things worse, they had the group "come full circle" and do every activity they'd done during week one to close out the month of January.

The couples padded into the indoor pool room, already in their swimsuits, where they were expected to compete in the same events they did on day 2.

Everyone groaned in mock protest, but made their way to the pool anyway, towels slung over their shoulders and nerves trailing behind them like steam.

The mood was lighter than it had been all week; for once, they all managed to laugh together.

Well… kind of.

The group had forgotten what they played before, so they came up with their own games- a bit of Marco Polo, then a float battle royale. Michael and Laney got winded quickly; Raven and Damien dominated- again.

She leaped on his back triumphantly after their win, wrapping her arms around his neck and laughing breathlessly. He smiled, but the smile didn't reach his eyes.

Selene could hardly stand to look at them.

"You know what this means, right?" Raven whispered, dragging her fingers down Damien's chest as they toweled off by the jacuzzi. "We earned that room. *Again.*"

Damien blinked at her. "Yeah… yeah, we did."

They headed to the exclusive room with the private jacuzzi, just as the hosts had arranged. Candles flickered from small holders, and a chilled bottle of champagne waited by the edge. Raven immediately peeled her bikini off, revealing her Greek goddess-like form, and lowered herself into the jacuzzi.

Damien followed her, his eyes hooded, his jaw painfully tight.

She swam over and sat in his lap, her nipple piercings brushing his chest. "You gonna keep looking like somebody died, or are we gonna enjoy this?"

Damien chuckled hollowly, resting his hands on her waist. "I'm sorry, Rae. I just… I ain't feelin' all the way here."

Raven froze, her eyes narrowing. "You've never turned me down before."

"I ain't turnin' you down. Just… ain't in the headspace. Can we just chill? Talk?"

Raven nodded, but her eyes were on him, studying him closely. Something in her shifted quietly. She kissed him and leaned her head against his chest.

The next day, instead of another murder mystery dinner like Day 3, the hosts switched it up. A golden envelope instructed them to dress up for "an elevated evening of memories."

The ballroom had been transformed into a photo studio. Black-and-gold drapes framed the walls. A vintage-style red velvet photo booth stood in the center, complete with props, filters, and a remote timer. Laughter filled the air for a while. The couples posed dramatically, romantically, goofily. Raven wrapped her leg around Damien's waist for one, nearly knocking both of them over. Laney and Michael kissed like teenagers. Caleb lifted Selene bridal style in one of theirs, but she was stiff in his arms. The moment Damien accidentally caught her eye, the air shifted.

Neither of them smiled for the rest of the shoot.

And then… the worst "memory lane" activity of all:

Telling the sunroom mirror if they saw anything different from Day 4.

Laney went first this time, hands holding her belly. She smiled at her reflection and said, "I see someone who confronted something she'd been avoiding. And she feels stronger for it."

Caleb smiled softly at his half-sister and then went next. "I see… the same thing. And… it wasn't easy. But some things poison you and… need to get out."

Michael said, "I see someone who thought this trip would help him, but… it just showed him he hasn't changed." Laney looked at him, brows furrowed.

Raven sighed. "I see a girl trying too hard to look like a woman who's not scared."

Selene stood silently, her arms crossed, eyes red. "I see someone who wants to do the right thing… but doesn't know what that is anymore."

Then it was Damien's turn. He hesitated at first, then stepped up. "I see a man tryin' not to make the same mistakes he promised he wouldn't. And failin' anyway."

Up until January 31st, the group continued through these activities, and Damien and Selene continued to not even glance at one another, to tell themselves alcohol had taken hold of them, that what happened wasn't *them*, but a mistake that should be wholly and quickly forgotten.

And then, at 3 a.m. on the dot, Selene woke with a jolt.

A savage crack of thunder split through the sky like a scream, and for a moment she couldn't tell if it had come from outside or inside her own head. The room was pitch black, save for the flashes of white lightning that tore across the ceiling, one after another, like flickering memories.

Her heart pounded, her throat tight. Her chest wouldn't rise fully, no matter how hard she tried to breathe. She pressed her hand to it, fingers trembling. Caleb lay beside her, undisturbed, face turned into his pillow, unaware.

Another **boom.**

It *shattered* the illusion of safety.

Suddenly, she was back there again. Her old living room. The awful, *awful* knocks on the door.

She squeezed her eyes shut, trying to push it all back. Just breathe. She had been teaching this to others for four years. *Breathe.* But the numbers were slipping away from her like water through her fingers.

Her legs swung over the side of the bed almost involuntarily. She needed air. Needed to move. Her slip was thin, barely covering her thighs, but she didn't care. She grabbed the golden key from atop the dresser, stepped into her slippers, wrapped her arms around herself, and opened the door into the hallway, hoping just to calm herself before she spiraled.

At the same moment, the next door opened.

Out came Damien, shirtless and rumpled, with the same haunted look in his eyes.

Damien drank- no- *chugged* from a bottle of Hennessy, wincing from the burn but sighing in satisfaction. His locs were chin-length now, his shoulders broader.

Raven, 26 now, quirked a brow at him from the bed, her silky robe falling down her shoulder. "You… okay, soldier?"

Damien looked at her, his deep brown eyes low-lidded. He put on the slowest, laziest smirk.

"Not e'en a lil' bit."

He then cackled, head tossed back, mind *gone*. Raven's face contorted in near-worry; she'd never seen him like this.

She went over to the armchair he was lounging on and plopped down on his lap. "You wanna tell me what's up?"

Damien sighed, taking one more swig.

"It's the 5th anniversary of the day Xan died."

He took another swig from the bottle without even thinking, swaying. "Been fuckin'… half a *decade* without my lil' bro."

It was quiet for one heartbeat. Two.

Then Raven took the bottle from him and chugged from it herself, making him quirk a thick brow.

She looked at him then, her green eyes somehow even more sparkly. "It's also the 5th anniversary of the day Kevin broke my heart. The worst night of my life."

They looked at each other.

And then-

They started *making out,* drunk and enamored.

Raven pulled back first, her face flushed. "We're really… fucking *soulmates*, aren't we?!"

Damien grabbed her face and kissed her again, clearly off his ass. "We fuckin'… *belong* together."

Raven put on the slowest smirk. "You thinkin' what I'm thinkin', soldier boy?"

Damien gave his signature crooked smile, his brown skin flushed.

"We on' live across a tattoo parlor for nothin'."

They both cackled, throwing on their jackets as they left their apartment building to brand themselves with each other for life.

)

**CRACK.**

Raven's eyes flew open like a shot, heart galloping in her chest. Another thunderclap rolled over the mountains, dragging her fully out of sleep. Her skin was slick with sweat beneath the sheets, her breathing shallow, ragged.

For a moment, she didn't know where she was.

Then she turned- slowly, carefully- and looked at the other side of the bed. Empty.

Damien wasn't there.

And instead of panicking, she let out a long, shaky breath.

*Relief.*

She sat up, brushing damp hair from her forehead. Her silky black camisole clung to the deep curve of her back, and the room felt too hot and too cold all at once. The flicker of lightning danced across the room, throwing ghostly shadows on the walls. A low rumble echoed behind it.

She stood, silent, careful, and crossed to Damien's top drawer. Pulled it open.

And there they were.

The pills the psychiatrist had prescribed him for his PTSD.

She popped the cap off with a practiced flick of the thumb.

Three bars.

He was told to take no more than one, but she knew that wouldn't be enough for her. She'd known since he'd been prescribed them, and she'd secretly taken them during storms like these.

She swallowed them dry.

Her throat burned for a second, but it passed.

What didn't pass was the feeling- the scratching, crawling sensation in her skull that told her she wasn't out of it yet. Not yet.

She sat on the edge of the bed and gripped the mattress like it was her tether.

But the flashes? They came anyway.

*The Jack Daniels bottle, sweat-slick in her hand.*

*Her feet, stomping against the carpet and then the concrete.*

*Her throat, raw from screaming.*

*The sound of tires screeching, of lightning flashing outside the windshield.*

And then-

*Blood.*

*So much **blood** covering the two of them.*

She shook her head fast, desperate to will the thoughts away. Her hands were trembling, her red-rimmed eyes shifting back and forth, uncoordinated.

But then- finally- the warmth started to spread. Slow at first, then heavy. She exhaled, and it came out in a long, whispery drag of relief. The tide pulled back from her body, from her mind. She blinked slowly. Her shoulders dropped. Everything... started to go quiet.

And the storm didn't matter anymore.

☽

Selene's back slammed against the wooden wall in the hidden tower room as Damien caged her into it, kissing and biting at her heaving cleavage as she gasped out, her body trembling from an aching mixture of guilt and want.

"Damien, we said we wouldn't, we *said-*" but her hasty, whispered words turned into one high-pitched moan when he dropped down to his knees and buried his head between her thighs. Her knees buckled, which he immediately rectified by looping her legs over his shoulders like nothing.

"I knew it," he began, words muffled against her heat as he held her writhing hips in place. "I knew you'd taste sweet."

Shame coursed through her like a shooting star, but it couldn't quite outrun the pleasure she felt as her hands gripped his locs for dear life. *Forgive me, forgive me,* she pleaded internally, desperately, before gasping as he stood up suddenly, carrying her to the couch so they could sin again.

# Chapter 25

*Retour a la case départ*

**25 October 2019- Pittsburgh, PA**

"Uh… Michael?" Laney, now 30, called out, squinting at her barely used laptop on the coffee table. "You gotta see this."

Michael was zeroed in on his own laptop, typing like he'd die if he didn't add a certain number of words per minute. "Give me… a second…"

"Michael, we could get paid a *hundred thousand dollars* to go on vacation in the mountains."

That made him stop.

In less than a second, he closed out the web window, shut his laptop, and was by his wife's side. On her screen was a photo of a gorgeous lodge, titled:

**The Evervale Lodge Experience: A Revolutionary Relationship Study.**

Michael's eyes skimmed over the words. "January 1st to March 1st… Utah… Homemade meals… fun activities…"

Laney couldn't help but perk up. "Michael… the baby is due like… *three weeks* after that. This could be our last hurrah."

Michael wasn't listening, though. Every part of him froze in place when he read the words:

**Full digital detox. No internet access.**

"Yeah, fuck no, Lanes, I'm sorry," he said, immediately going back to his laptop and reopening the window he had closed.

Laney gave him a look. "Are you kidding? That's *exactly* what we need for our final two months as a family of two."

Michael shook his head, still typing away. "Laney, I'm a programmer. My whole *life* involves technology. And what would I even do for work?"

Laney crossed her arms. "It's going to pay us in two months what you make in a *year*, Michael. I don't really think *work* is something to worry about."

Michael let out an exasperated sigh. "Fine- then what about the baby? What if it comes early or something?"

Laney rubbed her belly then- still tiny at just over three months along. "I'm sure there are *plenty* of hospitals nearby."

Michael squinted at her. "But why do you even want to *risk* it? Lanes, I don't understand why this is so important to you. Can't we just enjoy our final couple of months *here*? *With* a connection to the outside world?"

Laney looked down, then, a deep sadness settling behind her eyes. For a good ten seconds, it was silent- nothing but the sound of Michael avidly typing on his laptop keyboard, his glasses just barely reflecting chat bubbles.

Laney finally spoke:

"Because I'm getting tired of being married to someone who's more attached to his laptop than to me."

Michael finally stopped typing, then.

He sighed, almost... frustrated. "Lanes... that's not true. I just... I just like my game."

Laney looked at him sadly.

"And *I* like my husband."

Michael shut his eyes, thoughts running back and forth in his mind.

Then: "Fiiiiine, *God.* Let's apply."

Laney smiled then, running up and throwing herself on his lap. "I promise, we won't regret this."

He smiled at her, kissing her cheek lovingly.

She didn't notice him closing out the browser window before she came over.

## 1 February 2020- Evervale Lodge

The dining room was aglow with sunlight reflecting off the fresh snow beyond the windows, but that wasn't what made everyone pause in the doorway.

Balloons in gold, white, and soft blush floated gently above a decadent breakfast spread. On the wooden wall, a shimmering gold banner read:

**Happy Midpoint, Lovebirds!**

Michael gave a low whistle, swallowed in an oversized black thermal. "A banner, balloons, *and* champagne at 9 a.m.? God *damn.* They really went all out."

Selene blinked, almost in disbelief, her soft coils tucked into a lavender silk bonnet, her shame tucked somewhere deep within her.

She couldn't believe she'd *actually* gone through with it.

"Midpoint? Is it February already?"

Raven padded in barefoot, Gucci shades on, walking slightly off-balance, her jaw slack.

"Well, if *this* is the midpoint, the end better be a god damn Beyoncé concert. Fucking looks like a wedding reception in here." Her voice was slurred.

Damien stood near the doorway in a dark grey pullover, scanning the room like it didn't sit right with him. His eyes quickly found Selene's and then looked away just as quickly- quick enough to beat the memories of him gripping her ass as she rode him like her life depended on it on the tower room couch.

Gulping, she took the golden envelope. She read aloud:

"You're officially halfway through the retreat, lovebirds. You should be so proud. To celebrate, meet in the auditorium at 7 p.m. for a party you won't soon forget. We will be celebrating *you* with a film that just might bring tears to your eyes."

Everyone froze.

"…A film?" Laney asked slowly.

"Celebrating… us?" Michael added.

"Wait, hold up," Caleb said.

*"They've been filming us?"*

Selene looked up from the envelope, heart now pounding for a different reason. "They… never actually said they weren't."

There was a tense quietness then, one that rang in their ears.

### 25 October 2019- Atlanta, GA

Raven, 27, sprawled across their king-size bed, ring light positioned perfectly as she filmed another "Get Ready with Me." Damien, 25, sat in the corner chair, scrolling through potential security gigs while occasionally glancing at his girlfriend with deep pride.

"So, today's look is 'effortless goddess," Raven said to her camera, blending highlighter across her cheekbones. "Which, as we *all* know, takes about forty-seven products to achieve."

Her phone buzzed with a notification mid-sentence. She glanced at it, ready to dismiss whatever sponsored content the algorithm had served up, but then she paused- her eyes widening just so.

"Hold that thought, beautiful humans." She turned off the light and picked up her phone. "King, come look at this."

Damien glanced up from his own screen, turning the music off. "Another teeth whitening ad?"

"No, this is actually interesting." She patted the bed beside her. "Some kind of research study thing."

He moved over, settling beside her as she scrolled through the post. The images were stunning- snow-covered mountains, a lodge that looked like something from an old Disney movie, couples laughing by massive fireplaces.

"The Evervale Lodge Experience," Raven read aloud. "Digital detox relationship retreat. They're looking for couples to spend two months at this place in Utah, no phones, no social media, just connecting with each other." She paused. "And they pay you a *hundred grand.*"

Damien's eyebrows shot up. "You for real?"

"That's what it says. Plus, all expenses paid, gourmet meals, luxury accommodations." She clicked through to the website. "It's some partnership between a resort company and psychology researchers."

He scoffed. "Sounds like a scam."

"That's what I thought, but look." She showed him the credentials page, the professional photos, the detailed research methodology. "It's *legit*. They want to study three couples over eight weeks, see how removing digital distractions changes relationship dynamics."

Damien studied the screen with the same focused attention he brought to security assessments. "You really thinkin' about it?"

Raven looked at him now, excitement sparkling behind her eyes. "Think about our brand- we're the couple that's super online. They probably want to see what happens when all that goes away."

He sighed. "Two months long as hell, though."

"Two months where we get paid *ten brand deals* to live in paradise and focus on each other." Raven turned to face him fully, her green eyes dancing. "King, we could be *stable* with this."

He knew she'd been wanting that- stability, somewhere that was truly theirs. The influencer income was good but unpredictable, and his security work was project-based. The money from this could set them up properly.

"What would we have to do?"

"Share meals, play games, talk about feelings." She laughed. "Basically, what we do anyway."

He saw the genuine longing in her expression. For all her confidence and success, he knew the constant performance could sometimes wear her out. "You really want this."

"I think we *need* it," she said quietly.

Damien looked at the screen again- the cozy lodge, the promise of peace and privacy. "Alright. Let's apply."

"*YES!!!*" Raven squealed, peppering her boyfriend of almost two years in kisses. "God, imagine us in a mountain lodge. No internet, cozy fires, homemade meals…"

Damien smirked. "I'm finally 'bout to get my babies."

Raven snorted, rolling her eyes before kissing him again.

☽

The sky outside the tall, frosted window was painted in a dusky lavender, the mountains beyond looking like dark silhouettes against the settling evening. Inside their suite, the air smelled of Tom Ford Tobacco Vanille and Dior Poison- Damien's cologne and Raven's signature perfume mingling in a familiar haze.

Damien stood by the dresser, smoothing his blazer with slow, deliberate movements. Raven, across the room, was slipping her silver hoops in with practiced ease, but her eyes had been locked on him for minutes now.

"Alright," she said suddenly, her usually melodic voice crisp.

"What the hell's been going on with you?"

Damien looked up, startled, but only for a second.

He didn't respond right away. Just exhaled and turned, his jaw tight.

Raven's voice rose. "I'm not a *fucking* idiot, King. You think I don't know when you're off after two fucking years? You think I don't have eyes, ears, an *intuition?*"

Damien sat on the edge of the bed, rubbing his palms together. He let out a shaky sigh, his gut twisting nauseously.

Raven noted the tension etched into every inch of him, and her eyes narrowed.

*"Say it."*

Her eyes held something behind them, something that made his heart pound so hard he was scared he'd vomit right on the hardwood then and there.

Something scarily similar to *knowing.*

There was silence for a moment, the kind of silence that felt like something sharp was about to be said. Then Damien looked up at her, his dark eyes conflicted.

When his eyes met those of the woman he was supposed to love, to commit to, to *protect,* he knew he couldn't come up with a bullshit excuse this time.

"It's… It's Selene."

Raven felt her heart stop. For a reason she couldn't yet explain, she felt like that was the absolute *worst* answer he could've given.

He continued, brows furrowed, heart thudding. "She… she lost her baby sister almost seven years ago, on… on May 4th."

Raven blinked, then her eyes narrowed even further, heart pounding so loud she swore he could hear it.

"The same day you lost Xan."

Damien nodded once, jaw tight. "It started on the first day we was partnered up. It was stormin', and she just *broke,* cause storms reminded her of that day."

Raven's jaw ticked, her breath coming in a little faster. "...Just like they remind *me* of the night I caught Kev."

Damien nodded once, hands clasped. "And... and I never got to tell you this, because I was always focused on bein' there for you durin' 'em, but... they trigger *me,* too. They... they remind me of the blast."

Raven narrowed her eyes at him. "But you told *her,* right?"

He cringed, visibly, fully realizing now how completely and utterly he'd fucked up. What a complete and utter piece of *shit* he'd become.

He sighed, ultimately deciding to take the coward's way out. "Yeah, but it's just... It's just because she feels a lot of guilt about it, just like me, and we been talkin' about it, about *them.* I ain't mean to push you away, Rae, but that shit... I been *drownin'* in it."

Raven stepped back a little, slowly.

"So... you trauma-bonded. Just like *we* did."

Damien's jaw ticked. Raven was no idiot; he should've known *that* wouldn't work.

"I-it's not like that, Rae."

Raven's eyes narrowed. She pointed to the clean, clear script on her collarbone, the ink of his full name- the one that hurt like hell to get done, but she'd deemed the pain worth it.

"We went out and got each other's *names* tatted when we learned we had trauma on the same day. We thought it made us soulmates. And you're telling me it's *not like that?*"

Damien felt sick to his stomach, the ink of her name across his knuckles suddenly burning. But when he looked into her eyes and saw the pain she still held so dear to this day-

He swallowed and said:

"Yeah. We just been talkin'."

Raven stared at him, studying his eyes like she was trying to find the place where the lie began.

"Okay," she said finally, voice quiet. "Thanks for telling me."

She turned around to grab her boots and put them on, and Damien let out a shaky breath behind her.

He didn't notice the look of barely-held-in *rage* on her face.

## 25 October 2019- Brooklyn, NY

Selene, 24 today, sat cross-legged on their small apartment couch, laptop balanced on her knees, scrolling through her Instagram feed with half-interest as Team BS's "Case départ" played out of the Bluetooth speaker on the coffee table.

Caleb, 25, was, naturally, doing push-ups on the living room floor, muscles flexing with each rep.

"Babe," Selene suddenly said, pausing at a sponsored post, leaning in with curiosity all over her face. "Look at this."

The ad showed a stunning mountain lodge against snow-capped peaks, with elegant script overlaying the image:

**The Evervale Lodge Experience: Revolutionary Relationship Research Study.**

Caleb finished his set and looked up, breathing hard while patting his forehead dry. "What is it?"

Selene clicked through to the website, her voice taking on that slightly breathless quality it got when she was excited or needed to say something *huge*. "It's some kind of research study. They're looking for couples to spend two months at this gorgeous lodge in Utah with 'invisible hosts'. Digital detox, relationship exercises, gourmet meals..." She paused, eyes widening. "Caleb. They pay you a *hundred thousand dollars* to finish it."

He pushed himself up to sitting. "What's the catch? And what the hell are 'invisible hosts'?"

"It looks like legitimate research- a partnership between some hospitality group and the Center for Relationship Psychology. They're studying how couples connect without digital distractions." She scrolled through testimonials and photos. *"Look* at this place. It's like a fairy tale."

Caleb moved to sit beside her. "A hundred *grand?"*

"Fifty thousand per person." Her voice was soft, thoughtful, almost reverent.

Caleb snorted. "You gotta be honest though, that's *nothing* compared to what your aunt has in the bank, now."

Selene giggled, but her eyes lingered on the ad.

Taking note of his wife's interest, he sat beside her. "So, what exactly would we *do* there?"

Selene kept reading. "Participate in relationship-building activities. Share homemade meals. Do questionnaires about our connection and communication styles. Everything's provided- food, lodging, activities." She clicked on another page. "It says they're only selecting three couples from *thousands* of applicants, Caleb."

Caleb frowned. "Sounds too good to be true."

"The research is *real,*" Selene said, showing him the credentials page. "Dr. Diosa DeLuna has published *dozens* of papers on relationship psychology."

Caleb studied the lodge's images- the massive stone fireplaces, floor-to-ceiling windows, indoor pools, and cozy suites. "When would it be?"

"January 1st to March 1st. It begins on our anniversary!"

He could see how much she wanted this- the way her hands moved, the hope in her voice.

"What's the application process?"

Selene was already clicking. "Relationship questionnaire, lifestyle survey, video interview... ooh, and they want us to write down our food preferences so they can cook it!"

Caleb still looked skeptical. "How long do we have?"

"Applications close next week. But Caleb..." She gripped his arm gently. "This feels like *fate*. There's something about it. We didn't get to have a honeymoon. This can *be* that."

She smirked then, ever so mischievously. "And… It *is* my birthday. Don't you want to get me the best gift *ever?*"

He sighed, then, defeated. "Fine, God damn. You're lucky you just happened to find this on your birthday, or I'd *never* agree to this shit."

Selene squealed, jumping up to kiss him all over his face. "This is going to be so good for us. I just *know* it."

⟩

The zipper on Selene's high-neck baby-pink halter dress whispered shut as she stepped away from the mirror. She was putting on her favorite rose quartz earrings when she caught Caleb's reflection in the glass, tense and searching.

She turned to face him. "What?"

He didn't answer at first. Just kept looking past her like he wasn't sure how to say what was clawing at him.

Finally:

"Is there something you need to tell me?"

Selene froze, her heart immediately picking up. "What?"

Caleb stood, slowly. "You've been *different.*"

Selene blinked, her breath quickening. "Different how?"

"I mean, we haven't had sex in forever. You're always a million miles away. It's like I'm… reaching for you and you're not even there," he said somberly.

Her mouth tightened.

"Are you projecting?"

He tilted his head. "Excuse me?"

Selene crossed her arms. "Because, if I recall correctly, you not only hid the fact that you have a whole *sister* from me, but you blatantly *refused* to tell me why you hid it in the first place. So, if anyone is 'far away'… It's *you.*"

She felt bad for deflecting- cowardly- but she meant what she was saying, too.

Caleb looked at her, *really* looked at her.

Then, he dropped his eyes and exhaled through his nose. "You wanna know *that* bad?" he muttered.

"Fine."

He paced toward the window, his voice distant.

"I moved in with her and Michael over seven years ago. Just for a while. Thought it'd help me get on my feet after being stuck in my mom's shithole trailer."

Selene's breathing quickened as she examined his face.

He continued. "There were stories about that apartment. People said it was cursed, haunted, especially on July 1st. I didn't believe any of that shit." He laughed dryly.

"Until… it came July 1st."

He swallowed hard, his fingers twitching on his knee. "And… I got possessed. I don't know how else to explain it. I blacked out, lost control. I…"

Selene's breath caught in her throat. *'Is he **actually** going to tell me?'* her mind mused, her voice panicked even in there.

Caleb took a deep breath.

"I… I tried to kill Laney."

Selene froze, brows furrowing. "…Huh?"

Caleb nodded, eyes downcast. "Then… Laney got possessed, too. And… she tried to kill *me*. And then, she tried to blame me when it was *both* of us. And… and that's why we stopped talking."

Selene looked like a statue sculpted by pure disbelief.

Then:

"Let's… let's just go to the party."

# Chapter 26



*Challenge the Stars*

The auditorium had been *transformed*.

Candlelit sconces flickered along the tall walls, sheer drapes shimmered in soft amber tones, and a trail of rose petals lined the walkway between rows of plush velvet seats. Andro's "Иса" played out through the speakers overhead.

At the very front, a massive projector screen displayed in creamy white against black read:

**Happy Midpoint, Lovebirds!**

Selene stepped into the space first, thick curls half-pinned with a fresh white lily, her lips glossed in a soft mauve pink, her glittered skin catching every golden light, making her look *radiant*.

She'd hoped getting all dressed up would distract her.

It didn't.

Not when Damien entered just seconds after, looking crisp in a fitted black turtleneck and blazer, his locs tied back low, a gold stud glinting in his ear.

Their eyes met for a heartbeat. Just a heartbeat.

But Raven?

She felt it in her *bones*.

She didn't speak right away. Instead, she let her gaze flick between the two of them as her tall silver stilettos clicked across the floor with every effortless sway of her hips. She wore a blood-red satin gown that hugged her curves, a thigh-high slit showing off a milky thigh. Her hair, impossibly black today and freshly straightened, was in a sultry updo.

She looked *incredible*.

Not for Damien, though; for the first time in over two years, *not* for Damien.

Just for power.

Selene couldn't help but look at her, her heart thudding.

She looked away quickly, *too* quickly, but not before Raven caught her glance.

Caleb joined Selene's side a moment later, adjusting the cuff of his navy-blue suit jacket. He kissed her cheek with a hollow look in his eyes. Selene flinched ever so slightly from the contact.

Raven caught that too, her fists tightening so hard that her knuckles were white.

Michael and Laney entered last, hand in hand. Laney wore a silky pale-blue dress that highlighted her bump, her golden hair freshly straightened in a princess-like updo, and Michael, in a grey suit and paisley tie, had that familiar glow of a man too content to notice the chaos brewing.

"Can't believe they put together *this* kind of setup," Michael murmured as they found their seats. "They've really thought of everything."

Laney snorted quietly. "And to think we *still* don't know who these people are." Michael snorted in agreement, but Laney's jaw was strangely tense.

Everyone slowly settled into their velvet chairs, the low buzz of polite compliments and small talk circling around them.

The tension under it, though? Thicker than the carpet.

Selene's heart thudded despite herself when Damien sat only one row behind her.

She could feel his presence, the heat of him, without even turning around. She shut her eyes, trying to will out the memories of being utterly enveloped by his frame, of the two of them taking each other like there was nothing, *no one*, beyond that secret room.

Raven had one leg crossed over the other, her crimson dress spilling dramatically into the aisle.

Her eyes were narrowed on the back of Selene's head.

And just then-

**The lights dimmed.**

And the screen flickered on.

It's a static shot- grainy but clear. A fixed camera mounted high in the corner of a dim, unfamiliar room. There's no one in the frame at first- only silence, the kind that feels *pregnant* with something.

At the bottom of the screen was a date and time:

**January 10, 2020, 12:02 p.m.**

On the screen, Caleb enters, looking more tense than anyone, even Selene, had ever seen him. He's dressed normally in a hoodie and sweats, but the way his fists are balled at his sides shows that he is not *feeling* casual, not in the slightest.

Laney follows a second later, looking absolutely *exhausted*, tense like she'd come in reluctantly. She's also ironically dressed down in one of Michael's gaming hoodies and oversized sweats.

Finally, Caleb turns to her.

"Let's just… address it, Laney."

Selene, sitting beside Caleb, automatically looked over at him, gulping hard. She noted the absolute *petrification* in his eyes.

Michael also looked at Laney, brows furrowed.

Laney? She whispered, *"No, no, no, no, no, no,"* under her breath.

On screen, Laney tightens her jaw, refusing to look her younger half-brother in the eyes.

Then:

"We addressed it *long* ago, Caleb. The apartment building was haunted. We got possessed by whatever weird *spirit* was in there and did something fucked up. End of discussion."

Caleb crossed his arms then, his face annoyed.

"You're still using that stupid fucking *ghost* excuse?"

Laney looks up at him sharply, her fist tightening at her side. "It's *not* an excuse. It's the only thing that makes *sense.*" She steps toward him now, determination in her eyes.

"If we weren't possessed, then why would we have done it? Why did the bird fall and *break* when we did?" Her voice cracked as tears welled in her eyes.

"Why would it have lasted *six whole months?*"

Caleb's entire body tensed, shame coloring his features.

Then, he sighed. "I don't know. But it wasn't a ghost, Laney. That... that was something we *chose.*"

Laney's mouth trembles. Her jaw tightens.

"No. *No,* because if you're right, then I'm... then we're monsters. And we're not..." Her voice cracks, the tears pooling in her eyes audible.

"*I'm* not."

There is a long silence. The two siblings are facing each other but refuse to look at one another.

Caleb finally speaks, his voice lower now.

"I'm pretty sure whatever dark spirit that existed came *after* we slept together, Laney."

And the entire auditorium let out a horrified *gasp*.

## 1 July 2012- West Philadelphia, PA

"Close your eyes, birthday girl," Caleb, 18, said with a mischievous smile as he stood in front of his sister in the tiny kitchenette. Michael, never one to hold his liquor, was already asleep, passed out on the armchair like the end of the world couldn't make him stir.

Caleb hadn't baked once in his life, but he decided to attempt to bake… an *attempt* at a cake. It was covered messily in frosting so red it could *stain*, and stood lopsided on the counter.

Laney *loved* it.

She raised a brow, sucking frosting from her finger. "Caleb, you know you didn't have to get me anything. You being here and not with our demon of a mom? *That's* enough."

Still, Caleb reached up to open the tiny cabinet above the fridge- one he knew she wouldn't be able to reach on her own before he put the gift there.

He pulled out a small silver bag already stuffed with white tissue paper.

Laney *gasped*.

He handed it to her, his ocean eyes warming.

She looked at the tiny bag, then back up at him, and her hazel eyes twinkled. "Caleb…"

He smiled, sitting down on the pull-out sofa he'd been sleeping in for almost eight months now. "Open it."

Slowly, nervously, she sat down beside him and took the tissue paper out of the bag.

When she saw what was inside the little bag, she gasped a second time.

It was a beautiful glass bird- impossibly clear, its wings lifted in mid-flight.

Caleb's eyes softened as he reached out to squeeze her hand. "You always loved birds," he began, his eyes tracing her features. "Always talked about how amazing it would be if we could grow wings and fly away from mom's."

Laney squeezed the bird just slightly, a tear rolling down her face. "Caleb…"

His entire posture softened as he reached out and brushed her cheek.

"You've always been there for me, the only one in my life who ever was."

Laney looked at him, her eyes softer than he'd ever seen them. Then, she hugged him tight.

"I will always be there for you, Cabe."

He pulled back, slowly, holding her face tenderly. Then, without even thinking-

He kissed her.

Laney froze, heart thudding.

She knew she should push him away. Slap him. Ask him what the hell he was doing. Scream.

But for some reason… a reason she wouldn't be able to explain for years to come…

She kissed him back.

The auditorium fell so silent, it was as if the air had been vacuumed from the room.

Michael's brow was furrowed at first, his brain working slowly, still catching up to what he'd just heard, what he couldn't have *possibly* heard. His hand slowly left Laney's, resting limp in his lap. His mouth opened once… no sound. Then again.

"Lanes?" he croaked.

She didn't look at him; she *couldn't*. Her hand fisted her dress so tight, her knuckles were white.

Selene, a few rows ahead, was completely frozen- her breath stuck somewhere in the pit of her stomach. All the blood had left her face. She was shaking.

*We slept together.*

*Six whole months.*

She felt physically sick, her nerves affray. She stood up fast, her chair scraping behind her as she ran to the double doors, but-

**Click.**

They didn't move when she yanked the handles.

"Selene?" Caleb's voice came, low and uncertain.

Her body turned to face him before her brain decided to. Her eyes were wide and wet and completely unrecognizable.

"Is it true?" she whispered, her voice hoarse.

"Is that… real?"

Caleb's mouth opened, but no words came. He looked like a man underwater, suffocating, searching for air in a room full of people watching him drown.

"So, it *is* true." Michael's voice came from behind them. Laney had her hands over her face, sobbing into them.

"Lanes," Michael said again. "*Please* tell me this isn't-"

"It was *before* we got together! It stopped as soon as you asked me out, I swear to God, Michael," she choked out, her voice raw. "I didn't mean for it to happen. It was seven *years* ago, we-"

Michael suddenly stood, his voice cracking.

"This… this is the reason he *left*, isn't it?"

Caleb looked like speaking would make him vomit, but he tried. "Michael… She's right. It stopped right after you asked her out. We-"

"Don't you *dare* talk to me," Michael growled, pointing at him. "Don't you fucking dare open your mouth to speak to me."

No one moved. Caleb's head fell like the life was ripped out of it.

Selene just kept staring at him, eyes wet.

"When were you going to tell me?" she asked softly, almost childlike in its smallness.

"I wasn't," Caleb said, voice hollow. "I wasn't *ever* going to."

A bitter sound came from her throat- half laugh, half sob- and she nodded like it was confirmation of something she always feared. Then she sat back down slowly, eyes glassy, looking nowhere and everywhere at once.

Then-

**The screen flickered on again.**

It was the exact same date as the other one, this time at **12:11 p.m.**

And this time? It wasn't a confession room.

It was a room within the *gaming* room.

And in the center of the frame-

Is Michael.

He's sitting on a leather armchair, leaning forward, a wireless controller loosely in one hand.

But it's not a game on the screen.

The large, sleek Smart TV paints the dim room in blue light. The camera zooms in on what's on the screen- what Michael is typing in a message bar in real time.

And the moment everyone saw the chat bubbles clearly?

They *gasped.*

Raven's hand flew to her mouth.

Caleb blurted out, "Yo, what the fuck?"

Selene stumbled back like she'd been struck.

Damien's expression went deathly cold, like he could kill the programmer with his bare hands.

Laney, who was already shaking, *screamed.*

**And finally, the screen cut to black.**

And just when they were reeling, just when they thought the nightmare was over-

**The screen flickered on again.**

A new timestamp blinked in the top corner this time:

**May 4, 2013 - 1:03 a.m.**

Everyone leaned forward in their chairs, wondering what the hell the hosts could be showing from so long ago.

The date itself made Damien and Selene glance at one another and gulp.

Raven?

She began to *sweat*.

Grainy street footage filled the screen. A camera perched from a storefront captured the scene:

A storm rages, so heavy that it makes the palm trees whip. Wind rips through billboards; the rain falls hard and fast. Lightning flashes white across the screen.

Then- headlights come into view.

The car careens into the frame from the left, speeding through the intersection without pause.

No brake lights. No slowing down.

It sways and swerves, like the driver is entirely plastered or wants to kill themselves or both.

The street ahead glows faintly under the flickering lampposts- and there, barely visible at first-

Are two figures who appear to be holding umbrellas, as well as hands.

And the car?

**It slams into them without mercy.**

The entire auditorium gasped, horrified. Selene looked like she was about to vomit. Damien had seen a lot of things in war, including his brother's mangled body, but this made even *him* grip the armrest. Caleb covered his face immediately, and Michael/Laney managed to forget what they saw on the screen beforehand and held each other's hands on instinct (before dropping them just as quickly).

On screen, the Altima skids to a stop halfway down the block, finally coming to a halt after driving what looked like miles without even caring about red lights.

The driver's door opens-

And a woman stumbles out.

The camera is incredibly grainy, but she appears young, with red hair, a server shirt, and a posture of disoriented horror.

But what stands out most is the recognizable bottle clutched in her hand:

*Jack Daniel's Old No. 7.*

She looks. Just looks.

And then?

*She gets back in the car, slams the door, and speeds off,* leaving the two figures on the concrete, unmoving.

Everyone gasped, again.

Static ripped across the screen like a scream. Then, another cut. The new timestamp flashes in white letters:

**January 10, 2020, 12:01 p.m.**

The location is now back to being familiar-

The yoga studio.

Raven is sitting on a bench beside Michael, looking at a sheet of paper with three questions typed on it.

She appears to be thinking hard, biting the bottom of the pen almost nervously as she stares at the questions.

Michael looks calm- excited, even, a big smile on his face that seems almost sinister, knowing what he would do ten minutes after this.

But Raven? She looks *tense.*

She looks like she's considering whether or not she should write down the truth or not.

Eventually, finally-

Her pen touches the sheet of paper.

The camera zooms slowly, methodically, on it- so close that everyone could perfectly read every word on the sheet:

**What is the date your life changed?**
*May 4th, 2013*
**What is a symbol of that date?**
*Jack Daniels*
**When you close your eyes and think of that date, what is the first thing you see?**
*The two of them.*

### 4 May 2013- University of Central Florida

"Kelly, *wait!*" Kevin screamed, stumbling out with the comforter wrapped around his naked waist, but she didn't even hear him anymore.

Her legs shook as she bolted. She hit the doorframe with her shoulder but didn't stop. She moved through the dark apartment like she wasn't even in it, so fast that she'd look like a ghost on camera.

She didn't even remember grabbing her keys. She *definitely* didn't remember grabbing the Jack.

By the time she sat behind the wheel of the Altima she'd inherited from her mother-

She threw her head back and *chugged.*

The first swallow didn't register, but the second did. It burned all the way down.

She folded forward, elbows on the steering wheel, the bottle clutched between her knees. Her whole body shook.

Eventually, she sat back, face wet, curls wild.

Then, she drank again and turned the key in the ignition, her vision completely blurred with tears.

"Fucking piece of shit…" she slurred as she sped out of the parking lot, tears blurring her vision. "Fucking piece of shit…"

She didn't care where she was going. All she cared about was being the fuck away from *him*.

She took three more big gulps, crying harder at the burn, car speeding and swerving so fast through the storm that she could've driven off a bridge and not given a shit.

And then…

**A thick, sickening thud.**

Her windshield cracked. Her hood flew off. Her own reflection in the side mirror looked unrecognizable: pale, sick, *petrified*.

She could hardly even catch her breath, her thoughts running 100 mph despite how drunk she was. She could've vomited right on the steering wheel if her focus wasn't on whatever the fuck she'd just hit.

Slowly, nervously, she got out of her car, Jack still in hand.

And what she saw on the concrete chilled her to the *bone*.

She started hyperventilating. "No. No. No, no, no, no," she repeated over and over, her head spinning with more than just inebriation.

And then, quickly- more quickly than she'd ever moved-

She jumped back into the car, backed away, and sped off.

This silence felt *different.*

Selene slowly turned her head to look at Raven, her face pale with horror. Her belly felt ill in a *visceral* way.

Damien's eyes widened with dawning, sick realization.

He remembered her words to him after she kissed Caleb in truth or dare- eyes shifting everywhere, face pale.

*"I didn't tell you… everything.* **Everything** *that happened that night."*

Caleb's breath caught in his throat. He looked between the screen and Raven and whispered, "No fucking way…"

Michael, still reeling from his own exposé yet still affected, stared at her in disbelief, like he never even knew her.

Raven managed the wobbliest snort.

"I-I-I don't know what they're trying to sh-show. People hit things with their car and drive away all the fucking time!"

She forced out the loudest laugh anyone had ever heard her manage, her eyes going wild. "I- I-I don't understand what they're trying to show with this shit. They're obviously trying to pin it on *me*, but…"

But Raven, despite everything, was never much of a liar.

The screen went black, then *'Happy Midpoint Lovebirds'* returned, as if nothing had just happened.

Damien and Selene both let out a relieved exhale at once, shocked that either the hosts didn't film their… trysts… or, for whatever reason, they didn't feel the need to show anyone.

Until-

"Oh bullshit," Raven's voice boomed as she stood up so quick she could've sworn she'd faint.

"Bull fucking *shit!*"

She looked straight at Damien with venom in her eyes. He sat still, tense, like a sitting statue, as he saw the pure *fury* radiating from her, even with her cornered stance.

"You wanna judge *me?* You wanna judge *me?* Why don't you tell the class what *you've* been doing in this god-forsaken lodge behind all of our backs?!"

Damien and Selene froze at once, their hearts falling to the pits of their stomachs.

Quickly, still swaying from what she took last night, Raven swiveled over-

-and looked directly at Caleb.

"You're not the only one who had a fucked-up relationship, dude. Your *WIFE* has been fucking *MY MAN* this whole *FUCKING RETREAT!*"

Selene looked like she was on the verge of passing clean out, letting out a half-sigh, half-whimper.

Did Damien tell Raven? Did he actually *tell* her?

Caleb let out a breath like he'd been punched. His face was pale before, but now, he looked like the ghosts Laney used to blame for their… moments together.

He looked right at his wife.

The look on her face said everything.

She, a yoga instructor who was an *expert* in being present-

Couldn't even bear to *glance* at him.

"You…" His voice cracked.

"You did this. To me."

Selene didn't even try to explain, her small form trembling, her breathing so labored she thought she might faint.

Caleb's voice rose, dangerously, his eyes red at the rims.

*"YOU COULD **DO** THIS TO ME?!"*

Selene started trembling, tears filling her eyes. "It-it-it's not… it's not…"

But she felt like a fool even *trying* to lie when Damien's scent was still on her.

Damien? He sat stiffly behind them, jaw tight, eyes down. His girlfriend had the instincts of an oracle. He couldn't disrespect her further by trying to play this off.

Raven stared at him, giving him a look that resembled one of someone who'd been shot in the heart but still somehow kept living.

Then-

She let out a laugh.

One single, *bitter* laugh.

"So it *is* true."

For six miserable seconds, it was quiet, only sharp breaths and muffled sobs.

Damien managed to try to open his mouth, but she got out of her seat so fast that she got dizzy, reaching her hand back like she was about to either strike him or drag him out of his seat, and then-

**CLACK.**

The auditorium doors unlocked with a harsh metallic *groan*.

For a moment, no one moved.

Then- like something broke open inside them- they spilled out of the cursed auditorium.

Not together; not unified.

Like six shattered people tumbling into the lodge's dim living room.

Anger simmered off Michael in silent waves, his fists balled as he replayed what he saw on that massive screen on repeat.

Shame hung heavily on Selene, nails biting into her arms.

Laney looked pale, her arms wrapped tightly around herself, her belly somehow even rounder, poking out even more as if reminding everyone of the stakes.

Damien's jaw was clenched like steel, as if he let it go for one second, he'd *scream*.

He felt guilty for cheating; that couldn't be denied. But the guilt he felt for putting Selene in this situation? He didn't know how he could look himself in the mirror again.

Raven didn't even speak- wasn't even there. Her eyes suddenly gained 20/20 vision as she scouted for liquor.

Caleb wouldn't look at anyone, especially not Selene.

And then-

**CLICK. CLACK. THUNK. SNAP.**

Multiple doors slammed shut and locked at once- so loud that it couldn't be viewed as anything but intentional.

The couples scattered- each one rushing to a different handle, testing, pulling, rattling.

"The dining room is locked," Selene said, voice shaking.

"So is the ballroom," said Michael, voice the same.

Raven exhaled a trembling, angry breath. "Of course, the front and back doors, too." She kicked the front double doors with her steel-toed boots, her muscular legs usually able to do real damage, but the hosts seemed to have these doors almost bolted, the wood gathered straight from trees.

Damien stormed up the staircase, his dark eyes shifting side to side in panic. "All our bedrooms, too."

Caleb tried the hallway to the indoor pool. "Sealed off."

Laney let out a withering gasp.

"We're confined to the living room, kitchen, laundry room, and downstairs bathrooms."

They looked at each other, not knowing what the hell to say.

And then… they *saw* it.

On the coffee table, like it had always been there:

A single, matte-black envelope.

The same kind they got on January 10th.

The same kind that led to the nightmare that just played out in the auditorium.

Selene walked forward, hands shaking, and picked it up.

Inside was a glossy black parchment card with one sentence written in silver script:

*"Don't you feel closer, now?"*

# Chapter 27



*Tapping on the Table*


No one spoke. No one *could.*

The six of them existed in the same space, but they weren't together. They couldn't even *fathom* being together.

The same group who bonded over lavish meals, pool games, drinking games, club nights, and even built a damn tower with their bodies alone-

Could no longer imagine *existing* with one another.

They drifted off to separate corners of the still-gorgeous, still-luxurious living room like planets trying to find a place after a cosmic explosion.

The only sounds were the occasional crackle from the fireplace, which the hosts so kindly lit for them, and someone's muffled sobbing.

No one asked who.

Not when it could've been all of them.


Michael sat slumped against the arm of a plush couch, his glasses askew, his knuckles white around a throw pillow he hadn't let go of since the doors locked. His blazer was off, his white button-up crinkled and half-on.

He was completely torn between stewing over the sick past actions of his now-wife and brother-in-law-

And his worst secret- the "demon" he'd been fighting for years- being exposed for everyone to see.

Was he more betrayed or more ashamed? He couldn't even *begin* to quantify both feelings at once.

All he could do was lie his head back and chug one of the chilled beers that the hosts so very kindly kept in an ice-filled metal canister on the coffee table right beside that smug envelope.

Caleb stood by the kitchen island, head bowed low, hands flat on the counter. His blazer and white button-up were also off. He was only in a flimsy wifebeater, his muscles flexing and unflexing like he was working out in real-time.

He didn't know whether he wanted to hurt Selene, Damien, the 'hosts, or *himself.*

He couldn't control the images and sounds that looped through his mind like some kind of never-ending psychological horror film:

*Selene on her back, those flexible little legs wrapped tight around another man's waist.*

*Her soft, breathy moans- the ones Caleb used to **live** for- now spilling out for **him.***

*Damien's broad, dark shoulders moving above her, powerful and relentless, locs swinging with every deep thrust, acting like she was **his** to take.*

And then... maybe even worse...

*"You're still using that stupid fucking demon excuse?"*

*"Why would we have done it **for six whole months?"***

*"...**After** we slept together, Laney."*

*"It was something we **chose."***

He could've *screamed,* his fists banging onto the countertop in utter frustration.

Damien hadn't even *looked* at Selene since the auditorium.

All his inhales felt like betrayal, and all his exhales tasted like guilt. He was shirtless- basic training had long beaten out any shame over undressing in front of others out of him- and the dog tags he'd been faithfully wearing for almost seven years now, now felt *incriminating* against his chest.

Why wouldn't they? They'd felt the heat of Selene's skin just that morning.

Selene, despite everything, was glued to Laney's side, helping to elevate her swollen feet on a leather pouf.

"It's good for the baby," she said softly, her voice trembling. She wore a large white T-shirt she found in the laundry room and nothing else. "You should be around thirty-three weeks now."

Laney's face was blank, but she didn't stop her.

And Raven? Raven, for the first time this whole vacation, was *silent.*

She sat nearest to the fire, cradling a bottle of whiskey. She didn't give a fuck about the flashbacks it gave her anymore; she'd experienced worse, now.

Her heels were kicked off. Her hair was down, wild around her shoulders like a curtain of unraveling pride.

The hosts had lit the fire in the mantle and left behind a bin of thick comforters and soft velvet pillows, like some kind of fucked up silver lining.

So, they slept. Or tried to.

At 3 a.m., a sharp, sudden movement cut through the dark.

*Raven.*

She jerked upright, her breath catching in her throat. She was covered, *drenched,* in a cold sweat.

Her mind was set in a nightmarish loop:

*Damien,* **HER** *Damien. The heartbreakingly handsome bodyguard she'd seen in that theatre.*

*The fact that he wasn't in bed when we woke up in the middle of the night.*

*The fact that she felt relief because she could take his pills, not knowing he was* **taking another woman.**

Before she even knew what she was doing, she threw the blanket off herself, stormed across the floor, grabbed Damien by the wrist, and walked.

Her eyes were *wild.*

He startled awake instantly. "Rae- what the-"

**SLAM.**

She locked the wooden door behind them, chest heaving, breath loud and labored.

The bathroom was beautiful- stone walls, African paintings, marble countertops, and a golden sink.

It contrasted *too* sharply with the two soul-broken bodies who'd just entered it.

Damien blinked in the low light, sleep still on his face; he was never much of a sleeper, but now?

Now the thought of sleeping felt *impossible.*

Raven's face? There was no mistaking it.

She was *destroyed.*

"You cheated on me," she said, her voice trembling. Her hands were clenched so tightly her knuckles were white.

Damien's face went pale as he slowly digested the fact that what happened was not a nightmare, but their reality.

He gulped. "Rae…"

"Don't you 'Rae' me. Don't you fucking-" She shoved him hard in the chest, one, two, three times, making the large man stagger against the sink.

Her voice rose, a bass in it that he knew he'd have nightmares about from here on. "I told you how badly he broke me. Told you how I trusted *no* one. And you, you, *you-*" she said the last 'you' in a shriek- "were the one to go betray me?! With *her?!*"

She slammed her hand against the sink behind him so hard he could've sworn one of her rings cracked.

"With the girl you said was too polished? Too prim? *The bitch you didn't even* **trust?!**"

Damien flinched, both from the memory and from the venom in her tone.

"I- I never meant for it to happen like that," he said hoarsely, looking disgusted by his own body.

"You mean it just *happened?!*" Raven spat, sickened.

Slowly, with poison in her eyes, she sauntered closer to him.

"Tell me what it was about her that made it worth losing me. Was it those curls? That stupid little giggle? Or maybe it was the *yoga poses* that got you hard."

He looked like he had aged five years in five minutes. "Rae, it wasn't- it wasn't *planned.* I told you, we bonded over our siblings. I-It ain't like I set *out-*"

"Was it just once?! Or has it been going on this whole time?" Her voice cut through like a blade.

There was a deadly pause, then. So quiet that Raven's stomach dropped.

Her voice cracked, her shoulders shaking visibly, now.

"How long?"

Damien swallowed, expression *pained*.

He leaned back against the wall, shame stitched into every inch of his body. Shakily, he inhaled.

"The first time was-"

Raven's knees almost gave out. He instinctively reached forward, but she shoved his hands away like they'd burn her before leaning her entire body on the wooden door, her breath coming in raw and labored.

"The first time?! The *first* time?! You're saying it happened *more than once?*"

Damien stared at the ground, jaw tight, tears filling his eyes. He hadn't hated himself this much since May 4th, 2013.

"Say it," she barely managed to get out.

Damien met her eyes, guilt radiating like heat from every inch of him. And then finally, brutally:

"...Yeah."

Raven shut her eyes then, lips trembling.

When she opened them again, they were *deadly*.

"You were supposed to *protect* me."

"I know," he said, his voice hoarse.

"No, the fuck you *don't.*"

She turned around, putting one trembling, reddened hand on the doorknob.

"Congratulations. You just made *damn* sure I'll never trust anyone again."

Then, she left, leaving him to sink down onto the cold tile.

# Chapter 28

*Ça sert à rien de courir*

No one spoke that first morning.

They all woke up on the living room floor-some wrapped tightly in their gifted high-thread blankets, others sprawled out as if in defiance of comfort.

Laney was the first to stand, having slept all night beside a worried Selene on annoyingly comfy blankets and pillows, like the hosts were trying *hard* to make this situation 'okay'.

It wasn't.

She waddled to the kitchen, opened the fridge, and let out an irritated scoff when she saw the array of fresh fruits, veggies, meats, and ingredients.

"They stocked the kitchen, at least. How *sweet* of them."

Michael tried to follow, maybe out of habit, but Laney shot him a look that made his spine shrink. He walked back to his corner of the living room, defeated.

Damien kept rubbing the back of his neck, pacing like a caged panther. He and Raven hadn't been near each other since she dragged him into the bathroom hours before. Her voice still rang in his ears-her sobs, her screams, her disgust. Her *silence* was somehow the worst part.

Selene couldn't help but steal glances at him, guilt curdling in her belly. She put all her energy into making sure Laney was okay during this whole ordeal.

She found that only when she was preoccupied with that, did her brain not have time to reminisce about Damien's hands in her hair, Damien's mouth on her skin, *Damien* on *her.*

By the second morning, it was clear:

This was *punishment.*

Selene, of course, cooked breakfast, lunch, and dinner for everyone- humming Zaho's "La Roue Tourne" as she cooked couscous and stewed chicken tagine, blended and strained fresh strawberry-banana aguas frescas, and cut fresh honeydew into perfect little stars and crescents.

At one point, Damien got a plate from her.

He was disgusted with himself that being near her *still* made his blood drop low.

On Day 3, Raven couldn't treat Selene like scum that didn't deserve her attention anymore, though she'd sure been trying; even "accidentally" bumping into her once or twice.

But watching the elfin woman cook and clean like some perfect little housewife made her seethe in rage.

"Delusional of you to think any of us would want to touch *your* food when we know *exactly* where your hands have been," she said bitingly, begrudgingly wearing Damien's wifebeater now.

Selene had frozen in place, just slightly, but then went back to chopping up fresh grass-fed steak, not even bothering to turn around.

On Day 4, Michael tried to make a joke about the "cozy apocalypse" they were trapped in.

No one even *dreamed* of laughing.

Raven stared at him like he wasn't human, her usually perfectly sleek hair a wavy mess around her bare face. "You think this shit is funny?"

The disgraced programmer never joked again.

On day 5, Selene had cooked lentil-beef stew with spinach specifically for Laney, sitting beside her and urging her to eat.

"Iron is amazing for both mom and baby," she said, her voice soft but sure. She wore Damien's blazer over a short camisole dress, which would've sparked Raven's rage had she not drunk half a bottle of wine.

Laney looked at Selene with mild annoyance but took a spoonful anyway. "How do you *know* all of this, anyway?"

Selene smiled, her eyes twinkling with the beginnings of tears. "My mama taught me a lot."

Caleb looked at her then, fighting the urge to find her beautiful like he always did.

He knew the second he did, his brain would remind him that Damien had all but made her his.

At one point, he punched a bathroom mirror from the thought, knuckles bleeding as glass shards dropped onto the floor like hail.

Selene gasped, ran into the kitchen, and pulled out a fancy first-aid kit from a random cabinet, intending to clean and bandage him.

Caleb looked at her with so much disgust that she regretted even trying.

And the nights? They were the *worst*.

Blankets rustled under restless bodies. Breathing changed when one of them shifted in their sleep, which was extremely frequent. The fire crackled in the mantle, but even *it* couldn't thaw the bitterness.

Damien slept on the opposite end of the room from Selene, and it killed him. Not just because he missed her, but because he couldn't stand the situation he'd gotten them in.

On the morning of February 8th, Selene woke up early as usual to check on Laney, whom she always made sure to sleep beside, but when she bent down to check on the sleeping pregnant beauty-

She audibly *gagged*.

Laney woke up then, blinking up at the thick-haired yogi. All she could see was the pure exhaustion on her face.

"Selene?"

Selene swallowed, taking in a little gasp of air before forcing a smile, her hand unconsciously moving to hold her stomach. "It's that mushroom risotto I made last night. Dairy has *never* sat well with me."

But her face was pale, her eyes set in a squint.

Laney sat up from her array of plush blankets and pillows.

"Yeah, no. I'm a nurse. I know when somebody isn't okay. Look at you, you can hardly even *sit* straight."

Selene shook her head, though she winced a bit in discomfort. "Don't worry about me," she barely managed to whisper. "What do you want for breakfast this morning? It seems like they re-stocked the fridge in the middle of the night. I can make a really delicious country omele-"

Before she could finish the word, she suddenly felt the need to bolt to the bathroom.

She shot up, barely managing to avoid the of still-sleeping bodies as her small feet hit the bathroom tile.

She hunched over the toilet, throwing up for what felt like hours, panting hard as tiny stars began to cover her vision.

Later that same night, the silence of the past week shattered just like the mirror Caleb had broken.

Ironically, it started rather innocently. Caleb was scrambling eggs, absolutely *refusing* to eat Selene's dinner- but his tension was *volcanic*. A vein was visible and angry on his neck, his fist trembling on the wooden spoon.

Across the room, Damien passed behind him to grab a mug-

And their shoulders almost brushed.

Caleb froze in place so hard that everyone braced for impact, his head turning just so.

"Watch it, piece of shit."

Damien paused. "I ain't even touch you-"

Caleb slammed the spoon down and turned directly to the dreadlocked bodyguard.

"Yeah. Just my *wife*, right?"

Across the room, Selene stiffened. Raven looked up from her corner, eyes low-lidded from drinking.

"Don't," Selene said softly, bracing herself on a pouf. Her face was slightly green-tinted, as the sickness she'd felt that morning had persisted.

"No," Caleb snapped, stepping forward so that he was almost touching noses with the 2-inch-taller man.

"No, we're *not* letting it go. I wanna know how the fuck you could work out with me, spot me, and still be happy to *screw her under the same roof as me?*"

The words landed like grenades. Everyone, *everyone*, winced from the sheer *fury* in his tone.

"Caleb, please-" Selene stood now, her voice cracking. Her left hand clutched her belly, her eyes glazing over just slightly as she attempted to steady herself on the thick frame of a painting.

Raven stood then, her eyes narrowing.

"Don't act all pure, little Miss 'perfect'. Go on," she started, stalking toward her with pure poison in her green eyes. Her usually perfectly sleek hair was a mess, Damien's wifebeater loose on her frame.

"Go on and tell your *husband* it wasn't just once."

Selene gasped, both hands holding her stomach now.

Caleb stumbled in place, eyes widening with a mixture of devastation, disbelief, and *acrimony*.

Immediately, he turned to Damien-

-and punched him in the jaw so hard that blood splattered from his mouth and painted the cabinets behind them.

*"DAMIEN!"* Selene screamed out, lunging toward him, though Laney held her back protectively.

*"You disgusting piece of shit,"* Caleb hissed out, grabbing the large man's neck with one hand. Just as he drew his other arm back to punch him again-

Damien's fist collided with Caleb's nose, sending him stumbling as blood spilled out from his nostrils onto the hardwood.

Laney screamed, then. *"Caleb!"*

But Caleb was already lunging back, tackling Damien into the arm of the couch. They slammed to the floor, fists flying.

Michael rushed in, grabbing both men by the shirt. "Get *off* each other!"

"You pathetic fucking *snake!*" Caleb roared at Damien, blood still covering his face as he continued punching. "Acting like my fucking friend!"

"You made your god damn point," Damien said, wheezing slightly as he dodged the personal trainer's hits. "I ain't gonna sit here and let you put hands on me."

That's when Raven turned on Selene. Selene had never seen her like this- no makeup, eyes unhinged, hair red and curled at the roots.

"You act so damn *innocent.* The little healer, chef, maid, Whole time, it was just to mask what a *whore* you really are."

Selene's breath caught in her throat. "Raven..."

Damien turned his head toward the two women he'd touched in this lodge. "Rae, don't."

Raven chuckled then- a wicked sound.

"What an existence. Bones for a family, and an incestuous freak for a husband. I almost can't even be *mad* at you."

"Raven, enough!" Laney yelled, grabbing her belly.

But Selene didn't respond. Her breathing had gone shallow. She swayed where she stood, her eyes rolling back.

"Selene?" Damien shoved Caleb off to run toward her.

She couldn't answer him. She couldn't even *see* him.

All she could see were tiny black stars as her knees buckled.

Damien caught her just before her head hit the hardwood, his large hand cradling her as she went limp.

Everyone froze, even Raven, her hands still shaking in leftover rage.

Selene lay unconscious in Damien's arms, her lips agape.

"Fuck," Damien wheezed. "Selene- baby- Selene-"

The whole room fell into eerie silence.

# Chapter 29

*Perdu dans un brouillard*

It was around 3 a.m. when Selene finally stirred on the living room couch. Her eyes opened slowly, blinking up into warm, worried hazel ones.

"Hey," Laney said softly, crouched beside her on the living room rug, one hand on her swollen belly, the other over Selene's warm forehead. "Welcome back."

The large ceiling swam high above them. Selene's mouth was dry. Her hands felt like they'd been filled with sand.

"What… what happened?"

All she could hear was the station she'd constantly kept playing for some kind of warmth- on Maître Gims' "Zombie" now, ironically enough.

"You fainted a few hours ago," Laney said gently, moving a springy, damp coil from the sick yogi's forehead. "Your body just… gave out. Scared the shit out of all of us."

Selene struggled to sit up, only for the world to tilt again. One hand went to her stomach, the other to her head, where a migraine pounded with abandon.

Laney steadied her with a firm but careful hand. "Easy. I've got you."

Selene breathed through her nose, nodding faintly. "Where is everyone?"

"In the kitchen. I told them to give you space." She reached for a chilled water bottle and held it out. "You want a sip?"

Selene took it with trembling hands, her breathing still labored. A few gulps settled her nerves-

-until her stomach flipped without warning.

She turned to the side and vomited straight onto the floor, the chunky liquid seeping into the Beni Ourain rug.

"Oh- hey, hey, I got you," Laney murmured, grabbing a nearby towel and gently wiping Selene's mouth. "It's okay. Don't worry."

Selene panted, a hand over her chest. "I'm sorry," she said in the weakest voice.

Laney waved her off. "Shhh. Don't apologize."

There was a long pause.

Then-

"Selene… I have to ask…" her tone shifted, clinical but careful.

"When was your last period?"

Selene's face changed immediately. Her hands went from holding her belly to being limp at her sides.

The question hit her like a second fainting spell, only this time she was fully awake.

Her pulse quickened. Her mind flipped backward, then forward, then backward again.

She and Caleb had never *once* been together without a condom. They'd even held it under running water after each time like a ritual, having both agreed long ago that they wanted to enjoy the rest of their twenties together.

She and Damien, though? They hadn't used a thing.

They hadn't used a thing on a new moon- which Selene *knew* was when she usually ovulated.

She suddenly became *very* aware of how tender her breasts were, how they strained against her shirt in a way that wasn't usual.

Quickly, adrenaline filling her completely, she looked toward the tall window- the one she always stared through at 3 a.m., when her thoughts of Athena got too loud to bear.

The Snow Moon was as round as a coin.

Full.

*And she wasn't bleeding.*

Her throat bobbed. "I…"

Laney's gaze hardened. "I have a test in my bag."

Selene looked at her, small and scared. "Can you come with me to the bathroom?"

Laney nodded without hesitation. "Of course."

The two women supported each other to get up; one definitely carrying life, the other possibly doing so.

In the kitchen, the tension was already coiled like a snake with nowhere to strike. The air was thick, rank with shame.

Even at this time, no one had touched the food Selene prepared. No one had touched anything.

Then-

"You didn't have to come at her like that."

Damien's voice cut low through the silence. He stood stiffly against the counter, jaw tight, chest heaving slightly. He still had dried blood on his chin.

Raven didn't look at him. Her arms were crossed, hair disheveled, eyes bloodshot. "Excuse me?"

"I *said*," he repeated louder now, "you didn't have to come at Selene. *I'm* the one who cheated. You and her wasn't even close. That was me. So, blame *me*. Don't come at her like she tried to hurt you personally."

"Of course you'd defend her." Caleb's voice sliced in from the side of the room. He leaned against the fridge, bags deep under his eyes, dried blood still under his nose.

"You *both* have no honor."

Raven let out a sound that didn't even resemble a laugh. "No honor, indeed," she said, voice shaking with rage.

She turned to Damien with the darkest eyes he'd ever seen.

"He didn't even take off his dead brother's dog tags before he fucked her. It's like all he knows how to *do* is fail that poor boy."

The air *snapped*.

Everyone inhaled sharply at once.

Damien? His whole *demeanor* changed.

"You wanna bring up Xan?" he said, his voice deadly quiet.

Raven's eyes winced, but she held his gaze, balling her fists and tilting her head up.

"You right," Damien continued, stepping closer. "Xan wouldn't have liked that I cheated. He woulda told me I was wrong. He was always the better one of us."

He stopped right in front of her, those earth-rich eyes she always loved so much colder than she had ever seen.

"You know what he woulda *liked*, though?"

His voice cracked and then turned vicious. Raven's face started contorting in fear.

He crossed his thick arms.

"He'd have liked that I found a girl with *fire*. Not you. *Her.*"

Raven stepped back like she'd been struck.

But Damien? He wasn't even done.

"At least *she'd* never hit two people with her car, drive off, then change her whole *identity* to get away from the consequences."

Tears glittered within Raven's eyes now. Her breath was shaking so hard that it was audible.

There was nothing but a deafening silence, until-

"You have *no* right to say that," Caleb growled.

"Oh, Caleb, *please.*"

Michael, quiet until now, suddenly snapped. He stood from the barstool like he couldn't hold it in anymore. "You have no right to speak at *all.*"

Caleb turned slowly.

Michael, though? He wasn't anywhere *near* done.

"You're the guy who... God, I can't even say it. Your own fucking *sister.* While I was letting you stay in *my* apartment. I don't even care that we weren't together; you did that sick shit in *my* home. I'm tired of hearing your self-righteous bullshit. You're going off on Damien like you're better than him? What he did to you was *poetic justice*, in my eyes."

Caleb's face twisted into something dangerous.

He stepped forward- just a few inches- and his voice turned venomous as he puffed his chest out, fists balling like he was ready for damn near anything.

"Wonder why she'd prefer to fuck her own half-brother over you?"

Michael's breath caught in his throat, his skin reddening.

Damien winced just slightly. Even Raven snapped out of the pain she was in to brace for impact.

Caleb walked up so close that the strength difference between the two of them was obvious.

"Maybe it's 'cause her intuition told her she wasn't your type. That you'd prefer her a *dec-*"

Michael *lunged.*

He and Caleb flew into one of the lower cabinets, completely breaking it as the two men pounded at each other with the force of years of betrayal.

Raven, frozen for a second, suddenly turned to Damien-

And shoved him with all the force she had, eyes wild.

"You were supposed to be safe," she sobbed. *"YOU WEREN'T SUPPOSED TO BE HIM."* She pounded his chest with her thick-ringed fists, not wanting to stop until he felt a pain even *halfway* comparable to hers.

Damien just stood there, stone-still, jaw tight, not even defending himself as his large frame jolted back and forth.

And then-

*"STOP!"*

Two sharp cries came from behind them. Everyone turned, breathless and raw.

Selene and Laney had come out of the bathroom, both pale.

Selene's eyes were wide, stricken with nausea and something worse. She dropped her phone onto the hardwood at the sight of the group in complete disarray.

"I said *STOP!*" she cried again, trying to stop the vomit from rising in her throat.

But no one really did.

Michael continued shouting and punching at Caleb.

Caleb, mouth bleeding, continued punching at Michael blindly, cracking his glasses in the process.

Raven shoved Damien again, teeth gritted-

When Laney let out a petrified *gasp.*

One that sounded so full of fear that it silenced the room in an instant.

Everyone turned to the heavily pregnant woman, worry in their eyes.

And then-

**Every light in the lodge clicked off.**

Total *blackout.*

"Shit," Michael said immediately, scrambling from under Caleb. "Lanes? Lanes?!"

"Fuck, I can't see *anything,*" Raven panicked.

"No one move," Damien said, his bodyguard instincts kicking in. "And be quiet."

Just then-

**The lights flickered back on.**

Selene, with her hand still on her belly, *gasped.*

Michael's mouth dropped open.

Caleb scrambled to his feet.

Because Laney was gone. Vanished.

And her gasp still echoed in their skulls.

# Chapter 30

## *In the Breakdown*

"Laney?"

Selene's voice cracked as she called out, already hoarse from crying and vomiting and everything else the day had thrown at her. She stood in the center of the once luxurious, now destroyed kitchen, her eyes darting to every corner like she could will Laney's return just by staring hard enough.

"She was right next to me," she whispered, her voice shaking, unintentionally no louder than a whisper.

Damien slowly stepped forward, placing a gentle hand on her shoulder- hesitant, unsure if he even deserved to touch her after everything. Still, he couldn't deny how overjoyed he was that she was okay.

"Don't panic," he said, voice uncharacteristically soft.

Raven- still trembling from the fight, still seething from the betrayal- was the one to say what they were all thinking.

"She's gone," she muttered. "Like... *gone* gone."

Michael looked around the room as if Laney might suddenly appear behind a chair or something.

Caleb just stood in place, blood still drying on his lip, bruised knuckles twitching. He didn't look at anyone. Not even Selene.

Then-

**CLICK. CLICK. CLACK. CLACK.**

The sound echoed through the lodge.

One door unlocking. Then another. And another. Not just one. *Multiple.*

An entire *system* breathing back to life.

All five of them turned as the hallway lights flickered on. Every door that had been locked now… stood wide open.

The suites. The upstairs bathrooms. The gaming room. The art studio. Even the indoor pool room.

It was like the lodge was giving them a green light.

"Holy shit," Michael whispered.

"They want us to find her," Damien muttered, voice low. "They *invitin'* us."

"*Or* they want us to *see* something," Raven said grimly.

Damien went toward the ballroom, his fists tight, eyes scanning every inch of the room they'd once danced in. He called her name a few times.

Nothing. No answer. Just Frou Frou's "Let Go" playing hauntingly from Selene's Pandora station.

Selene went to the art studio. Her and Damien's painting was still there- storm, sun, stars. But no Laney.

Just the faint smell of old paint and dried sweat.

Raven checked the yoga studio. Then the spa room. The gym. She even kicked open closets. "Laney?" she called once. But her voice shook too much, so she didn't say it again.

Caleb wandered the hallway toward the sunroom. He didn't even realize he was crying until he saw a teardrop splatter on the wood floor.

He had a… complicated relationship with his half-sister. But knowing he might never see her again was a fate he wasn't prepared to meet.

Michael checked every bathroom. Opened every cabinet. He even lifted the toilet lid, as if he expected something *horrific*.

All he found was himself in the mirror—someone he barely recognized anymore.

Laney was simply *gone*.

No trace. No clues. No blood. No body. No belongings misplaced.

Not even a note.

On Valentine's Day, five sleep-deprived bodies slowly gravitated to the living room like magnets to metal. The couches were sunken now from too many sleepless nights; the coffee table was cluttered, and that damn black envelope still sat in the center like a smirking ghoul.

Caleb was the first to break the silence, his strong arms crossed, jaw still tight from five days of frantic searching.

"I think it's time we say it," he began, his Caribbean Sea-colored eyes narrowing.

"This retreat? This so-called 'relationship study?' It's a goddamn trap. Someone's got it out for us."

"Aren't *you* smart, Sherlock?" Raven muttered bitterly. Her fiery red roots were fully visible now. Since they had access to their suites again, she dressed comfortably in her own clothes, but she didn't *feel* comfortable at all.

Damien sat on one of the couches with his elbows on his knees, eyes on the floor, silent. Selene was curled beside him, unusually quiet, her hand resting on her still-sick stomach.

He noticed it, whispering "You ok?" in her ear every now and again. Once, he whispered, "You ok, moon girl?" and she felt heat rise to her cheeks despite everything.

She always whispered back, "Yeah, I'm fine."

She felt ashamed that even now, even after everything, she still felt the desire to hold him, to smell him, to kiss his skin, to feel his furnace-like body heat again.

"What even *is* this fucking place?" Michael said suddenly, voice so sharp it seemed to slice through the room like a knife. "It's supposed to be for 'research', but we haven't even fucking done anything worth researching. Those creepy black envelopes we got on January 10th were planned to get us to spill our secrets so they could *expose* us."

"It was their plan all along," Selene suddenly whispered, eyes distant, but still somehow sharp with knowing.

Everyone looked at her.

She sat up straighter. "I've been thinking about it. That black envelope?" She pointed to the coffee table. "It asked if we felt closer, now. It's like… they wanted each of us to know each other's darkest parts and just… sit with them. Like it would make us 'closer' in some messed-up way."

Damien's jaw tightened. "Yeah. But why *us?* Did any of us even *know* each other? Well, besides Caleb and Laney?"

Caleb's breath caught in his throat.

Then, he jumped up, a lightbulb clicking in his mind.

"Exactly. Me and Laney. It wasn't a coincidence that we both got selected. They knew. Whoever set this shit up? They knew about us when they picked us."

His face went pale as an even more haunting realization slowly came to focus in his mind.

"Maybe… even *before* that."

A huge weight dropped over the room, then. Everybody looked at each other like they were trying to find a pattern.

Selene suddenly tensed, eyes shifting like she was forming some frightening realizations of her own. "Did… did you and Laney tell anyone?"

Caleb froze as his brain went on a high-speed memory chase.

Then, he gulped. "I… I sent Laney an email. I… I don't completely remember *when,* but-"

Michael narrowed his eyes at him. "What do you mean, you sent her an email? Was it before… or *after* you left our apartment?"

Caleb's jaw tightened. Then:

"It was after."

Michael and Selene both looked like they'd been betrayed a second time. But just as Michael was going to ask "when"-

"She… she said she responded," Caleb stammered out. "But… but I didn't receive it. Maybe it… got out somehow and… I don't know."

He looked down then, his heart rate picking up.

Selene's eyes fluttered in thought before they focused on Raven, and then on Damien.

"But if it's just you… Why were Damien and Raven chosen?"

Damien glanced at her, his jaw tight, and then at Raven, who hadn't said a word to him in days.

Raven straight up froze, her pale face whitening even more.

"I… I hit them. I… I don't know if they died or not. But… maybe one of them, or one of their families…"

Selene gasped, clarity setting behind her eyes. "Set this whole thing up for revenge."

Damien leaned back. "But if it's about getting revenge on Raven… why the fuck are the *rest* of us here?"

Michael stood then, pacing the living room.

"So, whoever the hosts are knows about Caleb and Laney, *and* knows one or more of the people Raven hit?"

Selene nodded, jaw tight. "Exactly. Whoever planned this is someone who knew *all* of our secrets when they picked us."

Raven narrowed her red-rimmed eyes at her. "…And they somehow knew you'd end up fucking Damien, too? Unless you have *another* secret the class might wanna know about."

Selene looked at Damien then. He looked at her in return.

Their eyes lingered much, *much* longer than they needed to.

Raven scoffed, disgusted. "Oh, for God's sake."

Selene cleared her throat, looking away. "They *did* choose to partner us together. And… and…"

"They sent us to this secret room to 'talk'."

Damien's deep voice sliced through the room.

Caleb and Raven cut their eyes at them at once. "They…what?" Caleb asked slowly.

Selene cleared her throat, swallowing. "January 10th. Ours gave us a key and led us to… a secret room."

"And did you just… *talk?*" Raven said, eyes sharp.

Caleb cut his eyes at her, then. "You made fun of me for saying the obvious about this shit being a trap, but you say dumb shit like that? They were probably *excited* to be given a place to *finally-*"

Selene cleared her throat. "With all due respect… can we go back to the matter at hand? Clearly, the hosts had very… *specific* plans from the beginning. I'm not saying they *made* us have the affair, but-"

Michael clapped then, impatient. "Alright. So, let's get this straight. These people, one, know Caleb and Laney's shit; two, know about Raven's hit and run; and three, knew Damien and Selene would fuck."

He stopped pacing and then faced the others. "It's official; remember when we joked that we're in a Black Mirror episode? Well…we *are* in a Black Mirror episode. This *is* a simulation. We…"

He gasped then, his face going pale. "What if… what if…" Everyone looked at him intently, hearts thudding almost in unison.

"What if… we *are* Sims?!"

Everyone stared at him, frozen.

And for the first time in forever… they laughed.

"Bruh, I get shit's been tough," Damien barely got out through chuckles, "but let's not go off the deep end, here."

Michael didn't even crack a smile. "What else would explain Laney just... disappearing?"

Selene tried her hardest to hide her smile. "Michael... I'm pretty sure I'm real."

Raven scoffed bitterly. "And *I'm* pretty sure Sims fuck by rolling around under the covers. Not in *secret rooms* or wherever the fuck else y'all desecrated."

"Eh, *Wicked Whims* exists, to be fair," Selene said in the softest, quietest voice, making Raven cut her eyes at her.

Caleb stood up, annoyed. "You know what we're gonna do? We're gonna tear this whole lodge apart looking for clues. Whether we all have a common enemy or some weird psychological supernatural shit is going on, we gotta find out, because I'm *not* spending another night here."

Damien hummed in agreement, already rising, instinctively giving his hand to Selene, who took it and, again, looked at him for much longer than she needed to.

Caleb's lip curled in disgust. Then- "Alright. Damien and I will check the basement. Michael, check the main floor. Raven, check upstairs, even our suites and bathrooms, if you have to. Selene..."

He looked at his wife, whose face was still pale with nausea. "You look kinda sick, so stay here for now, I guess."

Selene nodded, and Damien looked at her intently, protectively, before Caleb motioned to follow him.

# Chapter 31

*Our Times Have Come*

The basement steps were narrow, steep, stone-lined, and colder than expected. There were no polished finishes or luxury designs down here- just raw walls and the scent of old earth and cold truths.

Caleb clicked his flashlight on. "Charming," he muttered.

They walked slowly, methodically, the stairs groaning beneath their equally solid weights as they descended into what felt like the ribcage of the lodge.

Once they reached the bottom, they paused.

Stone walls. Steel pipes. Empty wine racks.

And… silence.

A deep, suffocating *silence*.

Caleb swept the beam across the room, eyes narrowed. There were dozens of crates- old ones, covered in dust. Stacks of unused linens. Abandoned workshop tools.

But no bedrooms. No food. No signs of people *living*.

"Looks like a fucking dungeon," Caleb muttered. "But no beds. No toothbrushes. No used cups. No shoes lined up or jackets hung. No sign of anyone *being* down here."

Damien exhaled sharply. "Same with everywhere else."

They searched every corner of the creepy open space. They were relieved to not find Laney's body, but absolutely creeped out that she really did seem to just… disappear.

Caleb suddenly paused.

"These people gotta *live* here, right?"

Damien nodded once, jaw tight. "No way in *hell* they don't. They seem to know every damn thing at every damn time."

Caleb nodded. "They cooked a heavy ass breakfast, lunch, *and* dinner three times a day for a whole fucking month, yet we've never heard anyone come in or out."

Damien nodded in agreement, squinting as he looked around. "Yet, despite this lodge being fuckin' huge, the only bedrooms seem to be *ours.*"

Caleb scoffed. "I guess it makes sense we haven't found any extra bedrooms. Whoever these hosts are? They definitely never sleep."

Damien started to nod in agreement. But then…

He stopped in place.

His head stayed half-turned, frozen, his dreads grown out at the roots. His flashlight beam trembled slightly in his grip.

Caleb noticed. "Yo. You alright?"

But Damien didn't answer.

He just stood there, jaw tight, shoulders stiff.

His thoughts were running laps inside his head, and it wasn't just from sleep deprivation. He *wished* he could blame it on sleep deprivation.

His lips moved like they were trying to form something, like the air had thinned out just enough to make sound impossible.

He flat-out dropped his flashlight onto the cold concrete, making the room darker in the process.

Caleb looked at him quizzically. "Uh… dude?"

He still didn't answer. All he could do was breathe- *pant*, really, as the thoughts became clearer and clearer.

"Never sleep," he finally whispered, like the words were no longer Caleb's, but some kind of curse.

His heart started to thud, his stomach flipping in a way that made him feel sick.

And when they became too clear to deny anymore-

All of the color drained from his face. His eyes went wide.

And chills ran through his entire body as it finally *clicked*.


By evening, Raven was barely functioning. She had been tearing the entire lodge apart all day long and found no sign of… well… *anything*.

She stumbled into Caleb and Selene's suite, possibly for the 4th time; she had long abandoned counting.

The space was dark, the air heavy. The plum Echo Dot on the dresser played out soft music from Selene's linked Spotify- Blue Öyster Cult's "Don't Fear the Reaper" now.

"She *would* like this shit" Raven muttered, her makeup crisp and perfect. Despite everything, her "armor" became so comfortable for her that she put it on even now.

She stood for a moment, just breathing, just wondering if hitting two people with her car was worth *this* kind of nightmare.

Then, slowly, she dropped to her knees beside their bed.

Her fingers brushed along the floorboard until they caught the edge of something- smooth, firm, just barely hidden.

She squinted and reached beneath the bed.

Pulled it out. Unzipped it. Squinted, curiously, and then unzipped something else.

And then-

Raven Quinn went completely still.

Every drop of color drained from her face.

She didn't speak. She could hardly even *breathe*.

# Chapter 32

*Can You Keep a Secret?*

Damien gripped the stone wall like it was the only thing keeping him from collapsing, his strong chest rising and falling like it was all it knew how to do, Xander's dog tags clinking with every motion as he swayed where he stood, his head rolling despite himself.

His head spun. His heart thundered in his chest. And words… they wouldn't stop.

*Whoever these hosts are, they definitely never sleep.*

*They definitely never sleep.*

*Definitely never sleep.*

*Never sleep.*

**Never sleep.**

The basement was freezing, but a cold sweat broke over him. His labored panting was audible, now, and for a moment, Caleb forgot everything that had transpired between the two of them and placed a hand on the uncharacteristically shaken bodyguard's shoulder.

"Dude… you *gotta* tell me what's wrong."

Damien squeezed his eyes shut, not able to process Caleb's presence anymore. All he could process were the memories.

**January 3rd.**

He'd woken up in the living room at around 3 a.m., groggy and disoriented, the fire dimmed but still crackling. He and Raven had fallen asleep on the living room floor after game night, and they were covered in blankets and had fluffy pillows beneath their heads.

He'd heard a soft sound.

*Thock. Thock. Thock.*

He followed it to the kitchen.

Selene was there.

No makeup, hair tucked, in a silky robe she appeared to have just put on.

She was chopping fruit. But not just any fruit.

*Perfect shapes.*

Stars. Hearts. Crescents. Meticulously crafted like she'd done it a hundred times.

"You couldn't sleep?" he'd asked. At the time, he still didn't trust her and wanted to see what she could possibly be doing at that hour.

She had jumped, genuinely startled. He'd noticed her chest rising and falling faster, her pulse fluttering quickly beneath her skin.

Then, she giggled. The softest, most *practiced* giggle.

And she said:

*"I never sleep."*

He'd thought it was weird. Of *course*, he had. He'd even made fun of her with Raven afterward.

But he hadn't asked why her "hangover smoothies" needed fruit carved like gourmet garnishes.

He hadn't asked why the fruit looked *exactly like the fruit the hosts always put on the table.*

Wait.

The cooking.

The lavish homemade meals the "hosts" always cooked.

Soul food. North African food. Smoothies.

*The exact same kinds of meals that Selene cooked for the group after the auditorium.*

His eyes shot open, his pupils constricting in the dim light of the basement. He thought harder.

To the music that was always playing from her phone like constant background noise. From Pandora, Spotify, YouTube Music-

*And never offline or downloaded.*

His pulse pounded in his ears, but the thoughts wouldn't stop coming.

And then-

*The art studio.*

The night they painted each other, inside and out.

Selene had a remote to unlock it.

She already had the remote tucked into her dress pocket. Claimed she found it "while exploring."

She had a light clicker, too. She turned on the lights in there like she'd done it a thousand times.

She knew exactly where everything was. Exactly what to do.

Even that first time they entered the secret tower room behind the bookcase…

She led him there.

Like she already knew it existed.

The keyhole was hidden deep within the bookcase- yet she didn't even spend *two seconds* looking for it.

She'd just crouched down and turned it into the lock like it was the most natural thing in the world.

Damien's throat dried out. But it was the next memory-

The one that slammed into him like a truck-

That made his stomach turn.

**Murder Mystery Dinner.**

The lights had suddenly gone out, electric. Like someone had hit a button.

A *clicker*.

And when they turned back on-

Selene was playing dead. Lying on the bench, silent and still.

A new golden envelope had appeared on the table within the ten seconds that the lights were off.

There were also character sheets. A timer. A whole new *setup* on that oak table.

And no one, *no one*, heard the dining room doors open or close, lock or unlock.

He'd immediately looked at another door within the dining room, and when he realized it was locked, he figured the hosts were hiding in there.

He just… accepted that.

He didn't wonder why he never heard that door open or close, either.

He didn't even stop to consider that *the whole situation wouldn't have even been possible if someone who wasn't* **already in the room** *had orchestrated it.*

"Fuck…" he breathed out.

He still had the character cards, still stuffed in the pocket of the slacks he'd worn that night.

Selene had said her card told her to play dead. Whispered it with a knowing little smirk on that velvet bench.

He hadn't thought to read it. He hadn't thought to check.

He hadn't thought at all.

And now-now that line was screaming in his head.

*"I never sleep."*

The air around Damien turned razor-thin.

"B-be right back," he muttered to Caleb, voice distant, strained, already turning on his heel.

"Hey, wait!" Caleb called, but he didn't hear him even a little bit. He was busy sprinting up the basement steps two at a time.

He stumbled into his suite, chest heaving, eyes wild. The door creaked closed behind him, but he barely heard it.

In half a second, he was at the dresser. Bottom drawer. Into the pocket of those black slacks.

He reached into them and felt something with a hard edge.

The old character cards.

He pulled them out one by one- Caleb's, Michael's, Raven's, his own.

Then… Selene's.

Damien swallowed, bracing himself, and read each one. His stomach dropped.

His fingers tightened as if he might crush the card.

It was blank.

She was never told to "play dead."

She just *knew*.


Raven, on the other hand, was on her knees on the soft rug of Caleb and Selene's suite, pupils constricted as they fixed on something in her hand- something she'd pulled out of a closed zipped lining pocket within a large lavender suitcase.

*A Polaroid- slightly faded but well-preserved.*

Cold sweat began to bead on every square inch of Raven's skin. Her vision became blurry.

She felt the exact same sickening feeling she'd felt at 1:03 a.m. on May 4th, 2013.

In the Polaroid, Selene beams in a teal-colored knit hat stitched with a gibbous-cut moonstone, her smile brighter than she'd ever be capable of today, her eyes more innocent. And in her arms-

-a young teen girl.

Also wearing a knit hat- a lavender one with a moonstone cut into a crescent.

And those *glasses.*

Those same cat-eyed, purple-rimmed glasses Raven saw every time the thunder crashed.

*The same ones she self-medicated to forget.*

The girl's smile is lopsided; she has a dimple on one cheek and a small freckle on her nose.

Her face is beautiful, yet unique.

And that uniqueness was exactly *why* Raven recognized that face.

She'd seen it under streetlight.

She'd seen it on concrete.

She'd seen it in *blood.*

And now, despite the bar of Xanax she'd taken just a few hours before-

**The flashes came relentlessly.**

*A thunderstorm.*

*Whiskey in her belly, in her hands, in her blood.*

*A sickening thud.*

*Two young teen girls, lying motionless.*

*Matching bracelets on their wrists with heart pendants engraved with 'T&M Forever.'*

And now that same hat, and that same bracelet. Was being worn by one of those girls.

And she was in *Selene's* arms.

Raven's vision blurred.

Her breath left her body in a single rasp:

"Oh my *God.*"

Her pulse thundered. Her vision swam. Her lungs felt like they were filling with smoke.

And then-

*She ran.*

Down the still-gleaming hardwood stairs.

Barefoot, clumsy, her short boy shorts getting a hole in them from scraping against… she didn't even know, anymore. She just *ran.*

She didn't register the plush rug, the mahogany banister, the flickering firelight. Just momentum. Just panic.

Halfway down, her hip clipped the side table. A large lamp crashed onto the floor behind her, shattering into a million pieces.

The sound ripped through the lodge like a gunshot, signaling everyone to come to the source of the noise, worried and shaken, especially after everything.

Caleb was in there first, hauling up the basement stairs- already on edge from Damien's abrupt departure.

Then, Michael from his and Laney's suite, still hoping he'd find her and their baby asleep in their bed that now looked *mockingly* comfortable.

Then Damien, who looked like he knew *exactly* what was about to go down.

And then, calmly walking out of the kitchen after baking decadent heart-shaped chocolate-chip cookies iced with homemade strawberry icing-

Was Selene.

Her eyes flicked from the shattered lamp to Raven. Then to the Polaroid in her hand. She wore dark-wash jeans that showed off her shapely thighs, and a lavender sweater with sleeves that cut off at her elbows, revealing a tattoo that turned Raven's stomach.

She was still gasping, still shaking, clutching the photo like a live grenade. Her roots were visibly curly now, her face ghostly, even her freckles.

But she was looking at Selene like *she* was the ghost.

Her voice, when it finally broke free, came out shredded:

"It's *you.*"

She stood in place, shaking, a cold sweat shimmering on every square inch of her alabaster frame.

She opened her mouth again, her voice louder now, hoarse and gutted.

"It's *you,* isn't it?"

Her hand lifted, shaking violently, and she held up the Polaroid. She was shaking so much that the faces in the film could barely be recognized.

Damien's jaw tightened as he looked at the woman he bonded deeply with, the woman he'd broken a promise with, like she was potentially *dangerous.*

Selene looked at the Polaroid, eyes blank, a look that made every heart in the room stop.

Her expression didn't change; not even a flicker of surprise.

She simply… blinked.

Damien's eyes narrowed, his heart thudding even harder. He wanted badly, *so* very badly, to believe that he was just paranoid, that cabin fever had simply taken hold of his sanity.

That there was a different explanation for the array of realizations he'd just had.

But then, Selene slowly took her phone out of her pocket, her face still chillingly blank.

She tapped the screen with a freshly manicured nail; lavender with teal accents. The sound of a text message leaving played out.

*The kind of text message that requires an internet connection.*

Then she looked up-

Directly at Raven.

And for the first time since the beginning of the retreat, she didn't look gentle.

She looked *ancient.*

Like something that had waited nearly *seven years* to say this.

She took a slow step forward, her fitted sweater hugging her curves gracefully- *way* too gracefully.

"It's almost *amazing* how good your timing is," she said, voice eerily casual. "I was just about to call everyone for the Valentine's Day meal I made. Celebrate it together."

She walked up to her, close enough that Raven could smell her warm almond-vanilla scent- something that she'd always found comforting, but now felt *intentionally* so.

Close enough for her to see the *fire* behind Selene's gold-flecked eyes.

Selene lifted her small chin, her eyes narrowing just so beneath her thick lashes.

"Did you really think," she started softly, deadly, her voice firm in a way no one in the lodge had heard it before, not even Caleb.

Raven gulped, face pale, shivering so hard that her teeth clattered audibly.

Selene, though? She was *stone-cold.*

"That you could kill my sister and get away with it?"

# Chapter 33

*As the Music Dies*

Raven couldn't *breathe.*

Her throat convulsed as she wheezed for air, but it was like her lungs refused to open.

Selene didn't let up. Her voice was calm- *too* calm.

"She and her best friend, Imani?" she began, stepping toward the center of the room like she was addressing a jury.

"They were *13.* On their band trip to Disney. They stepped outside the hotel for late-night snacks. Giggling. Talking about gossip, boys. The convenience store was just across the street. Not even a thirty-second walk away."

Selene's voice darkened. "And then- **boom**."

Her hands slammed together with a sharp clap that made Raven flinch.

"A drunk driver swerved carelessly and *slammed* into them both."

Damien's brows furrowed. Michael whispered, "shit."

Selene's nostrils flared as she turned to Raven, her eyes sharper than broken glass.

"Just like the idiots who killed my parents."

She stepped toward the coffee table now. "And you?" she spat, eyes sizing Raven up like she was nothing.

"You couldn't even *own* it."

Raven staggered back, clutching the edge of the couch like she would easily collapse if she didn't.

Selene, though? She wasn't even *close* to done.

"You didn't call 911. You didn't check their pulses. You didn't try to save them. You didn't even so much as *scream.*"

Selene's voice was rising now, each sentence rougher, harder, more guttural. "You looked at their bodies-

-my sister's body-

-and you got back in your fucking car and drove away."

Raven started sobbing, shaking her head over and over like it would erase the memory.

Damien plopped down on the couch like he needed something to hold him.

But Selene *still* wasn't done.

"You ditched your Nissan." She stepped even closer.

"You bought a plane ticket."

She paused, now close enough to smell the petrified woman's perfume.

"And you dyed your hair and changed your fucking name like you didn't just-"

Her voice cracked. She pressed a hand to her chest. "Wipe out *two lives* because you were too fucking selfish."

Raven started hyperventilating, rage growing behind her eyes. "You're crazy. You're fucking *crazy-*"

"I spent *years* looking for you."

Selene's voice sliced straight through her words.

"My aunt and I, we were full of rage- beyond anything grief can explain. We had lost three people we loved the same way. And all we had to go off was a shitty storefront video. It took almost a year to even decipher the license plate."

Her jaw tightened. "Eventually, it led us to someone named Kelly O'Connor. Funny thing is?"

She laughed once, bitterly.

"Kelly O'Connor never existed after May 4th, 2013. Did she?"

Raven's fists balled at her side, voice trembling. "You insane fucking bitch. You *insane fucking-*"

Selene crossed her arms, unbothered. "And the police?"

She rolled her eyes. "Fucking useless. Wouldn't even label it a homicide. Just a tragic accident. No justice at all."

Selene backed up again, to the middle of the room, like a queen giving a grand speech.

"But I guess it makes sense. They *were* two little Black girls, after all."

Raven let out a disbelieving laugh, face wet with panicked tears. "What, you think your actions are *justified* because of that? I fucking got drunk and accidentally hit two people, shit that happens every fucking day, and *you* went and-"

"My aunt and I dreamed of saving up enough money to hire a private investigator to find you... I mean... Kelly. The most expensive, top-tier one we could." Selene's voice cut through like she hadn't even heard her.

She looked right at Raven, jaw tight.

"My aunt played the lottery numbers weekly for *five years straight*. Went to every bodega, every corner store, every-"

Raven became *hysterical* now. "*You're a fucking* **psycho!** There's no *way* you can *possibly* think you can get away with bringing us here-"

But Selene wasn't even looking at her anymore.

She had turned completely to Caleb.

"And then…" she said, her voice quieter now. "I met who I thought was my reward for everything I had been through."

Damien, Raven, and Michael- they had all frozen. The air had gone solid.

Caleb? He was trembling so hard that his *teeth* clattered.

Selene walked closer to him, now.

"I met who I thought my parents and my sister banded together in heaven to bring to me."

She took a deep inhale, her eyes glittering. "It felt *so* much like fate. I only started going to yoga to get over the unbearable grief I felt. Ended up loving it so much that I started teaching it."

She slowly walked back to the center, looking up at the high ceilings as if completely overcome by nostalgia.

"Once I started teaching, all I wanted to be was better, *stronger*. I wanted to be the *best* yoga instructor my students could ever have, because some of them could've been just like me. Doing that silly free 'fresh start' yoga class with my aunt on New Year's Day, just hoping it would make me not want to kill myself for once."

She looked at Caleb again. "So, I got personal training."

She then smiled, tears spilling free now. "And the boy who trained me became my first love, my first kiss, my first *everything*."

Her smile dropped just as quickly as it formed.

"And then… I saw that email he sent to his secret sister."

Caleb's face went so pale he hardly looked alive.

And Selene? She had *fire* behind her eyes.

*"On our wedding night."*

## 1 July 2018- The Plaza Hotel

When the just-weds finished, they didn't move. They lay in the plush bed naked, arms wrapped around each other like they never wanted to be apart.

Selene pressed her hand- her left hand, now adorned with *two* golden rings- to his cheek. "That was everything I've always imagined, baby."

Caleb's ocean eyes warmed as he kissed the toffee-skinned beauty for what had to be the hundredth time that day. "Glad I didn't disappoint you."

Selene snorted. "Please. Even if it were bad- which I can't imagine- I would still be happy. Since I was a little girl, I wanted my husband and me to lose our virginity to each other on our wedding night. I can't believe it's actually real."

Caleb tensed, a vein showing up in his neck just slightly.

Then, he forced a smile, moving a strand of straightened hair from her face. "I've always wanted that, too. I can't believe how rare we are. It's like… we were *meant* to find each other."

Selene looked at the handsome trainer, eyes warm, before hopping onto him and peppering his face, neck, and chest with kisses.

Caleb chuckled at the tiny woman's abundant energy. "Babe, we can't, you know, I need to check the condom."

Selene huffed while kissing his skin. "Right. Well, you'd better be quick."

Caleb smiled and kissed her cheek. "I'm gonna make use of the sexy ass rainfall shower in there too, if you don't mind. I smell like all kinds of wet dog. The sun was fucking *brutal* today, and wearing a tux really didn't help."

Selene snorted. "*You're* the one who insisted we marry on July 1st of all dates. Of *course*, you're sweaty."

Caleb smiled warmly, kissing her forehead one last time before he strolled into their ensuite bathroom. "Don't fall asleep while I'm in there. I plan to make you proud to carry my last name when I come back."

Selene winked at him, giggling, as he disappeared behind the tall door.

For a moment, she just lay in the impossibly comfortable bed. Inas had outdone herself, having booked the couple the most lavish room in the city for their wedding night.

That reminded the newlywed- Inas said the photographers already sent the photos to Selene's email.

Warm and smiling, Selene slowly got up from the bed and wrapped a fluffy cream- colored robe over her naked body. She was still sore, but in a way that made her feel proud, *claimed.*

Her white-pedicured feet padded over to the armchair where Caleb's laptop sat. From her phone, George Michael's "Careless Whisper" played, a song she made sure to play while they were sharing their first dance. She giggled at the memory, knowing her parents and Athena would've loved it, would've watched her and Caleb dance in the middle of that ballroom just like Lashawn and Youssef had always danced in the kitchen.

She picked the laptop up, almost reverently, and sat down, cooing at how comfy the chair was.

But when she opened Gmail-

She *froze.*

Caleb's email was open. The most recent email was sent just four hours earlier, unread, from a name she hadn't seen before.

**Delaney Davis.**

The subject being:

*"I didn't forget."*

Selene wasn't someone who pried. She trusted Caleb completely, wholly.

But something about this particular email sent *chills* down her spine.

Heart thudding, mind racing, she opened it.

And the chill spread to her *entire body.*

**Caleb…**

**I didn't even know how to feel when I got your email this morning.**

**Firstly, congratulations on the wedding. I am genuinely, so, so happy that you found love. You deserve it. Selene sounds like a dream.**

But to answer your question… No. I didn't forget.

I know I kicked you out when Michael asked me out. I have spent years feeling so guilty about that. But hopefully, now you understand why.

No matter how it felt at the time, what we did was fucked up. Point blank. I cared for you, I loved you, probably always will.

But I love Michael, too, and he is a good guy to me. He wouldn't have deserved to be with a girl involved with her own brother.

That's why I had to end things. I knew he deserved someone who was all for him. Just like you deserve a wife you don't have to hide, or come up with excuses for why you want her. I pray Selene is that woman for you.

Now that I know you're getting married, I think I'm going to start trying for a baby with Michael. You're entering your next chapter, so I guess it's time for me to enter mine.

Selene's heart was in her throat. She suddenly felt the urge to run to the bathroom. The next thing she saw was an attachment- one of a tiny glass bird mid-flight.

**I still have this, and I always will.**

**P.S. Laney- your 'lovebird'.**

Tears were in Selene's eyes now, her breath audibly catching in her throat.

But still, she scrolled down to the email this woman was responding to, sent eight hours ago-

*Thirty minutes before their ceremony began.*

**From Caleb.**

Dear Laney,

First of all, happy birthday. Hopefully, you and Michael are doing something fun today. I don't know if you're still together or not, but judging by everything that happened the last time we saw each other, I'm just gonna assume you are.

It's been a while since we spoke, but I couldn't start this day without sending you a message.

In 30 minutes, I will be getting married.

God, it feels so weird to say. I didn't see myself ever getting married, because I didn't see myself ever being with anyone but you.

After you kicked me out, I wanted nothing to do with who I used to be. I got a gym membership, moved to NYC, and got so good that I became a personal trainer. That's how I met the girl I'm about to marry.

Her name is Selene. She's super sweet. Can cook like some kind of celebrity chef. She was teaching yoga at the same wellness center.

I'm her first everything; she waited a long time to find someone to share herself with, and for some reason, she found me worthy.

She thinks she's my first everything, too. And honestly, it doesn't feel like a lie. Because losing you made me feel like a completely new person.

I proposed to her when the clock struck midnight on New Year's, just like how Michael asked you out. Figured if that was enough to make you fall out of love with me, proposing to her the same way would probably make her love me forever. So, thanks for the idea, I guess.

One day, Selene and I will have kids. That means you'll have nieces and nephews out there, and you'll probably never see them. I have no idea how to feel about that. Well, about anything, really. I don't even know if you and Michael have had kids by now. Knowing I may have a niece or nephew out there... It's wild. The thought is both surreal and a little depressing, but I'm trying to not let it get to me. You deserve a family that isn't fucked up.

Selene will never, ever know about us, and I can promise you that. I'd actually kinda like you to delete this email when you're done reading and hopefully responding. But before I marry her, I just couldn't say nothing to you.

I don't even know why I'm sending this, honestly. I guess I'm curious if you forgot. Or not.

Selene sobbed audibly now, legs shaking so hard that the laptop fell from her lap and hit the floor beside the wedding dress she became Selene Brown in.

◐

Selene laughed then, but it was entirely mirthless.

"And you want to know the funny part?" she said, her large eyes glittering with tears as she started stepping slowly toward him again. Everyone looked at her like she was danger incarnate.

Caleb?

He couldn't even *focus* on her.

Selene smiled, wiping her face. "I *still* loved you. Even after I saw it, even after I read every horrible, sick word, even after I checked Laney's socials and saw how *alike* you look-" she gagged quietly to herself.

Still, she shook it off and stepped forward, looking up at him. She was an entire foot shorter than he, but looking at them right now, you'd never guess it.

"I didn't want it to go this far. I hoped that if I had Laney right in front of you, you'd tell me the truth eventually. I waited a whole *month*, Caleb. I gave you *so* many chances. If you'd have told me the truth, this would've actually *been* our honeymoon trip. I would never have chosen to include you in the plan against Raven."

Caleb blinked, face pale as a ghost.

"Selene… what are you talking about? What plan?"

A weight dropped over the room. Everyone, *everyone* held their breath.

Selene smiled then, rolling her shoulders back like she'd been waiting to say this for weeks.

"This lodge?"

She gestured around the gorgeous living room- the Beni Ourain rug, the poufs, the Medina paintings, the Berber vases- every hint of Morocco that everyone had thoughtlessly brushed off.

"It belongs to Tatie."

# Chapter 34

*Une Colombe ou Corbeau*

## Independence Day 2018- Queens, NY

Inas stood at the counter, slicing figs with the precision of someone who could dice emotion if she tried hard enough. She wore a colorful muu muu and gold house slippers that covered her tiny feet. From the high-quality speaker on the counter, Zaho's "Un Peu Beaucoup" played out. From beyond the windows, fireworks were already going off like the sky itself was celebrating the news.

Selene sat curled in a chair at the breakfast table, her hoodie sleeves covering her palms, curls twisted into a high bun. The Maghrebi mint tea steeping behind them filled the room with something homey, perfectly complementing the paintings of souks and medinas hanging on the wall.

"So," Inas said, flicking a fig slice onto a plate. "*Raven Quinn*, hmm?"

Selene didn't look up, taking a tense sip of her tea. "Kelly O'Connor. Just... dipped in eyeliner and tattoos now. With cryptic captions about her 'eyes hiding more than we think they do.'"

Inas let out a sound halfway between a scoff and a snort. "*Hadi? Wesh bghat tensa?* She thinks hair dye and ugly jewelry can make people forget she killed two kids."

"She's got almost a *million* followers," Selene murmured bitterly. "A million people who don't know a thing."

She gave her own phone a look of near contempt. "She blew up on Tumblr in the summer of 2013, Tatie. She blew up *months* after killing Thena and Mani."

Inas made a look of utter disgust and spun around, holding the plate of figs like it offended her.

"Thirteen years, *ya binti*. And this- this Kelly, this *Raven*- ran like a coward. Changed every little thing about herself. *Choufi*, I bet she doesn't even *walk* the same anymore."

Selene's gaze was steady now. "But they found her. It took two months, but they actually *found* her."

"*Aywa*. They *did.*" Inas set the plate down and lowered herself into the pouf opposite her niece.

"And now we know every little thing about her down to who she sleeps next to at night."

Selene's eyes softened as she gazed out the window, a small, bittersweet smile tugging at her lips. "Damien King."

She paused, then added quietly, eyes wistful. "He lost his little brother the same day I lost Thena. The *same exact day*, Tatie."

Inas leaned forward, golden eyes sharpening with interest. Selene pulled out her phone and showed her aunt a couple of Damien's old anniversary posts- raw, vulnerable words about his brother Xander, the pain still fresh even years later.

Inas studied the photos and captions for a long moment, then let out a low, knowing hum.

"Mm. *Soulmates,*" she said, the word heavy with certainty. "Two people carrying the same pain on the same day? That is *not* coincidence, *binti*. That is *fate.*"

She tilted her head, a mischievous glint entering her eyes. "Plus… he sexy as heck, no? That man is *beautiful*. I can see in your *eyes* you attracted."

Selene's cheeks warmed at her aunt's ever-blunt words. But she didn't deny it.

Inas leaned in closer, her voice dropping with bitterness, now. "And it ain't like you staying with that *nasty* husband of yours."

It was true. After Selene found that email, she told Caleb she was extremely sick, cancelled their Greece honeymoon, and told him she needed to stay with Inas for the time being, as only *she* knew how to heal this specific sickness. She didn't know how to come to him about what she saw- not yet- but she *knew* she couldn't be in the same room with him yet.

Selene took a deep inhale. "So, what? I try to date Damien after we arrest Raven?"

Inas looked at her niece like she couldn't believe her naivety. "Arrest?! *Binti*, this *kelba* has spent *five* happy years getting away with what she did. She has seen riches, she has been in rooms with celebrities, she has laughed and danced and flaunted her body, while Thena lay still underground. And you think all she deserves is *arrest?!*"

Selene blinked.

"Tatie… what are you getting at?"

Inas smiled, the kind of glowing, fire-backed smile only five years of complete and utter *rage* can create.

"What was that movie Thena used to love so much?"

Selene quirked a brow, confused where this was going. "You're talking about… High School Musical?"

Inas nodded fast, too fast. "And where was that filmed, again? What state?"

Selene blinked, eyes narrowing. "Uh… Utah, I think?"

Inas smiled again, flipping her now entirely grey curls behind her shoulder.

"Remember how she used to talk about how she wanted to meet her soulmate in a mountain lodge New Year's party, like that boy and girl did?"

Selene couldn't help but snort a bit, then. "Tatie, I am trying my *best* to understand what this has to do with Rav-"

"Thena never *got* to go to a mountain lodge, and she never *got* to meet her soulmate," Inas interrupted, her voice cracking with genuine hurt.

Selene gasped, pain slashing through her heart at her aunt's true words.

Then, Inas leaned in, voice low, both hands pressed flat against the table.

"But… maybe we can do something in *her* honor."

Selene's eyes narrowed. "You're saying we… take Raven and Damien to a Utah mountain lodge?"

Inas' eyes sparkled. *"Yes."*

She moved quickly then, sitting directly across from her still-confused niece.

"The most *beautiful* lodge you can think of. When it's snowing, just like in the movie. Something romantic, something that'll make them feel like soulmates. I mean, really settle in, get comfy, eat well, have the time of their lives, and then?"

She clapped her hands together so hard that Selene jumped in her seat.

"It gets ripped away from them. Just like *she* got ripped away from *us.*"

Selene blinked. Once, twice, three times. But slowly… ever so slowly… The idea started to settle in.

She tried to hide how her eyes started to sparkle. "So, how do we do it? We rent an Airbnb for like a week, invite them, and then-"

"*Wash nti mhmouqa?!* A *week?!* Thena was in our lives for *thirteen years.* Raven need to be there long enough to feel at home. Only *then* can she understand our pain."

Selene knew the idea was crazy. She knew grief had completely enveloped her aunt's mind to the point that she wasn't mentally well anymore, to the point where reality no longer felt safe.

But she also knew how *good* it would feel to watch her sister's killer feel half of the pain they'd been forced to sit with since 2013.

She leaned forward, grip tightening on her lavender mug. She'd always made it a point to use lavender or teal things- little ways of honoring Thena and Mani.

"Okay. So, we rent the lodge for-"

Inas looked at her niece like she'd *lost* it.

"*Binti,* I won 75 *million.* We ain't 'renting' a damn thing."

Selene couldn't help but chortle, then. Her Tatie never, ever cursed, so she *knew* this was serious.

Inas continued. "We *buying* it. It can be a part of our family forever. We pass it down to your kids, and their kids, and their kids, and they will all know that, this?"

She slapped her hand on the table for emphasis, her gold rings clinking loudly, making her niece jump. Selene inwardly told herself she should've been used to her aunt's antics by now.

Inas continued with *fire* behind her eyes.

"*Generations* will know that this is the lodge where Athena Nasrin Armani got justice."

Selene couldn't help but smile then, her golden-brown eyes sparkling with tears at the thought. "Can we make adjustments to it? Maybe make it look like a castle? You know how obsessed Thena was with Disney *anything*."

Inas cackled, then. "We will add whatever we want to it. A pool, a theater, a gym, a spa, an art studio. And of course, a special little soundproof room for you, no windows. Just in case it storms."

Selene smiled at her aunt's consideration. She'd been hiding in the closet every time it stormed in hopes of running away from the sound, from the memories.

Then, as she pondered the idea of the Disney castle mountain lodge… Her eyes sparkled with excitement.

"Can the windowless room be like… hidden? Like, behind a bookcase or something?"

Inas laughed then, tears stinging her eyes. "Now you getting excited. *Haka bghit!*"

Selene leaned back in her seat, then, eyes dancing as she pondered the logistics. Then, her expression went from hopeful to doubtful.

Inas noticed it immediately, leaning in to study the grieving yoga instructor's face. "Tell me what you thinking, *binti.*"

Selene sighed then, her fingers tightening around the mug.

"The thing is, Raven and Damien are *rich.* Instagram pays a *lot* these days. She's always posting some new brand or tummy tea. An invite to a random lodge probably wouldn't entice them."

Inas just smirked, like she'd already thought this through a million times. "It won't be 'random', *binti.* You forget… *love* will be a big part of this."

Selene looked down into her empty tea mug, her brain slowly digesting what her aunt was getting at.

Then, she looked back up. "A couple's retreat?"

Inas smiled then, the hue of her golden hoops perfectly matching her eyes. "*Now* you understand."

She leaned back in the cozy seat, popping a fig into her mouth. "We make it just as romantic as Thena's daydream. Champagne, wine, chocolate, a nice jacuzzi. And a big bedroom that they never want to leave," she said with a wink, making her niece cover her face in embarrassment.

She continued. "And we can do little exercises and games and therapy stuff so it can feel like a real retreat, like the goal is to bring them *closer.*"

A pang went through Selene; but she couldn't tell if it was nerves or excitement.

"But Tatie… what if it doesn't work? I mean, I look *nothing* like Raven. Sure, Damien and I can bond over our grief, but what are the chances he'll actually be *attracted* to me?"

Inas looked at her niece like she'd just said the biggest load of BS there was. "Oh, please. You know *dang well* he gonna be attracted to you."

Selene couldn't help but snort, then. While she was humble, she wasn't *blind*. Lashawn had gifted her facial beauty and feminine curves, and the past 4 years of daily yoga and training had given her a physique that caught every eye in every room.

It was quiet, just for a bit, as the two petite women pondered this crazy idea of theirs.

Then, Selene couldn't help but smile. "So, after we buy it and fix it up… what do we *name* this lovers' lodge?"

Inas pursed her lips, mind racing. "It has to do with mountains, wherever it is."

Selene popped a fig into her mouth. "Or… *valleys*."

Inas looked at her sideways. "What, 'Lover Valley Lodge'?"

Selene giggled. "More like… Lover*vale*."

Inas gasped. "I knew I raised you to be smart. Lovervale Lodge~" she said it like she was christening a newborn.

Selene narrowed her eyes. "Ehh, but it's a *bit* on the nose. We need something that won't make it *too* obvious."

The two co-conspirators sat at the table, thoughts in their head, fire in their hearts.

And then, almost at the exact same time-

They looked up at each other at once with the most mischievous of smiles.

Caleb *thought* his breath had been taken away before.

Now? He could've fainted where he stood.

He shook his head in utter disbelief. "Selene… Selene, do you even realize how *crazy* you sound? Do you even realize how *batshit* this is?"

He gestured around the lodge. "You and T-Tatie; you guys are *criminals*. You-"

Selene didn't even so much as blink, her eyes eerily blank as she turned to Michael, who looked shell-shocked.

"We only planned for it to be me, Caleb, Raven, and Damien at first. But when I realized how easy you and Laney were to find-"

"Where *is* Laney?" Michael's voice broke through like a blade, his shoulders trembling.

Selene smiled, almost scarily casually, like she'd just remembered something pleasant.

She turned to look him directly in the eyes.

"Let me just say… You two were crazy as *hell* to choose to go on a two-month mountain retreat in her *third trimester.*"

"You crazy *cunt*," he growled, stepping toward the yoga instructor with rage in his eyes. She held a small hand up- not in fear, but in warning. He froze from her conviction alone.

She continued with the smallest smile. "It was *always* my plan to let her spend only a week here after the midpoint "party." While we were in the bathroom, I told her everything. Told her to let out the most *fearful* gasp she could. Then, I turned off the lights."

She pulled a clicker out of her pocket and clicked one of the buttons once-

**Making every light in the lodge flick off to darkness.**

Everyone gasped before she clicked them back on.

"While they were off, I let her out of a hidden exit." She pointed to yet another well-hidden trapdoor, this one connected to the kitchen.

From her back pocket, she pulled out her phone and unlocked it, swiping to a thread. She turned the screen toward Michael.

There were dozens of blue and gray texts. A photo of Laney at the airport holding a Starbucks drink. Another of her on the plane, blanket draped over her belly. Another on her and Michael's living room couch.

"Gave her the money she came for and more. Hopefully, she and the baby have a good life. They're home safe, now."

Her face hardened then as she looked at the glasses-wearing coder like he was the scum on the bottom of her shoe.

"Safe from *you*, that's for sure."

Michael flinched. His mouth parted- no sound came out.

"What's sad is… I *really* wasn't planning on inviting you guys, especially not after I saw she was pregnant. But then… the PI caught you sending those *disgusting* messages. I mean, you barely even hid it; you would send them on your *phone*, in *public!* And lord knows I couldn't let that slide. Not when I knew you'd make it so easy to expose. I gave you Wi-Fi for an hour, and that was the *first* thing you did," She scoffed.

And with that, she tucked her phone away, back into her pocket like a prized possession.

Selene stood a few feet away, tears already glittering in her large golden eyes. For the first time since the truth had detonated between them, her expression softened.

"Damien…" she whispered, voice trembling as she took one careful step closer. "Yes. I planned to get close to you. I planned all of it. But I swear on everything I never expected to feel… *this.*"

Damien's breath hitched. He stared at her like she was a stranger, betrayal carved deep into his face.

His hands clenched into fists on his thighs, knuckles white.

"I trusted you with my brother's memory. I opened up to you. I broke a *promise* for you. And it was all a part of some sick fuckin' *game?*"

Selene gasped, heart pounding, the look of pure disillusionment in his eyes hurting more than she expected it to. "It… at *first,* it was. But I swear to God, I-"

"I *trusted* you," he reiterated, voice breaking. "I *wanted* you. I thought- fuck, I thought maybe this was somethin' *real.*"

"It *is* real," she whispered, voice cracking with raw honesty. "Everything I felt for you… everything between us… that was *real,* Damien."

Selene took another shaky step forward, then reached into her pocket with trembling fingers. She pulled out the small white stick and held it out to him.

Damien stared at it for a long, agonizing second before slowly taking it from her palm.

The words were unmistakable.

His breath left him in a rush. The test trembled in his large hand as he looked up at her, eyes wide with shock, pain, and something dangerously close to *awe*.

"Damien…" Selene whispered, voice cracking. Fresh tears spilled down her cheeks.

"You're going to be a father."

The room *exploded* into silence.

Raven stumbled back like she'd been punched. Her face contorted, tears brimming in her red-rimmed eyes as she clapped a hand over her mouth. Caleb strained out a curse.

Damien, still staring at the stick, slumped slowly onto the back of the couch like gravity had finally won.

He blinked once. Twice.

His chest heaved. "Selene…" he said at last, and it sounded like it came from the deepest part of his soul.

"You're pregnant?"

Selene nodded, tears sliding down her cheek. Damien looked at the Clearblue test again.

**Pregnant, 2-3 weeks.**

He let out a breath that sounded like something cracking.

Raven stared at the stick still clutched in Damien's hand like it was a knife, her breath shaking, her eyes glazed.

Then she dropped the Polaroid. It hit the floor with a whisper-soft thud.

Selene bent and picked it up with all the grace of a woman who knew *exactly* who she was now.

She turned and walked slowly to the front double doors. She rested her hand on the doorknob, then looked back-

Straight at Damien.

"You don't have to be with me, Damien." Her voice was soft. She turned the knob, then, looking over her shoulder. "I'm more than happy to raise this baby on my own."

Then, her voice firmed up. "But if you want to be involved…" She turned the knob again, almost opening it.

"You *might* want to come with me in the next thirty seconds."

The whole room *froze*.

Raven hissed.

"Damien… don't you fucking dare. Not after everything. Not after she did this to me. To *us*."

Damien's body was wound tight as a wire, his face tortured. The stick trembled in his hand.

For one breathless second, it looked like he might stay frozen there forever.

Then he spoke, voice low and hoarse, his eyes locked on that door like it was both the end and beginning of everything:

"I can't let my blood down a second time."

# Chapter 35

*Isn't This Exactly Where You'd Like Me?*

For a while, they just stood on the porch- silent- beneath the purple sky lit by a bright waning gibbous moon.

Selene, for the first time, wasn't looking at it, though.

She was looking at the stars.

With her free hand, she clutched the Polaroid to her chest.

And then-

**Wind.**

Loud, heavy, sweeping across the trees.

A helicopter sliced through the night. Its blades thundered above them as it descended onto the expansive driveway.

Within seconds of touching down, the doors flew open-

*And out came a rush of police officers.*

Inside, chaos *erupted.*

Caleb was the first to be dragged out, his eyes wild. "You can't! We were… we were *young! SHE* wanted it, too! And wh-what about Selene, she *fucki-*"

Selene closed her eyes, still holding the Polaroid.

Then came Raven.

Her heels scraped against the gravel as she screamed, wet-faced, messy, her red-rooted hair flying. "I had just caught my boyfriend of *fifteen years* cheating! I wasn't in my right mind!"

Selene's hand tightened on the photo.

Michael was last- face pale, shirt soaked. He tried to run.

Didn't even make it two steps. A cop pinned him down like a roach.

"Yeah, nah dude, you ain't getting away with pretending to be a teenager and sexting minors online."

Selene exhaled, her eyes soft but sure.

She knew this would happen; the warrants had come from *her* clean evidence; but watching it was something else.

Damien stood beside her, eyes wide, form frozen.

"You set them up," he said beneath his breath, looking at the woman he'd impregnated like she was a monster.

Selene smiled, eyes twinkling with tears.

"I set *justice* up."

That's when it appeared.

A black Mercedes-Benz Maybach.

*The same one that had picked them up from the airport on January 1ˢᵗ.*

The tinted window rolled down. And there she was.

Inas.

Elegantly dressed in a cream silk turban and oversized sunglasses that couldn't hide the sharp beauty of a matriarch who had waited a long, long time for justice. P!ATD's "But It's Better If You Do" played loudly from the Bluetooth speakers.

"So good to finally see you in person, Damien," she purred, lowering her sunglasses to bare her aureate eyes.

"Wah, you are a *gorgeous* man. You deserved better than some *sakra* who killed kids."

Damien blinked, letting out a breath of pure disbelief.

Inas' eyes dropped to Selene's belly, still small but energetically glowing, and her lips curved warmly. She smiled like a queen who had claimed her legacy.

"*Yallah*, this kid will *model.*"

Selene looked up at Damien with twinkling eyes, tears falling down her cheeks again. He still looked shell-shocked.

Inas beckoned them with a gold-ringed hand. "*Wallah*, what are y'all waiting for?! I've been sneaking through that trapdoor to cook and clean and write envelopes for a month. I'm ready to go to a *restaurant!*"

Selene snorted. "Tatie, *I* was the one who came up with everything the envelopes said; you just had to copy the texts I sent you."

Inas raised her small, chubby hand, revealing ink stains. "*A hmar!* You think this was *easy* for me?!"

Selene laughed- bright and genuine- a laugh she hadn't heard herself make since 2013.

She got into the car and motioned for Damien to follow.

He looked back at the driveway, at the sign, at the helicopter his girlfriend of two years was handcuffed in.

Then, with a tight jaw-

He climbed into the back seat of the Mercedes. The door shut behind them with a soft, final click.

The car pulled off- gliding down the mountain road, headlights slicing through the night-

And Selene rode off into the moonlight.

# Epilogue

*Tell Me You're That Somebody*

## 19 June 2020- Rex, GA

The yard was alive with music and laughter, Aaliyah's "Are You That Somebody?" playing loudly through a retro boombox Uncle Jr. had brought just for the vibes.

He and Andre King, both bald now, were tending to the grill, smoke curling into the hot, almost-summer air, while kids ran wild with sparklers. Aunties passed out foil-wrapped plates heavy with ribs, mac and cheese, collard greens, and peach cobbler. Big Mama rocked in her chair, tending to her new granddaughter and great-grandson as the babies' mothers- Shanice and Kiki- smiled brightly beside her.

The whole block knew: the King family Juneteenth cookout was the one you didn't miss. Even Miss Bertha showed up with homemade cornbread.

As the sun dipped low, Damien stood near the fire pit, his dog tags warm against his chest, dreads reaching his collarbone, now. The family gathered, falling quiet as Andre lit a special firework in memory of Xander. The crackling glow shot skyward, exploding into silver against the darkening sky.

Cheers broke out, but Damien's throat was tight.

Then, in the hush that followed, a ripple went through the crowd. Heads turned.

"Lord have mercy…" Tonya, her auburn wig perfectly laid, whispered, a bright Kente-style mask over her nose and lips.

Walking through the yard, dressed simply in a flowing white sundress, but still unmistakable-

Was Jasmine Campbell.

Damien froze, his breath catching audibly in his throat. For a second, he wondered if he was seeing things.

Jasmine was just as gorgeous as he remembered; if not even more so. Her dark hair, long and high-quality, flowed with the light wind. Her caramel-toned face was extra glowy from the sun. She still kept the fitness she'd developed as a cheerleader throughout high school and college, but her curves were even more pronounced now, her legs impossibly soft and shapely beneath her dress.

Tonya's face broke into a smile as she crossed the yard and pulled the now 27-year-old beauty into a hug. "Baby girl!" she said, eyes watering. "Look at you!"

"Mrs. King," Jasmine said through a leopard-print mask. "I missed you so much."

Andre ran from the grill to hug her. "God, you grew up! I remember chasin' after you and Mo when y'all was in kindergarten."

At the mention of his nickname, Damien froze even further, his face visibly floored.

Later, after the greetings and stares, Jasmine found him near the edge of the yard. She gave him that same smile he remembered from childhood- soft, dimpled, *too* familiar.

"Can we talk?" she asked gently.

He nodded stiffly and followed her a little way down the street, away from the crowd.

Jasmine stopped, crossing her arms nervously.

"I heard about… what happened with Raven," she said quietly, the Jamaican flag pendant around her neck glittering. "I'm so sorry, Damien. You two were like… a power couple online. To have her ripped away from you in that way… it must be *so* hard."

He said nothing, staring down at the cracked pavement, hands shoved into his pockets.

Her jaw tensed as her eyes shifted. "I-I mean. She's in *jail,* not *dead,* so I probably shouldn't act like she is. You might still be together-"

"We ain't." He interrupted quickly and coldly.

She took in a deep breath, then, trying hard to hide the relief that bubbled within her chest. "Oh… I see."

For ten seconds, there was nothing but the sound of fireworks still going off.

Then, she drew a deep breath. "And… I need to say something else. I'm sorry for what I did to you," Her voice cracked with regret. "It wasn't worth it, D. He cheated on me just weeks later. And by the time I tried to call you, you'd… you'd already gone off to the Army. And then… Xan…" Her voice cracked.

He maintained his calm appearance, but his breathing came a little shaky, now.

Her large brown eyes took him in. "How've you been?"

He finally looked at her. His eyes were tired, older.

"I got twins on the way."

It felt like a heavy weight had dropped on the pavement.

Jasmine's brows lifted, a pang slashing through her. "Oh. By Raven?"

Damien shook his head no. She could tell from the look in his eyes that he didn't want to discuss it further.

She managed the tiniest smile, then. "Congratulations, D. You always wanted twins- boy-girl ones like your mama and Uncle Jr. I remember when we used to talk about our future family, our kids' names…"

Her voice cracked as the memories started flooding in.

Damien took a deep, labored inhale. "Ain't no 'congratulations'. I mean, I love 'em, and I'm excited to raise 'em, but…"

Jasmine's beautiful face suddenly held deep concern. "But what, D?"

Damien's jaw tightened, his expression turning cold.

"Ion' want *shit* to do with they mama."

His words, brutal and final and true, sliced through the almost-summer air.

She gulped. "If you don't mind me asking… what happened?"

He gave a bitter laugh, though nothing about it was funny.

"You wanna know why I'm so fine talkin' to you right now, despite how *bad* you broke my heart?"

Jasmine winced, the guilt filling her all over again.

He continued with a cold, mirthless smile.

"'Cause what you did to me? It don't even *compare* to what *she* did."

Jasmine gasped, tears filling her eyes. She hated the thought of Damien being hurt by not just one woman, but *two*. He didn't deserve it. Not D.

She looked down for a long moment, then lifted her eyes to his. They shimmered with unshed tears, raw and vulnerable in a way he hadn't seen in years.

"D… I've missed you," she whispered, voice cracking. "I've been missing you for eight years. Not a single day has gone *by* that I don't regret what I did to you."

Her breath hitched, self-disgust plain on her face. "It wasn't worth it. Not even a little. No one I've been with since- rappers, athletes, whoever- has even come *close* to comparing to you. They never even touched what we had. You were always… my *person*."

Something deep in Damien's chest twisted painfully.

He searched her face- the impossibly smooth caramel skin, those big, expressive eyes with lashes that still made his stomach flip, the endearingly upturned nose, and those full lips he used to kiss for hours.

For the first time, he noticed how much she and Selene actually favored one another.

The realization made his stomach turn.

Jasmine kept going, tears slipping freely down her cheeks now.

"I don't expect you to forgive me. I don't expect you to want me back. But… I'd love- God, I'd *love*- to at least be friends again. To not be strangers carrying all this *history* between us."

Damien was quiet for a long time.

He could still smell her perfume- Dolce & Gabbana's *The One*- the exact scent he'd saved up for months to buy her when they were seventeen.

Everything came rushing back in a flood:

Elementary school recess when she'd shared her juice box with him. Middle school when he realized he was in love with his best friend. High school stolen kisses behind the bleachers. The way she used to fall asleep on his chest like she belonged there.

He hadn't realized until this moment how much of his heart had stayed locked away with her.

"Yeah," he said finally, voice thick. "I think I'd like that, Jas."

## Los Angeles, CA

The day was quiet in the way only lockdown days could be. Caleb- now *Corbin Kai* to the world- moved through his morning ritual in the spotless apartment: eggs sizzling in the pan, resistance bands neatly coiled on the counter, his phone buzzing with brand collabs and training inquiries.

From the outside, it looked like he'd rebuilt himself. A new name, a new city, a new life.

And then-

"Kai!" a bright, lilting voice called from down the hall, carrying that effortless charm that had made her a household name.

Barefoot, a glass water bottle in one hand, Saoirse Sullivan strolled into the kitchen. The sunlight caught on her long flaxen-blonde hair, her sculpted legs glistening. She wore a sports bra and high-waisted leggings from her latest sponsorship deal.

Caleb froze for just a second, the sizzle of the pan filling the silence.

Somehow, this angel-looking woman stood barefoot before him, stretching her toned arms overhead like it was the most natural thing in the world.

She crossed the room, kissed his cheek casually, and snagged a strip of turkey bacon from the plate. "You didn't burn breakfast this time," she teased, flashing him a grin.

The image was almost surreal. To the outside world, she was a Boston-bred fitness influencer with millions of followers. To him, she was the woman he cared for, and he now lived with, quarantined together in her luxury high-rise.

He forced a small smirk, masking the storm in his chest. "Guess I'm improving."

But as she moved through the kitchen, radiant and trusting, Caleb's thoughts twisted darker.

No matter how definitively he'd changed his name or how bright the California sun was, the shadow of his past followed him. The arrest. The headlines. The word *incest* stamped onto his soul like a scar.

The charges had been dropped- Pennsylvania's statute of limitations had saved him- but the stain remained.

And sometimes, when he watched Saoirse laugh in the glow of her ring light, he wondered:

*What happens when the world realizes who I really am?*

For now, he kept his secrets buried. For now, he let himself believe this new life could last.

He glanced at the wall mirror, quickly fixing his perfectly dyed jet-black hair.

He attempted to smile.

The cottage glowed like something from a dream. Ivy climbed the stone walls, flowers bloomed in planters along the windowsills, and the wraparound porch twinkled with strings of fairy lights that Selene had insisted on leaving up year-round. Inside, every corner breathed warmth- crystal prisms catching sunlight, stacks of books, and handwoven throws draped over chairs. It was a home built for comfort, for love, for family.

But tonight, it felt unbearably *empty*.

Selene nestled on the velvet settee in the living room, her curls, even thicker now from prenatals, brushing the center of her back, the golden glow of the lamp softening the shadows. Her phone rested in her hand, open to Instagram.

Picture after picture scrolled by: Saoirse radiant in sunlight, Saoirse doing partner yoga in her luxury high-rise, Saoirse laughing over organic avocado toast with someone Selene knew too well.

Caleb- now "Corbin Kai".

Her fingers lingered on the screen, over a picture of Caleb and Saoirse kissing, both of them smiling as though the world had never ended.

Her throat burned. Not because she still wanted her now-ex husband, but because she wished, *craved*, that she could have someone, too.

A certain towering someone with locs, tattoos, and a heart that held the same pain hers did.

Even after the paternity test confirmed he was indeed the father, Damien had made it crystal clear he wanted *nothing* to do with her- only the babies. He'd even hired a third party to get updates from her about them because he didn't want to hear anything from her.

He would never, *could* never, forgive her using his brother's memory just to hurt someone else.

Although Inas had a cottage that looked like it belonged to an enchanted fairytale built for her in Atlanta, and it was everything she *and* Athena had always dreamt of, it didn't really *feel* like home. Not when it was close enough to Damien's high-rise to co-parent with him easily, but far enough that he wouldn't experience the displeasure of running into her.

She rose slowly, her hand resting on the curve of her 23-week belly, and walked down the hall. The nursery door stood open, the walls glowing faintly.

Inside, the room was split into two halves.

On one wall hung the name **Artemis Athena King**. Tiny stars glimmered on the ceiling, and a mobile of clouds and moons hung over a crib lined with pale pinks and dusty lavenders.

On the opposite wall was the name **Apollo Alexander King**. Paper lanterns that glowed with fire-shaped bulbs hung above his crib, and dusty teal constellations lined the wall.

Selene stood in the center of it all, her arms wrapping protectively around her bump. She cradled it, imagining what they'd end up looking like. Would Apollo, whom she already called "Pols", be tall like his father? Would Artemis, whom she already called "Tems", have dimples like herself? Vice versa?

Would Pols like fire like his late uncle? Would Tems love the moon like her late auntie? Vice versa?

Just then- a *kick*.

Selene gasped, a tiny smile on her face now as she rubbed her belly tenderly. "I love you," she said softly, tears glimmering in her eyes. "So much already."

Sniffling, she headed to the side of the room, admiring a framed canvas painting on the wall: silver stars falling from dark clouds, with a hopeful sun peeking out from behind.

### Kissimmee, FL

The fluorescent lights buzzed faintly overhead. Raven, her hair fully red again and cut to her chin, sat at the metal table, her jail oranges loose over the curve of her pregnant belly.

She hadn't wanted visitors. Most days, she ignored the list, preferring to keep her chin high and her mind sharp. But when the guard told her someone unexpected had signed in, curiosity dragged her here.

The door clanged.

And who walked in made all of the color drain from her already-pale face.

Tall. Broad. Short chestnut-brown hair and eyes so blue you could get lost in them for days.

Kevin Murphy.

For a second, she thought she was hallucinating. The years had aged him- lines cut deeper into his face, his once-boyish charm dulled- but his eyes were the same. The same deep blues she loved for fifteen years.

The same ones that set her down the path that killed Athena Amrani and landed her *here*.

"Kells," Kevin said softly, his voice breaking. His eyes were hollow, like he'd been living in sheer *regret* for the past seven years.

He sank into the chair opposite, eyes pained as he observed her belly. "God… look at you."

She didn't carry the same emotion. Her face was *stone*.

"You got some nerve showing up here."

The jail wasn't quiet- not by any means- but the air felt so silent it was *painful*.

Kevin winced, guilt etched into each of his features. "I know. I *know* I'm the last person you want to see." His hands trembled slightly.

"I'm sorry. I swear to God, Kells, I am so damn sorry. For everything. This? This mess?" He gestured vaguely at the walls. "It's on me. If I didn't… do what I did… You wouldn't have gone out and…"

He couldn't finish, his eyes downcast.

She stared at him, her jaw tight. Even though she had her red hair back, she looked nothing like Kelly. Kelly had hope in her features. Dreams.

Raven? She just had reality.

"I'll do anything," he pressed, his voice almost pleading. "Anything to make it right. I swear to God, I'll spend the rest of my life making it up to you. Just… tell me how."

She let his pleading words settle over her for a couple of heartbeats.

And then? Her mind flickered like a slideshow.

Selene, the bright-eyed yogi. Selene, who was pregnant by the man she loved for two years of her life. Selene, who had orchestrated her downfall in the slowest, cruelest way.

Selene, who had *yet* to burn for her crimes while she herself sat there, locked up, alone, pregnant by a guard whom she'd seduced in hopes that they'd let her out if she had a baby on the way.

They didn't.

And then... Raven smiled. Slow. Menacing. "Anything?" she asked, her voice dangerous as glass.

Kevin didn't hesitate for a second.

*"Anything."*

Her hand smoothed over the swell of her belly, nails digging lightly into the fabric of her oranges.

And, for the first time in over four months, her green eyes glittered with something besides just rage.

# Acknowledgments

First and foremost, I want to acknowledge my parents, who loved me more than anything in the world and nurtured the creativity and confidence that made writing this even possible. Did I tell them to skip certain chapters? Many times. Did they listen? I doubt it. But if they read those scenes anyway, I hope they see them as proof of the…um… *very* vivid imagination they helped cultivate.

To my husband- thank you for supporting me in every way possible throughout this journey and for introducing me to the beautiful Moroccan culture that shines through the pages of this story.

To my sister- your presence is the invisible heartbeat of this novel. Siblinghood plays a central role because losing mine is my worst fear. A part of me needed to explore what it means to survive such a loss, to find some kind of hope after. Even if by… um… *unseemly* means.

And finally, to the writing program at Georgia Southern University: thank you for giving me the tools to write this story in my own voice, at a time when that voice matters more than ever. Oh, and also for introducing my parents to each other; I, and this book, wouldn't exist otherwise (no, seriously; I don't think anyone else would have a mind messed up enough to come up with this, lol).